Pasko Na, My Love

A HOLIDAY ROMANCE ANTHOLOGY

ELLE CRUZ

MAAN GABRIEL

MAIDA MALBY

MIA HOPKINS

SARAH SMITH

TIF MARCELO

EOT *Publications*

Copyright

Acknowledgments

We have so many people to thank for this, our first Filipino American romance anthology, to come into being.

- •Our families for their unconditional love and support;

- •Vania Hardy for the gorgeous artwork of a cover;

- •Our beta readers, editors, and proofreaders, especially Linda Hill, for looking over the party scenes. The authors shoulder all responsibilities for any inconsistencies that remained after their careful perusal of the stories.

- •Preslaysa Williams for the financial contribution;

- •And you, our dear readers, for appreciating our efforts to bring our stories to life. We hope to hear from you through reviews and by engaging with us on social media.

Table of Contents

Last Minute

SARAH SMITH

Last Minute

SARAH SMITH

Blurb:

Twenty-eight-year-old Ruby is in charge of catering the 100th birthday party of her grandmother. As the baby of her family, Ruby has grown up in the shadow of her older, more successful cousins, so she's determined for her catered dinner to go off without a hitch. But when her head chef calls out with food poisoning the day of the party and sends chef Mason Waller as her replacement, Ruby is pissed. She's loathed Mason ever since he screwed her over in culinary school five years ago. There's still plenty of fire between these two … in more ways than one.

Content Note:

Profanity

RUBY

"Ruby. Please don't freak out, but I've got some bad news."

I halt in my tracks, nearly skidding into the massive metal prep table and almost dropping my phone. Crap. That's not what I want to hear from my best friend and the head chef of my catering business hours before we're due to cater Lola Naty's 100th birthday party.

"Bad news? Bad news? What do you mean bad news?" I sputter like a broken record.

Abby sighs before coughing, then gagging, then I hear a muffled retching noise on the other end of the phone line.

"Abby, are you okay? What's going on?"

There's a gurgling noise, then another sigh. "No. I'm not okay. I have food poisoning."

Dread swirls in the pit of my stomach. A stress-cramp needles my right side.

"Food poisoning? What…how?"

"I think it was the wings at that dive bar." She makes a groaning noise. "God, I'm going to kill my sister for insisting we try someplace new last night instead of sticking with the Thai restaurant we know is amazing and always order from. But no, we had to 'switch it up.'" Her voice hitches up as she mocks her sister's tone. "I feel awful, but I'm not gonna be able to make it to the venue today. I can't cook like this, not when I'm vomiting every two minutes and can barely crawl out of bed."

My eyes prick with unshed tears. This cannot be happening.

I force myself to close my eyes and take a slow, deep, cleansing breath like I learned in yoga class. Ujjayi I think it's called? A low rumbling noise emanates from my throat.

"Whoa, what was that sound?" Abby asks.

"My attempt at a cleansing, soothing breath. I learned it in yoga," I mumble.

After three slow, deep, cleansing breaths, I'm still a wreck. My heart races and my brain is a muddled mess of thoughts as I scramble to try and figure out what to do.

I catch one of the servers giving me a strange look before darting out of the kitchen to the dining area. Way to go, Ruby. Way to seem like a total weirdo to the staff of the Hacienda Luz. I bet the chefs and caterers they normally employ at this high-end venue in the heart of Napa don't have to force themselves to take calming breaths to avoid a meltdown. I bet they're unflappable in a crisis, unlike me.

I catch my reflection in the high shine of the stainless-steel walk-in. My brown eyes are wide and my mouth is hanging open. I look like the character that gets off-ed first in a horror movie: completely and utterly horrified, caught totally off guard.

"I'm so, so sorry, Ruby." Abby sniffles and I can tell she's on the verge of tears. I instantly soften. Here she is stressing about me all the while puking her guts out.

I tug at the messy bun I threw my hair in this morning. A chunk of my wavy black-brown hair comes loose, and I tuck it back up. "It's okay, Abby. You can't help that you're sick."

For a second, I mentally take stock of the situation. I'm in charge of catering the single most important event for my entire family. Today is the one-hundredth birthday of Lola Naty, the matriarch of our family. For my entire life, she's been our collective heart and soul, showering her kids, grandkids, and great grandkids with love and hugs from the minute we were born. She hosted holidays, birthdays, and parties for my family ever since I can remember. Today is a tribute to her, to show her just how much she means to all of us.

On top of that, today was going to be my chance to prove myself. As the baby of my entire family—the youngest grandkid due to the fact that I was a surprise baby for my parents in their mid-forties—I've always been looked after and taken care of by all of my relatives. Which is wonderful honestly. I was constantly being held and cuddled by my older cousins, aunties, and uncles. My ates were always told to, "look after Baby Ruby!" and "be sure to hold Baby Ruby's hand when you're walking together!" and "save some dessert for Baby Ruby! She's the littlest, she's not as fast or as strong as you!"

It was all well-meaning and kind of course, but at twenty-eight, I still hold that place in my family. Still the baby, still the helpless one, still the one to coddle and look after when there's any big event. That's why I offered to cater this party when my cousins started planning it a year ago. I still remember the shocked looks on their faces when I spoke up.

"You sure you can handle it?" my eldest cousin Vida said, eyebrow raised. She's Lola Naty's right hand woman and holder of the purse strings when it came to paying for the party.

"One thousand percent sure," I said with a wide smile, excited at the prospect of honoring Lola Naty with my food.

"You're still a new company, Ruby," my cousin Ollie had said. I didn't miss that scoff he tried to hide when he cleared his throat.

"I'm aware," I said in a polite yet firm tone.

I was on the verge of pointing out that as the family screw-up he had no right to question my company or me—especially not when he ended up flaking out completely when we had to plan the party. I've had a more stable work history and a far less dramatic personal life, unlike the walking train wreck that he is.

"I've catered several big events in the two years since I started this company," I said to everyone. "I'm certain I'll do an amazing job for Lola Naty. Let me do this?"

I tried not to flinch at the chorus of sighs from my cousins. Clearly, they had zero faith in me. But that made me all the more determined to prove them wrong.

"Okay," Ate Vida said with a forced smile. "You're the caterer."

My chest aches at the thought that I'm on the verge of ruining this whole party now that I've lost my head chef.

Another retching sound echoes from Abby's end of the line. She clears her throat. "Don't worry, Ruby. I'm not going to leave you high and dry. My replacement is on his way."

I gasp. "Oh my gosh, you sent a replacement? Oh Abby, thank you! You are seriously the best, most amazing friend I could ever..."

I drift off when I see a familiar tall and broad figure step into the kitchen clad in a white chef's coat, holding a cloth bundle of kitchen knives. My jaw plummets to the ground.

Mason Waller.

I haven't seen this guy in five years—he's the one person I hoped I'd never have to see again because he's my culinary school enemy and the person I despise most in this world.

He starts to smile, and I make a disgusted noise into the phone while looking right at him, not bothering to hide it. Why should I? After what he did to me, after how he completely screwed me over five years ago, he has no right to expect anything less from me.

"Abby, what the hell? You sent Mason as your replacement?"

He crosses his arms over his broad chest and glares at me.

Abby makes a groaning noise. "I know! I know! Look, Ruby, I'm sorry, but he was the only chef in my contacts list who was free at the last minute. Plus, he owes me a favor."

She mentions something about how the walk-in of his restaurant short-circuited one night months ago, causing all of his produce to spoil, and she saved his ass by offering up half of the produce from the small restaurant she co-owns with her cousin, who is friends with him.

"He owes you a favor, huh?" I say while looking right at him. He smirks.

I roll my eyes in full view of him before darting past him out of the kitchen. I scurry down the hall to a darkened corner where I'll have at least a bit of privacy.

"Abby, how could you? You of all people know how he screwed me over."

"Ruby, I know. Believe me, I know how awful this is. But he's an amazing chef. You know he is."

I huff out a breath, my silent acknowledgment that Abby is right. We're still friends with a lot of the folks we went to culinary school with and meet up regularly. Some of them are friends with Mason and have mentioned him when we catch up. He's a two-time James Beard Award nominee the last two years in a row after he opened his French Bistro-style restaurant here in Napa. Not sure how he pulled that off given the fact that he dropped out of culinary school after he completely screwed me over.

Even now my stomach bottoms out when I think back to that day in culinary school. We were assigned to be partners for our final pastry project: baking a wedding cake. We didn't know each other well, but Mason seemed nice enough. He was polite and an incredible cook. I remember his red wine reduction was the most flavorful I've ever tasted, better than I've had at any restaurant, ever.

But then, the day our cake was due, he no-showed. He didn't call, didn't text, didn't tell a single person where he was. He just stopped coming to class. And because our pastry instructor was a hardass, he failed me even though I showed up and finished the cake on my own.

"This was a group project, Ms. Moore," the instructor said. "That means it will be evaluated as such. It doesn't matter that you did all the work; half of your group didn't show up. You failed the most fundamental part of this project."

A handful of days later while I was wandering through campus, wallowing in my "F," I saw Mason looking disheveled and dazed outside of a coffee shop. I was so upset I walked up to him and started to lay into him for missing class.

Instead of apologizing, he lashed out at me. "God, Ruby. You think I give a shit about some stupid cake at some stupid school? I've got a million more important things going on in my life right now."

After that he stormed off, leaving me speechless.

"Yeah, Mason is a jackass and totally deserves a kick to the nuts for how he caused you to fail your pastry final and how he lashed out at you afterward," Abby says, pulling me back to the present moment. "But…"

When she pauses to take a breath, I worry she's still vomiting again, but thankfully she doesn't.

"Mason is the one person other than me who I know will execute your menu perfectly for today," she says. "I know how much Lola Naty means to you. I know you only want the best for her birthday. And Mason is the best. More importantly, he's available."

I let out the weakest, saddest-sounding chuckle that perfectly illustrates just how defeated I feel at this moment.

"You're right," I finally admit. "Get some rest, okay? And drink lots and lots of water."

"I will. Call me tomorrow and let me know how it all went, okay?"

"Promise."

"And try not to kill Mason."

"I can't guarantee anything."

We say goodbye. I hang up and walk back into the kitchen only to be greeted by Mason's lethal frown.

A beat later he swallows, and the intensity of his expression fades. He still looks angry and annoyed though. And ridiculously handsome.

I scold myself internally for making that silent observation about his appearance. But anyone can see what a stud Mason is. He was the hottie of our culinary school class, what with his six-foot-two leanly muscled frame, thick head of chestnut hair, mesmerizing hazel eyes, and sharp-as-hell jawline. I had a bit of a crush on him in culinary school—everyone did. I mean, he was drop-dead gorgeous *and* could cook. A guy like that is worth his weight in gold in this day and age of man-children, so many of whom can't seem to master basic tasks like cooking and cleaning.

Though now he looks a bit more rugged—more weathered. His hair is shaggier and messier, and his square jaw sports a healthy sheet of stubble.

My favorite…

"So, is gawking at people in disgust before storming out on them some new kind of greeting?" he says. "Call me old-fashioned, but I prefer a 'hello.'"

"And call *me* old-fashioned, but I prefer when people show up when they're supposed to. Like for group projects."

Recognition flashes across his obnoxiously handsome face. "Wait, you're still mad about that? Ruby, that was, like, five years ago."

"Of course, I'm still mad," I bite.

He shakes his head before looking off to the side. I catch the tail end of an eye roll before he aims an exasperated stare at me. "Fine. I'm sorry."

A bitter laugh falls from my lips. "No way. You don't get to give me some half-assed apology after this long. I know you don't mean it."

He lets out a sharp sigh. "So, are we gonna prep and cook or do you need to spend more time chatting on the phone or rehashing ancient history?" he asks. Now I'm the angry and annoyed one.

"Fine. Let's cook," I mutter while walking past him.

"Don't sound so thrilled. Not like I'm saving your ass or anything."

I spin around at him. "Excuse me?"

He jerks away the slightest bit like he's shocked I'm reacting this way at his obnoxious comment.

"Let's get something straight," I say. "The only reason you're here is because you're my last resort."

He snorts a chuckle and grips his hand to his chest. "Ouch."

"Oh please, don't act like you want to be here…"

I trail off and force myself to take a moment. I close my eyes and pinch the bridge of my nose, willing the patience to work with Mason so I can pull off this catering feat for Lola Naty.

When I look at him, those thick eyebrows of his crash together and he tugs a hand through his wavy chestnut hair. He's frowning like he's taking issue with what I've said.

"You're right. I'm only here as a favor to Abby," he says curtly.

"Great," I mumble as I grab the paper copy of the menu. "Let's get this over with."

I start to gesture for him to look at it on the metal table with me, but he holds up a hand. "Wait. Let's have a truce, okay?"

"A truce?" I almost laugh.

"A time-out, a break, whatever you want to call it. Then you can go back to hating me for something that I did five years ago."

I grit my teeth, ready to go off on him, but he speaks before I can. "We have to at least try to get along. This is for your grandmother, right? I want her to have the best party."

His hazel eyes go warm when he mentions her. So does his tone. Like he actually cares about doing a good job for her, even though he doesn't even know her. It's so disorienting that for a split second I'm heartened. I shake my head slightly and refocus.

"Right," I say. "I want everything to go as perfectly as possible for her."

He nods once and sticks his hand out at me. "So, truce?"

I squint at his hand, then up at him. "Temporary truce."

This time his chuckle comes out at a low, teasing rumble. I'm thrown off at just how much I like hearing it.

God. What a sexy laugh.

I banish the thought from my brain before gripping his hand. I shake it once and start to let go, but his hold on my hand remains.

"Wait." His gaze is on me, and his brow quirks up. With his free hand, he reaches for my other hand, which I just now realize I've positioned slightly behind my back.

When he wraps those long thick fingers around my wrist and pulls it gently forward, I shiver. Holy … hang on, are those goosebumps flashing across my skin right now?

I take in the expression on his face, the look in his eyes. His gaze is focused for sure, but there's also something else there…like, teasing? Actually, playful is a better world. Like he's enjoying this back-and-forth between us.

Like he's enjoying holding my hand.

I swallow and follow Mason's eyes as they land on my free hand. The corner of his mouth quirks up, and his stare cuts to me. "Just wanted to check and make sure that you weren't crossing your fingers behind your back. That voids the truce, you know."

The start of a smile pulls at my mouth. Both corners start to make that familiar journey upward, but I bite it back before it fully takes hold. I don't know what game he thinks he's playing or if he's trying to throw me off, but I won't fall for it.

I yank both my hands out of his grip and rest my hands on my hips. "Nope. No crossed fingers. We're in the middle of a temporary truce. Now can we please stop with this ridiculousness and get started?"

That playful gleam in those piercing hazel eyes dissipates. He blinks and nods once. "Of course."

* * *

"Wow. That's a lot of pork."

I glare up at Mason, who's standing next to me, frowning down at the paper menu of tonight's service. He doesn't seem to notice. Or care. He just keeps gawking at the menu with the most confused look on his face, like he's trying to decipher ancient symbols.

19

"It's a normal amount of pork," I say defiantly. "Besides, pork is delicious. And Lola Naty's favorite food. It doesn't matter if you think it's too much."

He scoffs. "I was just commenting."

"Well, I don't need your comments. I just need you to familiarize yourself with the menu and ingredients and help me prep for the next few hours until the party starts."

He holds up both hands like he's surrendering. "Okay, okay. Forget I said anything. Jeez."

He leans his tall frame down and studies the menu. Even though I'm the one who planned this menu, I give it another once-over too: pork adobo, chicken adobo wings, lumpia, pancit, bacon fried rice, roasted whole pig, and sautéed vegetables.

I explain that I arrived early this morning to start the prep.

"Pork adobo is slow cooking in the ovens. So is the whole pig." I gesture to the trio of stainless-steel ovens on the far side of the kitchen, then point to the deep fryer. "The chicken wings are par-boiled and drying out on paper-towel-lined trays so they'll be extra crispy when we dunk them in the deep fryer. And we've got two thousand lumpia in the freezer that we'll fry for tonight too."

Mason's eyes go wide. "Two thousand? How big is your family?"

I let out the first genuine laugh since he's been here. "Have you ever tasted lumpia? It's delicious. And impossible to eat just one. People eat it by the truckload, just you wait and see."

"Fair point." He grins and for a moment I can't help but soak in just how handsome he looks when he's flashing a genuine smile.

I go over the veggies that I'm planning to serve along with how long it'll take to cook the rice. When I finish, Mason is gazing at me with a dazed look in his eyes. "Wow. You've planned this down to the last detail."

I shuffle my sneakered feet against the super shiny terra cotta-hued tile floor, feeling the slightest bit self-conscious. He probably thinks I'm a nutcase. "Yeah, well. I like to be organized."

I catch him looking at the menu again. "Cake for dessert," he says softly.

I can tell by the way he refuses to look at me and the slight strain in his tone that he's thinking about our pastry project.

"Yup. Ube and passion fruit crème cake. Lola Naty's favorite. But don't worry, I made it yesterday so it's chilling in the fridge. You won't have to help with it."

I know I sound snarky, but part of me can't help it. I'm still angry at how Mason ditched me all those years ago, how he was the sole reason I failed that project, how even now he refuses to acknowledge how he hurt me, how he can't even muster a genuine, "sorry."

I pause for a moment. I'm not doing a very good job of holding up our truce to remain cordial and professional.

"I just mean that the cake is taken care of. We won't have to worry about it," I say.

"Got it," he says curtly. "Abby told me you've been planning this party for almost a year."

"I have, with my family. It's a big deal, this birthday celebration. I mean, how many people make it to one hundred, you know? We wanted to go all out."

"That's amazing. Your grandma making it to this milestone, I mean. That's really cool that you and your family still have her around." He clears his throat. I observe how the parts of his cheeks that aren't covered in stubble flush pink, like he's embarrassed at what he's said. I don't know why. It's one of the nicest things he's said to me since he's been here.

"It is," I say softly. "Um, can you help me make a couple of batches of the adobo glaze for the wings?"

"Sure."

For the next hour, Mason and I work in surprisingly companionable silence. We chop and pour and simmer, ending up side-by-side at the stovetops, only talking to clarify measurements and ingredients. Despite our tense history, I have to admit that Abby was right—Mason really is a professional, dedicated to helping me crank out this menu.

I dip a spoon in the sauce and make a satisfied "mmm" noise. "Wow, that's good. Could use a bit more acid though."

I'm about to tell him to add a few more splashes of vinegar, but he walks off. When I look up I expect to see a bottle of vinegar in his hand, but to my horror, he's carrying a bottle of fresh-squeezed lemon juice.

He moves to pour it into the pot. "No, don't!" I shout before moving to grab it from him. But I lose my grip and knock the bottle over, all over the front of his chef's jacket.

Mason hunches over to look at the soaking wet mess on his coat, his arms hovering at his sides. "What the hell is your problem?"

I stomp my sneaker against the floor. "What the hell is *your* problem?"

"Um, how about the fact that I'm wearing an entire bottle of lemon juice because of you?" The side of his jaw bulges as he clenches down. "God, you acted like I was adding arsenic to the recipe. What is wrong with you?"

"Look, I'm sorry I spilled lemon juice all over you, but this is *your* fault."

His head snaps up and he aims that glare at me. "What the…how is this my fault?"

"You were deviating from the recipe! I told you when we were going over the menu that all of these dishes are family recipes. My relatives are expecting everything to taste a certain way. You can't just add whatever you want."

His mouth hangs open as he stares at me, as if I've just offered the most nonsensical explanation possible.

"It was a few splashes of lemon juice, Ruby. Way to overreact."

My skin pricks with frustration. "How would you feel if someone in your kitchen decided to throw a random ingredient in one of your recipes that you've spent years perfecting?"

He stammers before clamping his mouth shut.

I stand straighter, feeling ten feet tall at having rendered Mr. Bigshot Chef speechless.

"Okay, fine. That's a…fair point," he mutters, throwing up his hands in defeat before gesturing to his soaked chef's coat. "I can't wear this."

He steps back and yanks it off, revealing a white t-shirt that's also soaked in lemon juice.

I run to the back and fetch a clean chef's jacket. It's the least I can do for soaking him. When I make it back to Mason, I almost trip over my own feet. Because there he is, standing shirtless in front of me, looking like a living, breathing marble Roman statue.

A strangling noise escapes my throat. I cough in an attempt to cover it up, but even if I manage that, it's pretty clear from my wide-eyed and unblinking stare that I'm completely and utterly mesmerized by Mason's body.

Jesus Mary and Joseph, he's *hot*. I scan his entire bare torso, taking on how it's a perfect combination of hard mass and lines. Well, that's the sexiest six-pack I've ever laid eyes on. And his chest hair…

My mouth waters as I observe the burst of dark hair at the center of his chest, how it thins out and trails down his waist underneath his jeans.

Mason doesn't look like those polished images you see in advertisements—he looks a million times better. Sexier, more authentic. Something about his body looks real— deliciously, unabashedly real. Like he earned his physique through the hard work of physical fitness and an active lifestyle, not through airbrushing. His light-tan skin glows underneath the fluorescent kitchen lights above. I almost scoff. No one should look that good under the least flattering lighting on planet Earth.

When I make it back up to his face, I realize his lips are moving.

"Um, sorry, what was that?"

He frowns. "Can I have that?"

He juts his chin at the lump of fabric I'm holding.

"Oh! Sure! Um, s-sorry, I um…"

He takes the jacket out of my hand as I struggle to formulate words in the aftermath of witnessing the sizzling hotness that is Mason Waller's torso.

Just then my phone rings in my pocket. I've never been so happy to receive a phone call.

"Hello?"

"Ruby! Oh, thank god you picked up."

"Who is this?"

"Your cousin Ollie."

I bite back a groan. Of course, he'd get a hold of me the night of the party after going MIA when it came time to plan and pay for everything. It's been several months of no contact and he has the nerve to call now?

"Look, you won't believe what's going on with me right now, but I'm literally on a plane and just landed …"

The smell of something burning captures my attention from my rambling cousin. And that's when I notice that the pots of adobo glaze are boiling over on the stove.

"Shit!"

I drop my phone on the metal table, run over to the stove, and flip off the burners. With two kitchen towels wrapped around my hands, I slide one massive pot off the burner. Beside me Mason does the same.

My heart feels like a battering ram in my chest. I take a steadying breath before dipping a spoon in the cloudy dark liquid and nearly gag at the bitter flavor coating my tongue.

"Damn it. The sauce is overcooked. We have to start over."

"Start what over?"

I look up at the entrance to the kitchen and see Ate Eden standing there.

Shit.

I bite my tongue to keep from yelling a curse word. Despite the madness unfolding at the moment, I have to stay calm. I can't let Ate Eden see me flustered. She's the event planner at this venue and is in charge of all the party planning for tonight. Yeah, today is turning out to be an utter shitshow since I've lost my go-to chef due to food poisoning and I'm burning dishes in between arguments with the replacement chef who's my sworn enemy.

But Eden can't find out. She'll lose total faith in me and think the birthday party is doomed. Must play this off as coolly as I can.

"Nothing!" I say quickly.

Eden aims an inquisitive look at me before turning to Mason, who is still standing there shirtless. Oh god. That definitely doesn't make it look like things in the kitchen are under control.

I make a mental note of what a perfect juxtaposition this is—my girl boss cousin donning a designer pantsuit and heels looking as polished as possible and standing just a few feet from my half-naked culinary school classmate.

My cousin's deep brown eyes bulge. "Oh my—"

"It was a spill!" I blurt before I let out a nervous chuckle. "Just a little spill of lemon juice on his chef's jacket. Right, Mason?"

I pivot my gaze to Mason, who I hope can tell by the pleading/desperate look I'm giving him that I want to minimize this fiasco as much as possible.

He nods while quickly pulling on the jacket. "Yup. All good now." He holds up his hands at his sides and grins, like he's presenting himself to Eden. "You know how important it is to spot-treat stains. Gotta do it immediately or the stain stays forever."

"Yup. Forever!" I repeat in a pitchy tone.

Eden narrows her gaze at me before her expression eases and she flashes a professional smile. "Well. As long as everything is under control."

"Yes. All good, Ate. Promise!" I give her a thumbs up, my lips shaky as I grin wide. God, I bet I look like a deranged clown.

Mason steps forward and reaches out his hand. He flashes a suave smile. "I'm Mason Waller, the chef helping out Ruby tonight. I'm honored to be cooking for your grandmother."

And just like that, my cousin's pinched smile is gone, replaced by a giddy grin. "Oh my, that's very kind of you." Her gaze on him turns thoughtful. "I feel like I've heard your name before. Have we met?"

"Not sure. Have you heard of Atout here in Napa?"

Eden's perfectly shaped brows hit her brown-black hairline. "*That's* where I know you! I read the feature about Atout in Food & Wine magazine! You're the chef and owner!"

"In the flesh."

For a minute my cousin is too busy fangirling over Mason to notice the chaos in the kitchen, which goes a long way in easing the tension gripping all the muscles in my neck and shoulders the slightest bit.

She turns to me. "Ruby, you didn't tell me you had a famous chef cooking Lola Naty's birthday dinner with you." She gently bumps me with her elbow.

"It was a surprise," I lie.

"Well, I don't want to interrupt the culinary genius happening in here." She squeezes my hand. "You're doing a great job, Ruby. I'm so impressed."

I smile and tell her thanks despite the nerves twisting my stomach into a knot.

I hope you're right.

"How are things going for you?" I ask.

Eden's smile twitches slightly. "Good overall. Just dealing with Mr. Kawolski's usual … unpleasantness."

I make a face and nod in agreement. Mr. Kawolski is the insufferable manager here at Hacienda Luz. He micromanages every aspect of this venue like his life depends on it. Ever since I got in this morning, he's popped in a half-dozen times to make sure I'm doing everything "up to code."

"You're the best of the best, Ate. Even he can't bring you down."

Eden pulls me in for a quick hug. "Thanks for that," she says.

"Oh, and not sure if there's anything you can do about this, but Ollie called me a few minutes ago. He said something about being on a plane that just landed."

Eden's pretty face pulls a frown. She mutters a Tagalog curse word. "I swear to God, he is the biggest pain in the ass. He thinks he can disappear during the entire planning process and just show up whenever he wants to."

"Sounds like Ollie."

"Yeah. It does," Eden mutters. "Nice to meet you, Chef Mason."

Eden pops out, leaving me and Mason standing there. I look up at the clock and see that it's less than two hours before people start to arrive and we have to start serving. I can't screw anything else up if I want dinner service to start on time *and* go smoothly.

I bite my bottom lip, feeling overwhelmed.

"Hey." I turn to Mason, surprised not only by the softness of his tone but at how gentle his expression is as he looks at me. "You're right, I shouldn't have questioned your recipe. I'm sorry."

I nod, too upset to say anything for fear of breaking down. The last thing I need right now is to burst out crying in front of Mason.

He surprises me yet again in the space of a few seconds by resting his massive hand on my shoulder. "We'll fix this. I promise."

And then he spins around and moves faster than I've ever seen anyone move in a kitchen. He dumps out the pots, washes them clean, and starts dumping the ingredients into the fresh pots.

"Come on, Ruby. You've got this." He flashes the most beautiful smile. It's exactly what I need to see.

I get back to work right alongside him.

An hour later, a new batch of the glaze is simmering. I dip a spoon in, blow on it, and take a careful sip.

"Good?" Mason asks.

"So good."

He flashes a devastatingly gorgeous smile before checking on the adobo simmering on the stove. With the help of one of the cooks who just arrived, we head into the walk-in and carefully place a dozen fresh flowers on each tier of the cake. I thank the cook before he leaves to continue with the food prep. When it's just me in the walk-in, I take a moment to look at the gorgeous towering layer cake encased in pearl-white buttercream frosting. Each layer is dotted with a delicate cluster of bright pink roses, Lola Naty's favorite flower.

I start to tear up just thinking about what her reaction will be when she sees it. The most special cake for the most special woman.

"I hope she loves it," I say in a quiet voice.

I also made a smaller, simpler cake for Ate Vida, who's celebrating her fiftieth birthday today but didn't want to take the spotlight away from Lola. It's mango cheesecake, which is Vida's favorite fruit. The mangoes are even flown in from the Philippines.

When I'm back out in the kitchen, my phone buzzes with a text.

Sophie

Ruby! You won't believe whose
car I'm in right now!

Me

LOL is this a guessing game?

Paris Hilton?

Barack Obama?

Jesus?

The Pope!

A string of eye roll emojis follows.

Sophie

Oh my gosh, Ruby. I'm with Travis!!!

Me

…Travis who? Am I supposed to
know who that is?

Sophie

Yes!! Travis is the guy who I hooked up
with in the Bahamas five years ago and
ghosted, remember? Ron's best friend.

I gasp.

Me

Oh my gosh, really?

Wait, is this the Travis you said
was the best sex you ever had?

Sophie

YES

Another gasp. One of the cooks turns around and asks
me if I'm okay.

"Oh yeah. Just fine." I step out of the kitchen and call
Sophie.

"Wait, so you're bringing Travis to the party with you?"
I ask as soon as she picks up.

"Why are you calling me?"

"Because this is some juicy stuff and I wanna talk about it, not text."

"Well…I'd prefer texting…seeing as I'm in the car right now…with company."

"Come on! We can talk in code," I tease.

"Ruby!"

"Okay, okay. I'll text you."

I hang up and quickly type out a message to her.

Me

So let me get this straight. You're in the car with your older brother's best friend and you're bringing him to a huge party with your entire family? After hooking up with him five years ago and having zero contact since then?

Sophie

Yeah. It's a long story.

Me

You'd better fill me in!

Sophie

Promise I will later! How's everything going in the kitchen? You need help?

Determination hits, and I stand up taller even though my cousin can't see me.

Me

Nope. I've got it all under control.

Sophie

Can't wait to taste the menu you put together! I've been talking you up to Travis, he can't wait to eat some of your yummy food!

I'm heartened and nervous all at once.

Me

Aww you're the best! See you soon!

I check the time on my phone. Guests are due to arrive in the next half hour.

I dart back into the kitchen where the cooks and servers are gathered and waiting for me.

"Okay, everyone. Let's plan on putting the food into the serving warmers in about twenty minutes."

Everyone nods their agreement.

"Then in about an hour, we'll bring out the cake for the big reveal, which will be right before everyone starts singing happy—"

A crash sound rattles from inside the walk-in.

"What the…"

When I throw open the door, I'm frozen in shock. Because there's Lola Naty's beautiful cake mushed against the wall of the walk-in.

For a second, all I can do is stare. One-half the cake is perfectly intact. But the other half is smashed against the side of the refrigerator, completely ruined.

I can't even blink, I'm so stunned. My brain is struggling to process that the image in front of me is real and not a nightmare.

"Ruby. Shit, Ruby, I'm so, so sorry."

I glance over to see Mason standing just a few feet away, his face twisted in a pained, horrified expression.

My heart thrashes in my chest and my throat is aching with the urge to sob, but I swallow it back. "What. Happened?"

Mason blurts something about losing his balance while trying to grab the container of minced garlic from the top shelf.

Then he says something about me not having to worry, he'll figure out a way to fix it.

And that sets me off.

I ball my fists at my sides and step up to this guy who's easily a foot taller than me. He jerks back like he's terrified of me.

"Just stop, Mason! Stop! You can't fix this. You ruined the cake and I can't...I can't even..."

The sound of someone clearing their throat jerks my attention off the side. That's when I notice the door to the walk-in is open and the entire kitchen staff is staring at us.

I grab Mason by the arm and lead him to the back corner of the kitchen. In my peripheral vision, I see everyone scurry away from us, clearly trying to stay out of the line of fire.

I throw open the door to the storage room and slam it shut once Mason and I are inside. And that's when I fully let myself go. No more fake smiles, no more pretending like everything is okay. No more shoving down my anger and irritation for the sake of working together like professionals.

The most important part of this dinner is ruined. Because of Mason.

"Of course, you'd ruin another cake for me. God, it's like the universe sent you to mess up all the important events in my life. First, you no-show on our pastry final in culinary school, causing me to fail the course. Then, you destroy Lola Naty's birthday cake, and I … I just … I can't …"

I take in the look on Mason's face. It's a mix of shock and terror. Like he's observing some strange wild animal and is freaked out about getting mauled, so he's staying as still and as quiet as possible.

I shake my head. "You know what? I don't have time for this. I have to make a whole new cake now because of you."

I spin around and reach for the doorknob. But when I try to open the door, it doesn't budge.

"No. No, no, no …"

I twist and tug at the doorknob as hard as I can, but still nothing.

"Here, let me try."

At the sound of Mason's soft, skittish tone, I move to the side to let him have a turn. But even with his height and muscle, he can't open it.

I let out a laugh of disbelief that sounds more like a sob. "This can't be happening."

I tug my hair free of the messy bun it's been in for the whole day and watch as Mason starts to kick at the door. In my panicked brain-haze, I vaguely recall Mr. Kawolski mentioning something earlier about how the lock on the door to the storage room is broken so it automatically locks when you shut it. Crap, why didn't I remember that?

"Hey! Hey, you guys! We're stuck in here! Let us out! Please!"

Mason pounds on the door and shouts a few more times. I hold my breath, hoping that someone, anyone will come and free us.

But a minute passes and no one comes.

Mason finally gives up. He's panting, shaking his head while staring at the door. "It must be too loud in the kitchen to hear us. We're all the way in the back. Wait, I can call someone to come get us."

He shoves his hand in the pocket of his chef's jacket before muttering a curse.

He turns to me, his eyes sad. "I think I left my phone out there."

Frantic, I check the pockets of my jeans and my jacket, but they're empty too. I must have left my phone on the metal table in the kitchen. I shake my head and my shoulders slump forward.

My heart is thrashing in my chest. It feels like my lungs are on fire, like I've sprinted a race even though I'm standing in place.

I tug both my hands through my hair, hoping that pulling against my scalp will help me refocus and figure out a way out of this. But my mind stays blank. Hot tears prick my eyes.

I fall against the nearby wall, knocking a broom over. It lands with a sharp clank that causes Mason to flinch. But I'm too sad and drained to react. I slide down until my ass hits the dingy tile floor, prop my elbows on my knees, and cover my face with my hands. And then I finally let myself cry.

"God, look at me." I sniffle. As pathetic as I feel, part of me feels…relaxed. The stress knots in my shoulder and upper back feel loose. It's like crying helped release all of the anxiety and nervous energy I've been holding in the run-up to this day.

"I, uh, think you look great."

I let out a sad, snotty chuckle at Mason's quick response.

"No, I mean…I'm such a failure. I tried so hard to make sure that the catering for this party goes off without a hitch, and it seems like every single thing that could possibly go wrong is happening. I suck at this. My cousins were right."

I hear the sound of Mason's footsteps around me, then the shuffling of fabric. I look up to see him plop down next to me. He kicks his long legs out in front of him and rests his hands on the tops of his thighs.

"What do you mean your cousins were right? They told you that you'd fail?"

The concern in his expression is weirdly comforting. He looks like he cares about me in this moment. How strange. And wonderful.

I shake my head. "No, not like that. It's just that I'm the baby of my family. I'm the youngest of all my cousins because I was a surprise baby for my parents when they were in their forties. My whole life my parents and aunties and uncles told my older cousins to look out for me, to take care of me. Which isn't bad. It's wonderful honestly, to have your whole family looking after you like that. But it also made them view me in a certain way. I'm 'Baby Ruby.' Always the young one, always the baby, always the one that people are checking on and second-guessing because they think I'm too naïve and too inexperienced to handle anything on my own. This was going to be my chance to prove to them that I could pull off something impressive. But I've gone and locked myself in the storage closet the night of Lola Naty's one-hundredth birthday. Typical Baby Ruby."

"Hey. Don't say that."

I'm startled by the conviction in Mason's tone. It sounds like he's defending me. Wait, is he?

"Ruby, there are a lot of things that I need to apologize for and explain."

I'm taken aback. What is he talking about?

"But first I need you to know that you're not a failure. You're not a baby. You're amazing. You're in charge of catering this huge event for your family, and you're doing an incredible job."

"Yeah, right," I mutter.

"No, listen to me, Ruby." He touches his hand to my arm. "You. Are. Amazing. In the hours that I've been here cooking and tasting the food, I've been blown away. This is the most incredible catered menu I've tasted. You're such a talented chef."

"Wait … Are you serious?"

The corner of his mouth quirks up. "Dead serious. Actually, that's a lie. There's another catered event that I attended where the food blew me away."

"Okay…" I'm not sure where he's going with this.

He flashes a wide smile. "It was that gala at the aquarium last month. The food there was just as delicious."

"I catered the gala. You were there? You liked the food?"

"I loved the food. I arrived late because I had a full dinner service at my restaurant, but the hors d'oeuvres were mind-blowing. I'm still fantasizing about those prawn canapes."

He runs his tongue along his perfectly plump bottom lip and my stomach does a flip. Well, that's sexy as hell.

"I asked who did the food for the event and when they said it was you…"

"You couldn't believe it?"

"No. I absolutely could believe it because you were incredible in culinary school. I'm in awe of your skills, Ruby. I always knew you'd be a huge success, whatever you decided to do."

I feel my insides go warm and gooey at the praise Mason has just showered over me.

"I know we're stuck here right now and that really, really sucks, but try not to panic," he says after a second. "The cooks are out in the kitchen. So are the servers. The food's all ready to go, you've already given them instructions on how to serve everything. It'll be okay."

He's right. The hard part—the cooking—is done. The one remaining stress cramp in my stomach eases the slightest bit. That sharp pain now feels like a dull ache. It feels easier to breathe now too.

He gives me a soft squeeze on the arm before pulling away and resting his hand in his lap. My arm suddenly feels cold at the loss of his touch.

I clear my throat and try not to think about just how good Mason's hand felt on my body…and just how much I want him to touch me again.

He looks off to the side, his expression twisted slightly, like he's thinking about something painful.

"I owe you an explanation. For why I no-showed our pastry final in culinary school." His chest heaves as he pauses to take a deep breath. "My dad had some health issues for a lot of my life. When I started culinary school, it seemed like he was doing well. But then he had a heart attack the night before our pastry final. He almost died. That's why I no-showed."

I cup my hand over my mouth as I gasp. "Oh my gosh. Mason, I'm so sorry. I had no idea."

"It's okay. I didn't tell anyone. I didn't want anyone to know what was going on in my personal life. When he had a heart attack, I kind of lost it. My family came so close to losing him and part of me broke inside…"

His eyes shine with unshed tears. He blinks them away. "I was a total mess. I could barely function, barely remember to eat and drink. I couldn't sleep. I didn't care about anything or anyone. I just wanted to be by my dad's side for every step of his recovery. I quit going to class. Eventually, I missed so much time that the culinary school contacted me to say that I was unenrolled. I didn't even bother to call them back. I didn't care. Nothing mattered other than being with my dad and making sure that he was okay."

I squeeze Mason's hand. "Of course. Anyone would have done the same in your shoes. I know I would have."

"I probably overreacted. My dad told me a million times that he wished that I'd go back to school instead of babysitting him at home," he says. "But I couldn't. Nothing else mattered—nothing was as important as spending time with him. Almost losing him made me realize what should be my priority in life. I'd never forgive myself if I were away at school and something else happened to him…"

Mason's eyes go glassy as his voice trails off. He closes his eyes for a long moment and gives my hand a gentle squeeze, like he's savoring the contact. When he opens his eyes, his gaze is clear. "He's okay now, thankfully. He's in a lot better health."

"That's such a relief to hear."

The smallest smile tugs at his lips. "When I moved back home to take care of him during his recovery, I took over all the cooking. I made him eat only the healthiest stuff. He hated it."

"I'm sure deep down he loved that you cared enough to look after him like that. That's such a wonderful thing you did, Mason."

"I don't know about that. He'll never forgive me for making him give up fried food."

We both chuckle.

"Seriously, Mason. That's amazing how you put your life on hold to be with your dad, to take care of him."

The smallest smile pulls at his lips. "He was so happy when I finally went back to culinary school. When I told him, his exact words were, 'it's about damn time.'"

His expression sobers. "If I could go back in time and do things differently with you, Ruby, I would. I wish I could. And I know you would have understood had I told you what happened. I just… it's hard to explain. It was like

I was in this panic haze. I couldn't think straight. I don't even remember parts of my life during that time, I was so stressed and worried about my dad. I was spending night after night in the hospital obsessing over his progress and every little setback he had. For the longest time, it felt like I couldn't breathe. Not until we got him home and he started to get some of his strength back. That took months though."

I lace my fingers in his hands, hoping he can tell by that little gesture just how much I feel for him.

"I didn't realize the instructor failed you because I didn't show up," he says. "After a week of me no-showing, the administration at the culinary school called me a bunch of times, but I ignored all calls and messages back then. I was holed up at the hospital, focused on my dad. If I had known our instructor planned to fail you on account of me, I would have contacted him or the school. I'm so sorry. And I'm sorry I was such a jerk when I first got here and saw you today. When you brought up my no-showing at our pastry final, I thought you were being petty. I had no idea you failed because of me. I'd be pissed at me too if I were you."

"It's okay, Mason. Truly. I don't care about that anymore. Yeah, I was angry, but that was before I knew the whole story. I understand why you didn't show up. And I'm so, so relieved your dad is okay. That's all that matters."

This time when he smiles, his eyes are brighter. He looks a million times lighter. "Thank you, Ruby."

For a long moment, we just sit there quietly and look at each other. It's like the air in the room has shifted now that we finally cleared this up.

I breathe, and immediately the scent of Mason's spice-rain cologne fills my lungs. His palm feels hot to the touch against my skin. The look in his eyes is different too. It's like his gaze is deeper, more focused. Like he's looking right through me, to the deepest part of me. It makes me feel giddy and at ease all at once.

He blinks and glances to the side. A deep red flush creeps up his cheeks. "You know, I had a crush on you in culinary school."

I make a choking sound. "Um, what?"

"Yeah." He looks down at our hands, our fingers interlocked before rubbing the back of his neck with his free hand. Is he nervous?

"I was gonna ask you out after our pastry final," he says, a sheepish look on his face. "Obviously that didn't pan out."

"You were?" I'm blown away. Hottie chef Mason had a crush on me? Me? Okay sure, I'm cute. And when I'm not wearing a cooking smock and covered in sauces—when I take the time to dress in something pretty and put on some makeup, I can look sexy. But in culinary school, I looked like a mousy Vanessa Hudgens. Cute for sure, but I didn't think I ever registered on Mason's radar.

"I was into you, Ruby. Big time. I was amazed by your talent. You were so creative and true to your roots. I loved how you incorporated Filipino ingredients into a lot of our cooking assignments. Plus, you're hot."

I let out a very silly, very un-hot-sounding giggle. "I wasn't expecting to hear you say that."

He shrugs. His smile doesn't budge. "Just speaking the truth."

Feeling suddenly bold, I shift to fully face him. "Well, my truth is that I think you're super hot, Mason. I always have."

It's cute the way his brow ticks up like he's shocked. I'd assume someone as devastatingly handsome as Mason would get used to being called hot. I guess not.

He leans closer to me and cups my face with his hand. "So, we think the other is hot. That's good news."

I chuckle. Our faces are barely two inches apart. Mason's gaze lands on my mouth. When he exhales, I can taste his breath on my tongue. Goosebumps flash across my skin.

I start to lean forward but stop myself. "Wait, you're single, right? I mean, I guess I should have asked before moving to crawl in your lap, but we weren't exactly getting along earlier today, so I didn't think to…"

He takes my chin gently in his hand, grinning at me. "Yes, I'm single. You?"

I bite my lip and nod before gently pressing my lips against his. We move our mouths slowly against one another, taking our time, savoring the feel of our lips on each other.

Soon our tongues are licking and teasing. I move to straddle his lap and my hands end up tugging through his hair. He grips my waist, moaning into my mouth.

"Mmm. I know," I say between kisses.

"God, Ruby. You are…this is…"

Just then the door swings open. I yelp and nearly fall back, but Mason pulls me up.

"There you two are!" one of the servers—Carmen, I think?—says while standing in the open doorway.

"Yeah, um, we, uh…got locked in…"

"The door wouldn't open."

Carmen frowns down at us talking over each other to explain why she just found us in the storeroom making out.

Then she starts to smile. "Locked in. Right." She winks. "Can you save it for later? We've got a party to cater."

We quickly stand up and dart back into the kitchen, which is bustling with servers darting in and out and cooks prepping food.

"How's it all going?" I ask Carmen.

"Great! The guests are loving the food."

I let out a quiet squeal and pump my fist in celebration. Mason gives me an encouraging pat on the arm.

Carmen winces. "We're gonna need to figure out what to do about the cake though."

Mason and I look at each other. Raw determination bubbles up inside of me. I can tell by the look on his face that he's feeling it too.

"I have an idea," I say.

"I'm all ears. Let's do this, chef."

An hour later the destroyed cake is salvaged. It looks pretty damn good. Mason and I stand at the metal table, surveying the new design we improvised for the cake. Since half of the cake was totally fine, we decided to make a clean cut along the ruined back side of it and re-frost it with buttercream. Now it looks like an avant-garde asymmetrical cake. And we rearranged the rose clusters to look like they're cascading from the back to the front.

"Wow. We did it." I let out a laugh of disbelief.

"We really did. And damn, it looks incredible. Artistic, even." Mason looks at me. "This was one hell of a cake redemption. Our culinary school instructor would be proud of us working together."

I elbow him playfully before gazing at the cake once more. "Lola Naty is gonna love it."

Mason pulls me into a hug before dusting a kiss on my lips. It's not till we pull apart that we realize everyone in the kitchen is staring at us.

"Looks like you two are getting along just fine now," one of the cooks says, smirking down at his saucepan.

"We are. We just had to, um, work out our differences."

"What's what we were doing earlier," Mason adds. "In the storeroom."

Carmen flashes a thumbs up and winks. Mason and I chuckle.

I check the time. We're running a bit behind schedule, but it's all okay. Thankfully there's been loads of stuff going on at the party—karaoke, tributes, dancing, and a visit from Santa Claus—that kept everyone busy and distracted from noticing the blip. "Cake goes out in five minutes," I say before getting everything in order to deliver it to Lola Naty. I turn to Mason as he starts to walk off. "Will you present the cake with me?"

His brow raises slightly, like he wasn't expecting me to ask him that. "You sure you want me to? That's a really special moment for you and your family."

"And you're part of it. You helped salvage the cake."

He beams at me before leaning down to give me a quick kiss on the lips. My face is hot as I step back, flustered. I use the nearest shiny stainless-steel surface to check my appearance. Yikes. My makeup is faded and my hair is a mess. I pull the mini makeup kit I packed in my purse from the shelf where I set it when I first walked into the kitchen today and do a quick swipe of lipstick, mascara, blush, and highlighter. I'm in the middle of smoothing back the million flyaways in my hair when I feel Mason's hand on mine.

"Hey. You look beautiful."

There's a fiery spark in his gaze. I'm about to melt into a puddle on the floor, but then realize I have to change too.

"One sec," I tell Mason before stepping out of the kitchen and into the nearby hallway. I stop at the tiny closet where I stashed my dress and heels earlier this evening and do a quick change. It's a challenge in the small space, but I manage to do it in just a couple of minutes. When I step out, I'm clad in a gold cocktail dress and nude pumps. I smooth my hair over one shoulder and pop back into the kitchen. Mason's eyes bulge out of his head when he sees me.

"Holy …"

"I look okay then?"

He shakes his head. "Okay isn't allowed in your vocabulary when you look this good, Ruby. Try stunning."

I bite my lip. "Thank you."

I walk over to the wheeled metal cart that holds Lola Naty's cake and take a breath. "Let's do this."

Together Mason and I grip the handle of the massive cart and roll it carefully to the entrance of the ballroom. I spot Eden standing just a few feet away and give her a thumbs-up before I light the single candle on the cake. She nods and signals everyone to start singing happy birthday to Lola Naty, who's sitting in her wheelchair at the center of the low stage. While everyone sings, she smiles.

Mason and I roll the cake over to her. Her eyes go as wide as her grin. "Oh my."

"Happy Birthday, Lola Naty. We love you so, so much." I lean down to give her a kiss and hug.

"Wow! It's beautiful, apo. Like a work of art."

I tear up at the awe in her voice. The musicians on stage start playing, "Pasko Na, Sinta Ko," her favorite song. The hopeful instrumental echoes in the massive space. Lola Naty closes her eyes like she's savoring the song, the moment.

I bend down to give her another hug before Mason and I start cutting the cake. As the party winds down, people come up to me to rave about the food.

"Everything was so yummy, Baby Ruby."

"Best food I've ever had."

"I'll be dreaming about your lumpia forever."

"Oh my gosh, this cake! It looks like it belongs in a magazine!"

"You're so talented, Ruby! Wow!"

"I gave your name to all my friends who have big events coming up and need a caterer."

"Me too!"

I beam at all the wonderful comments from my family.

Eden walks up to me. "Amazing job, Ruby. I can't imagine anyone else catering Lola Naty's special day."

She hugs me before walking off.

"Well damn," Mason says. "You're a hit."

"I think I am."

Someone calls my name and I start to walk off, but Mason grabs me gently by the hand, pulling me back to him.

"I know I'm five years late with this, but you wanna grab a drink sometime?"

I beam up at him. "A drink?"

"Or dinner." He wags his eyebrow. "If you're in the mood for more."

I tip-toe up and kiss him. Around us my family cheers and whistles. "I'm definitely in the mood for more with you, Mason."

THE END

ABOUT SARAH SMITH

Sarah Smith is a copywriter-turned-author who wants to make the world a lovelier place, one kissing story at a time. Her love of romance began when she was eight, and she discovered her auntie's stash of romance novels. She's been hooked ever since. When she's not writing, you can find her hiking, eating chocolate, and perfecting her lumpia recipe.

Booklist:

linktr.ee/authorsarahs

Social Media

@AuthorSarahS

Volcanic Love

ELLE CRUZ

Volcanic Love

ELLE CRUZ

Blurb:

Sophie is a thirty-year-old with a wildly successful sex podcast. She has secretly been in love with Travis, her older brother's best friend, for years. A mistake from the past tears them apart. Sparks fly when they when they see each other five years later during her grandmother's one-hundredth birthday celebration. Sophie will have to put aside her insecurities to win back Travis's heart so she can finally have the happily ever after she's always dreamed of. Fans of turtles, volcanoes, and forbidden love (not necessarily in that order) will enjoy this lighthearted contemporary romance.

Content Notes:

Profanity

Sexual themes

CHAPTER ONE

Sophie

December 23, 1:15 p.m.

If you'd told me I was going to make a career out of talking about sex in a filthy, over-the-top way, I would have told you to seek professional help. And yet here I was, living this dream I'd cultivated from the ground up.

People were spilling out of the tiny café and lined up along the narrow sidewalk. I'm pretty sure Java Jane had never seen this kind of crowd before, and it was beyond shocking to think they were all here because of little old me: a professional sex podcaster who'd grown up in this small town of Napa, California.

I sent out a silent thank-you to Jeannie, the event manager, who'd specifically instructed me to forgo driving. Instead, I headed over on foot and came in through the back entrance. I had to walk around the parking lot and strip mall, but the extra two minutes was worth it to avoid the crowd.

"Sophie! Hey!"

Jeannie squeezed me in a tight hug, her spindly arms pinching me. "Did you see the turnout? It's amazing!"

"Yeah. Uh, it's surreal," was all I could say.

"Surreal? This is more than surreal. It's phenomenal." Jeannie swept me in through the back entrance and stopped me in front of a stack of boxes. "Our very own celebrity has returned! Everyone's so excited to see you again."

My heart fluttered. It really was a different experience coming home after everything I'd accomplished. This job, which had all but robbed me of my time and taken me away from my family for three years, was a source of immense pride. A brand that empowered women and made them stronger by harnessing their beauty and sexuality. I was redefining feminism in a new way and, as a result, had gained a million subscribers.

All this from a podcast where I talked about everything raunchy under the sun, pretty much nonstop.

Not sure how my Filipino family perceived it, because I'd avoided seeing them in person for the past few years. I was pretty sure I was going to find out very soon though.

The surreality of the situation continued.

From the moment I stepped into the café to rousing cheers to when I sat down on the stool next to my interviewer, I still couldn't believe my life. You would have thought I'd be used to it by now—getting invited to parties with celebs and influencers, getting big sponsorships—but none of it compared to coming home not as yourself but as someone else entirely.

Someone famous.

Freddie B was my interviewer. He was also from my hometown but a few years older than me. He'd made a name for himself too and now lived in Oakland as a DJ. I settled on the stool across from him. I waved to the crowd and waited for the applause to die down.

Freddie started the interview by reading my bio. I tried not to listen too closely. For some reason, I always had trouble accepting accolades. I spent so much time uplifting others and getting them to prioritize self-love, yet I couldn't really do the same for myself. Why? I wasn't sure. Maybe that was the reason I worked so hard and liked to push myself past my limits: because I had high expectations. Perhaps I was afraid that settling into happiness would take away my drive to succeed. It was a ridiculous notion, but I couldn't help feeling this way.

"It's so nice to see you again, Sophie." Freddie had a warm smile and kind eyes that lit up in a genuine way. "I heard you haven't been back home all that much since you moved to LA."

I threw him a grin and shrugged.

"Yeah, it's true," I said.

"How long has it been?"

"Since I moved to LA? About three years."

"Wow. So how does it feel finally coming back? I'm sure your family's been eagerly waiting for your return."

"I'm excited to be back. It feels great."

"I heard you came back for a special occasion," Freddie said. "Tell us about it."

"Yeah. I figured it was about time I came back home during the holidays, but there's another reason. My grandma's turning the big one hundred and my whole family's coming to town to celebrate. As a matter of fact … I see some of my cousins in the crowd."

The sight of them filled my heart with joy. My younger cousin Dean was there. His older brother, Manny, and Manny's wife, Jessica, were also present…along with their one-year-old daughter, Maggie. I cringed internally, even though I knew Maggie was too young to understand my profession and the kinds of things that could come out of my mouth at any moment. But still…maybe there was a conservative auntie buried beneath the wild child inside me. When I'd turned thirty, was there some sort of magical thrall I'd fallen under that had morphed me from a carefree young soul into a stern, finger-wagging mother figure? The thought unsettled me.

"It's nice that your family supports you. Well, I hope they won't mind if we get to the nitty-gritty of the day. Sophie Palacio, host of the infamous *She Vibes* podcast, what topics are off the table?"

"Hmm …" I'd played this little game before. These interviewers knew what I was going to say; they were just going through the motions. Whatever they wanted to talk about … I was prepared.

"Nothing," I said. "Be my guest."

"Really? So…we can talk about relationship advice?"

"Yes."

"Sex?"

"Yes."

"Favorite and least favorite positions?"

"Yes."

"Body count?"

"Of course!"

Laughter filled the room. I dug my fingernails into my knees to stop my legs from jiggling. Even though I didn't really like getting interviewed (ironically), I couldn't help but smile. The energy in the crowd was infectious.

"I think I know a topic that might make you squirm a little bit," Frankie teased.

"I don't think so," I taunted back. "I don't shy away from anything. I'm the one who came up with that segment on my show called *What's in My Butt?*"

More laughter and giggles erupted in the room. Freddie laughed too, then his eyes narrowed mischievously.

"So…we can talk about anything."

"Yes, Freddie! Anything."

"Who's Magic Mike?"

I could practically feel the blood drain from my face. And just like that, Freddie found the one topic I did not want to discuss.

I'd sorely underestimated Freddie B. The guy had balls. Maybe that was what the *B* in his name stood for. Beneath the jovial exterior was a ruthless interviewer who went straight for the soft white underbelly. And yet I only had myself to blame. The cozy safeness of my hometown had lulled me into a false sense of security. I should have been on high alert.

A few seconds of awkward silence elapsed. I made the mistake of looking into the audience. Everyone was rapt, waiting for my reaction.

I decided to play it cool. Giving away any real inkling of how Magic Mike made me feel would be a huge sign of weakness. And as Sophie from *She Vibes*, I could not show anything less than strength and infallibility.

"It was a great movie," I said. "Channing Tatum gave a brilliant performance."

"Uh-uh, you know exactly who I'm talking about," Freddie scolded me, wagging a finger. "Come on. Fess up. Who is he?"

Before I could answer, a few whispers filtered up from the crowd. I noticed some confused looks, and finally someone raised their hand.

"Can you remind us about Magic Mike?" they asked. "Some people are new here."

"Ah. Great point," Freddie said. "Sophie. Care to enlighten us? Or at least give a rundown for the newer listeners?"

I cleared my throat and sat up a little straighter.

"Okay. No problem. Magic Mike is the guy who gave me the best sex of my life. It was mind-blowing. Everything he did was perfect. The way he talked and communicated…asking me what I liked, how I wanted to be pleasured…no other guy has come close to the level of Magic Mike's sexual prowess." In my head, I also added a silent, *and no one will.*

"Yup," Freddie said. "You've had a quite a few sexual exploits in addition to Magic Mike. Like Mr. Darcy, Boomer, Shagaholic, and Big Johnny. You've spoken about all your wild experiences with them ad nauseam. But Magic Mike was different. Even though you vowed you'd never settle down, you said something about Magic Mike that really caught our attention. What was it again, Sophie?"

I pasted on a brittle grin. I was a professional podcaster. I had no problems discussing any topic, but Magic Mike was different, especially being back in my hometown. Just talking about him in the place we'd grown up together hit me in a different way. It made me feel vulnerable…and maybe a little bit scared. Honestly, I didn't want anyone finding out his true identity. It would be a complete disaster.

"That … he was the one who got away," I murmured. "I said that if hell were to freeze over and I decided to settle down…that he's the only one I'd do it for. I'd give up the single life forever for him."

My voice had practically dropped to a whisper. I'd talked about him dozens of times on my podcast, so why did it feel so different now? What kind of magic was working in the air that made my feelings so much more potent…as if I could just utter his real name and conjure him from the ether?

But who was I kidding? I'd treated him like shit. I'd loved him since I was eight years old, and the moment I'd had a chance to make him mine, I'd blown it.

And now he was long gone.

"Sophie? Sophie, are you okay?"

I rapidly blinked away the unshed tears burning behind my eyes. I pasted on another bright smile and switched gears. I had an audience waiting, and I couldn't disappoint my fans.

"Of course I'm fine." I waved off Freddie's concern. "You guys are not going to believe the Bumble date I went on last week. Strap yourselves in. It's going to be quite an adventure."

CHAPTER TWO

Travis

December 23, 7:45 p.m.

I walked into Slither Heaven on a Friday night. No, it wasn't a strip club. It was the only exotic pet store in all of Napa. Correction: It was the only exotic pet store in a fifty-mile radius.

Some people would have been put off by the smell. Unusual pets such as lizards, snakes, chinchillas, and ferrets in an enclosed space didn't make for a very pleasant-smelling environment. However, it felt like home to me. I loved pets. Especially the kind you could keep in a glass terrarium. The nerdy little boy I'd used to be loved the idea of keeping my furry and scaly little friends close by in my room. Talking to them and caring for them calmed me down. Lucky for me, my mom and stepdad had let me keep so many pets. At one time, I'd had seven snakes, an iguana, several hamsters, a bearded dragon, and a tankful of freshwater turtles. And don't even get me started on the tortoises. I'd had a whole hoard of those as a kid.

"Travis De La Cruz! Is that you?"

Mrs. Lockhart scurried out from the back room and walked up to me. Her eyes looked huge behind her Coke-bottle glasses. Was she aware she could get laser surgery on her eyes? Or was she so old she was no longer a candidate for that kind of surgery?

"Yes. It's me," I said.

A big smile spread across her face, and she gave my arms a firm, affectionate squeeze. Her smile faded into an *O* of surprise as she squeezed my arms again.

"Oh my," she said. "Have you been exercising? My goodness. When did little Travis grow up into such a hunk?"

"I'm glad you approve, Mrs. Lockhart," I said with a grin.

"Well, it's so nice to see you again, honey. I remember you used to come in all the time when you were a kid. I think the last time I saw you was when you were in high school. What brings you in? Are you in the market for a new lizard?"

"Well, not for me," I replied. "I'm here to purchase a gift for someone special."

"Excellent! Do you have anything in mind? What's the occasion?"

"A centenarian birthday."

Mrs. Lockhart didn't answer. All she could do was blink a few times in confusion as she contemplated my weird request.

"Let me explain," I said. "My best friend Ron's grandmother is turning a hundred. I'm going to her party tomorrow, and I wanted to get her a unique gift. I remember Ron telling me that her favorite animal was a turtle, but she never had one because they were too high maintenance. So, I'm here to see if you would be willing to sell Jeremy to me as a gift for Ron's grandmother."

"Jeremy?" Mrs. Lockhart's eyes went impossibly wide. "But...why?"

"Because Jeremy's a tortoise. Close enough to a turtle but easier to care for. And he's about the same age as Ron's grandmother."

Mrs. Lockhart wrung her hands. Her gaze darted back and forth as she struggled over the proposition.

A part of me felt bad for asking such a thing. Jeremy was her pet tortoise. She'd had him since she was a child, and I was sure he held sentimental value. But I was a lawyer. I had a winning mentality. A losing scenario was not an option.

"I can see you're conflicted, Mrs. Lockhart," I said. "Name your price."

"But…Jeremy isn't for sale."

"I'll give you a thousand."

The number made her gasp.

"Oh, you must be messing with me," she said, wagging a finger at me. "You've always been a peculiar boy, Travis."

"I'm serious. I will give you a grand for him."

She paused. I could see the gears turning in her head. Mrs. Lockhart stepped back. She looked me up and down, then crossed her arms over her chest. She'd been running this pet store for almost thirty years. It was successful but in a modest way. I would guess that a thousand-dollar sale in the span of minutes was a rarity for her.

Suddenly the gleam of a shrewd businesswoman filled her eyes.

"All right, boy, if you really want Jeremy, I'll let him go for five thousand."

I sucked in a sharp breath between my teeth.

"Two thousand," I countered.

"Deal!"

We shook on it.

While she scurried off to prepare Jeremy, I contemplated my decision. Jeremy was a standard Russian tortoise. The ones with rare color patterns could certainly run into the thousands, but Jeremy, even in his extraordinary old age, shouldn't have fetched more than a few hundred dollars.

Contrary to my actions, I was not a big spender. Living in San Francisco with the primary goal of retiring early threatened to dismantle my sanity every damn day. But I loved my job as a corporate litigator. I suppose I could have retired now or transitioned into a job that conveyed significantly more joy, but I loved to work. It was what I did best. It helped distract me from certain things.

I turned and looked out the window at the quaint little café across the street.

Java Jane Café. Suddenly, thoughts of deep-set brown eyes and a sexy, raspy laugh filled my head.

There'd been an event there earlier today revolving around someone very important to me, but I'd missed it. I'd gotten out of work too late.

"Come with me to the counter and I'll ring you up," Mrs. Lockhart said.

I peered into the small plastic crate. Jeremy was in there, his head and limbs tucked tightly into his shell. I would be cranky too if I were a hundred years old and forced to move to a brand-new place out of nowhere.

"I don't think I have to tell you to take good care of Jeremy," Mrs. Lockhart said. "I have no idea why you would pay an arm and a leg for an old tortoise, but I hope he's worth it."

I handed her the payment and picked up the crate by the handle. I held him at face level. Jeremy's beady black eyes gleamed in the dim lights. My heart filled with nostalgic adoration, and another emotion I hadn't felt in a long time: hope…hope that this gift would not only bring joy to the birthday celebrant but help mend two broken hearts in the process.

"Yes," I agreed. "I have a feeling he's going to be worth it."

~*~*~*~

CHAPTER THREE

Sophie

Christmas Eve, 4:01 p.m.

I was in love.

My two-year-old niece, Kali, squirmed in my lap as I lavished her with tickles. It was her fault. She'd woken up the napping auntie, and tickles were the consequence. Her adorable laugh made my heart swell exponentially. And I swear to god, my ovaries did the same thing. It scared the hell out of me because I'd vowed I would never be a mom. I'd convinced myself I was a free spirit and would never be tied down to a husband and children.

But things had changed when I'd turned thirty. Even a couple of years before the milestone birthday, I was growing tired. Well, weary was more like it. The years of dating, partying, and traveling had started getting old. Not that there was anything wrong with that life. I had embraced it, and every wild adventure had contributed to the person I was proud of becoming.

But I found myself wanting something different. I found myself thinking of him.

Magic Mike. And whenever I thought of him, dreams of settling down and having a family followed naturally.

My tickles faltered, and little Kali had no patience for an auntie with waning energy. She clambered off my lap and walked over to her tablet device plugged into its charger.

"Sophie, are you tired?" My sister-in-law, Aditi, walked into the room, her hair in curlers. Her pregnant belly peeked out from beneath her bathrobe. It made my motherly instincts flare up even more.

"No. I was playing with Kali. I was just pretending to be asleep," I said.

"When are you going to get ready for the party?"

I glanced at my phone.

"We still have a couple hours," I said. "My dress is ready, and all I have to do is throw on some makeup."

"Okay," she said. "Let me know if you need help."

I nodded as she walked back into the hallway leading to her room.

I chose to stay with my brother, Ron, and his family while in town. I could have stayed with my parents, but let's face it: I was too damn uncomfortable. Believe it or not, they didn't quite understand how big of a deal I was. They knew I was a podcaster, but they didn't listen to my content because they'd heard it was "racy." Basically, I wanted to avoid an awkward situation. It was safer to stay with my Kuya Ron.

"Hey. Why aren't you ready yet?"

Speak of the devil. Ron appeared in the living room, fully dressed in slacks and barong Tagalog, looking at me as if I'd grown a third nostril. The moment Kali saw him, she screeched in joy and held her arms out to him.

"It's only four o'clock," I said. "Why are you in such a hurry? Looking sharp, by the way."

He swung Kali up into his arms and gave her a loud kiss on her cheek.

"You're a girl, and girls take forever to get ready," he said.

"First of all, I'm a woman. Second of all, you shouldn't assume I take forever to get ready for a party just because I'm a woman."

"Assume? You think I've forgotten that we shared a bathroom for years?"

I always had plenty of ammo in the chamber when we started bickering, but I just couldn't bring myself to fire back. Returning home, doing the interview yesterday, and coming face-to-face with emotions brought on by Magic Mike all started wearing on my soul.

"Something's bothering you." Ron assessed me as he put his squirming daughter back down.

Immediately I felt uncomfortable under his gaze. His big-brother appraisal was too accurate. I could never really hide anything from him. Where it was easy for me to bend the truth and sneak around behind my parents' backs, I could never put one past Ron.

"It's not a big deal," I said.

Ron walked over to the family room and sat on the love seat across from me.

"Soph. We haven't seen you in three years," he said. "Well…we've chatted on Skype and Zoom over the years, but you refused to come home. I know your career took off and you were busy getting your life together and moving down to LA. That part I understand. But three years? Not even a single Christmas or birthday or Mother's or Father's Day was worth coming back for just one day? Soph, you're old enough to know that if something is really important to you, you'll make time for it."

My heart dropped into my stomach. Not only did he fish my insecurities from the depths of an unfathomable ocean, but he plunked my heart on the ground and beat the shit out of it with a stick.

"Kuya, today is Lola's birthday, and I don't feel like having this discussion. If I wanted to talk about this, I would have stayed with Mom and Dad."

Kali toddled over to the couch and reached for me. She had her mother's gorgeous eyes and Ron's smile. I gathered her into my arms and breathed her amazing baby scent into my lungs, hoping it would ease the worries bubbling up inside.

"You missed the first two years of her life," Ron said. "See how much she loves you? And she has a baby brother on the way. It would be nice if you would come by more often. Be more involved with the family despite your career. It's important, Soph."

I frowned and averted my gaze. I would have crossed my arms over my chest, but I couldn't because Kali was on my lap. I did the same thing every time I was the target of a self-righteous lecture. It wasn't the most mature reaction, but zoning out was a defense mechanism. It helped divert my attention from the real problems I kept buried deep inside. But I couldn't hide anymore. Ron was right. It was time to come face-to-face with the consequences of my actions.

Suddenly the doorbell rang. Grumpy, my brother's corgi, started barking up a storm.

"Ah, he's here early," Ron said.

Kali squished my face between her hands. I must have looked hilarious because she started laughing hysterically.

"Who's here?" I asked, caught in Kali's infectious fit of giggles.

"Travis."

The world stopped spinning.

Baby laughter vanished. My heart disappeared through a trapdoor I hadn't even known existed.

"*Who*?" I hissed, my eyes wide with horror.

"Travis," Ron repeated, completely oblivious to my reaction. He made a beeline to the front door but stopped cold when he saw my face.

"What's the matter?" he asked.

"Wha—how—why is Travis here?" I demanded, my voice pitched far too high. "I thought he moved to San Francisco!"

"He's back in town for the holidays." Ron gave me a strange look. "And we invited him to Lola's birthday. Why?"

Alarms went off in my head. I shot to my feet with Kali still in my arms.

"What is your problem?" Ron demanded.

"Nothing." I forced a smile and laugh, which probably did not help the situation. "It's all good."

Ron shook his head, probably wondering what had gotten into me. He turned his back on me to resume his steps toward the front door. I took that opportunity to flee down the hallway to the master bedroom, where Aditi was still getting ready. Luckily, the door was cracked, and I could see Aditi still in her robe. She was standing by her bed, looking at her phone.

"Aditi, I'm so sorry to bother you." I knocked while simultaneously entering. "I, uh…think Kali needs to go number one."

I handed Kali over to her mother and backed out of the room.

"Okay, I'll check," Aditi said, peeking into Kali's pull-up diaper. "Did you see who was at the door—Sophie?" She did a double take when she spotted me trying to slink away.

"I forgot something," I said, ignoring her question. "I'll be right back."

Then I did something I wasn't proud of. I borrowed a page from the cliché rom-com handbook. I went to the bathroom in the hallway, closed the door, and snuck out of the house through the window.

* * *

I had no plan. Here I was, a thirty-year-old woman, walking down the street on Christmas Eve, with literally no direction. I wasn't even wearing my own shoes—I had on a pair of my brother's old tsinelas I'd found in the backyard. Ron called me and demanded to know where I was, and I came up with some pathetic excuse that I had to buy feminine products at the drugstore.

I looked at the time. One hour till Lola's birthday, and I was a mess.

A text I received from my cousin Ruby made me feel even worse.

So…did you get a present for Lola?

I slapped my forehead so hard I was sure it left a mark.

Damn it, Ruby. She knew I was a horrible gift giver, and this text was just her way of helping jog my memory. But it would have been nice if she'd asked this question way earlier than just an hour before the birthday.

I had no right to be upset with Ruby though. This was my MO. I was the world's worst gift giver…if I could even manage to remember to get a gift at all. I relied on old gift cards and personal checks as last-minute resorts. But I was back in town, completely unprepared. I had absolutely no present to give my grandmother for her one-hundredth birthday.

"Fuck me," I whispered.

During my aimless walk, I had found myself back in the downtown area of Napa. Everything was in the process of closing early because of the holiday. Like a complete idiot, I wandered into the CVS drugstore and scoured the aisles. After a few minutes, I left, completely appalled. Did I really think I'd be able to find anything appropriate to get my one-hundred-year-old grandmother in a store that sold fake eyelashes, lube, and condoms?

I headed back to Ron's house. It was a good thing I knew these streets well, because I was on autopilot as I let the memories come streaming back.

Five years ago, my brother and Aditi had gotten married in the Bahamas.

It wasn't a conventional wedding where only a small handful of people went because travel was a hassle. Not even close. About one hundred guests traveled down there to attend the wedding. It was unlike any wedding I'd ever attended or seen. Joy and love were in abundance. We were in a tropical paradise, witnessing the union of two people madly in love, with one hundred guests matching that same intense, happy energy.

The whole place was electric. It was hard to describe the feeling there. I went there with every intention of flirting and hooking up with someone new and hot and exciting. However, fate had other plans.

Enter Travis De La Cruz. Ron's best friend since the sixth grade.

I'd had a crush on Travis since day one. It had started out completely harmless. For years, I was the annoying little girl not worthy of any attention or time.

But boy, did I keep my eye on Travis. And he'd grown into a gorgeous, thirst-worthy man, just like I'd known he would.

Years had passed. As adults, we'd see each other in passing, mainly at Ron's parties. We acted cordial toward each other. I would engage in polite small talk with him every now and then, even though all I wanted to do was tear his clothes off and act out every dirty fantasy I had of him.

That was why it came as no surprise that all the inhibitions vanished in the Bahamas. Like I said, there was some kind of magic in the air. The way the sun soaked every surface like butter melting on warm toast, the caress of the tropical breeze, and the scenery straight out of paradise—it was no surprise every desire was heightened to unbearable levels.

Travis was no exception. He looked good enough to eat. Combine my ever-living thirst for him and plenty of drinks from my brother's open bar…

And we'd had one explosive night.

Correction: Three explosive nights.

Hopelessly lost in my daydreams, I practically floated all the way back to my brother's house. The late December chill did nothing to thaw out the hot memories from five years ago. I received a text from Ron the moment I used my spare key to open the front door.

> We left for the party early. Sorry but you weren't responding. Don't worry, Travis will give you a ride.

WHAT. THE. HELL.

Even before I saw him, I felt that same inexplicable magic that transported me to another time and place. Sea salt air. Balmy Bahamas breezes. The heady scent of fresh, crisp cologne.

I looked up. There he was. Travis Michael De La Cruz, the object of my desires, and the man who'd given me the best sex I'd ever had.

Magic Mike had found me, and there was no escaping this time.

CHAPTER FOUR

Travis

Saint Vincent and the Grenadines, Bahamas

Five years ago, October

It was late. No one would have guessed how late it was because the party was still in full swing. The wedding of Ron Palacio and Aditi Wilson had been a raging success. The open bar might have had a little something to do with it.

Despite the series of doors open to the stunning view of the beach under a moonlit sky, the heat pervaded. All those bodies packed onto the dance floor of the resort ballroom intensified the humid summer night atmosphere. Travis wandered outside with an ice-cold bottle of water in his hand. He had intended to take a brief walk down to the shore, dip his feet in a little, and then maybe head back to his bungalow.

The sight of a woman lying motionless under a cluster of palm trees drew his attention. Fear thundered in his heart, but once he drew near, he could see the gentle rise and fall of her chest as she took in steady breaths.

It was Sophie.

His heart twisted in agony. God, she was everything. She was beauty and vice. Joy and terror. Pleasure and ruin. She was his best friend's little sister and therefore stood for everything forbidden to him. If that was true, then why did he find himself coming closer instead of walking away?

She opened her eyes and stared up at him.

"It's you," she said.

Travis didn't respond. He looked down into her face, trying to ignore the way the deep neckline of her dress and the short skirt affected him in the most inappropriate of ways.

"Are you okay?" he asked, fighting his dirty thoughts with every inch of his being. "Do you need me to walk you back inside?"

It was Sophie's turn to pause. Instead of answering, she held out her hand. Travis grasped it and helped her to a sitting position. He loosened his grip, but Sophie didn't let go.

"Sit with me," she said.

Travis sat. They were about six inches apart on the sand, their legs extended in front of them. Travis handed her the bottle of water.

"Took advantage of the open bar, huh?" he said.

"It was my idea, you know." Sophie twisted the cap off and took a dainty sip. "Ron didn't want it at first. He's super kuripot, but with a lot of threatening, I finally persuaded him."

Sophie was buzzed. It was unlike her to use Tagalog words, especially ones describing her brother's frugalness. She was a pleasant, happy kind of drunk who swayed gently back and forth in her seat. She wasn't the kind that went off on slurred diatribes and stumbled around everywhere, threatening to topple over with every precarious step. No. Despite her hooded eyes, joy illuminated them from the inside out. It made Travis happy knowing she was in the moment.

She scooted closer and leaned her head on Travis's shoulder.

He froze. Everything in his rational mind told him to put distance between them. Unfortunately, the rest of his body wanted nothing more than to get as close to Sophie as humanly possible. His rational mind was effectively outnumbered.

"Aren't you afraid of being on an island?" she asked. "Did you know that islands were formed by these huge, cataclysmic volcanic eruptions? Aren't you scared that could happen to us while we're here?"

A grin broke across his face.

"No. I never thought about it," he replied, trying to hide his amusement.

"How could you not?" Sophie demanded. "People will tell me I'm being paranoid, but it's bullshit. I don't believe for one second that all these volcanoes are dormant. They're just waiting to explode, and we'll all be caught by surprise."

"Did you have a bad experience with a volcano or something?" Travis asked.

"Not necessarily," Sophie said. "But that doesn't mean it won't happen."

She shifted in the sand, easing up even closer to Travis. She wrapped her hand around his bicep. Her face was very close to his, but she was so animated she didn't seem to notice the way her proximity affected him.

"You wanna know what I got for my brother for his wedding? A personalized table runner. And it's silver. With green-and-red bead accents. God, what a shitty gift. Do you think that's a shitty gift?"

"No. That's a nice gift." Travis's voice almost cracked when Sophie brushed her bare leg against his thigh.

"No. It isn't." Sophie gasped, her eyes lighting up under the soft glow of the night sky. "You know what would have been an amazing gift? A volcano eruption survival kit."

Travis turned his face toward her and looked her in the eye.

"Really?" he asked. "What does that entail?"

Sophie scooted in closer. She was turned toward him, her breast pressed against his arm and her leg halfway slung over his. Travis was not a religious man, but he found himself imploring the Virgin Mary to give him strength to banish every sinful thought running through his head.

"Maybe…super heat resistant personal protective equipment." Her excitement persisted. Travis was relieved she seemed oblivious to the way she made his pulse race like a flood bursting through a dam. "Some kind of hazmat-looking suit, except it was designed to resist superhot temperatures. And then an inflatable raft made of the same kind of heat resistant material so that you could ride on it instead of getting buried under a river of deadly, fiery magma."

Sophie paused for a second. She appeared to ponder her thoughts, then a smile of disbelief materialized on her face.

"Oh my god!" She laughed, burying her head against Travis's arm. "You probably think I'm the most ridiculous person you've ever met. For real though…I don't know why I give such terrible gifts. It's a weakness of mine."

Travis felt a lump in his throat. He gazed at her profile. He wanted to ease her worries…to make it so that he could right any wrong in her life.

"It's not about the gift," Travis murmured. He gently brushed aside a lock of hair obscuring her face. "It's the thought. No matter what you get someone, no matter how small, your intent shines through."

Sophie's smile faltered. A darkness rushed into her eyes, eclipsing the soft, starry illumination from the moon above. It was darkness and…heat. Travis recognized its pull, and he paused too, wondering what Sophie would do next.

He watched, transfixed, as Sophie's lips parted slightly. The tip of her tongue peeked out as her eyes trained on Travis's mouth.

"What do you think my intent is now?" she asked, her voice suddenly husky.

With his heart near to bursting, he could no longer fight the urge. Travis reached out, cupping her cheek with a gentle hand. Sophie's eyes fluttered closed as she leaned into his palm.

"I hope to god your intent matches mine."

"There's only one way to find out," Sophie replied.

She leaned in and kissed him.

He'd imagined what this moment would feel like a million times, but nothing compared to the real thing. The power of her kiss overwhelmed the voice of his conscience. It didn't matter that she was his best friend's little sister. She had a hold on him he hoped would never break.

Travis closed his eyes and lost himself in her. He knew from that moment he would never be the same.

CHAPTER FIVE

Travis

Napa, present day

Christmas Eve

I learned something important five years ago. All you need is three days to know if you're in love with someone. Day one begins with physical attraction. Not the toxic kind that gravitates toward some unnatural, unsustainable standard of beauty. No. It's as simple as a look in the eyes. A smile. The way they walk, or even the shape of a knee, or the hollow of a dimple, no matter where it is on the body.

Day two is the afterglow. Once the crush settles in, there's a rush of euphoria that follows. Their mere presence, a mere thought, or even an object can trigger those heady feelings of adoration.

Day three is the most important. It's the goodbye. Humans say farewell to each other all the time. It's the effect of the farewell that tells you if your feelings are real. It's natural for goodbyes to trigger some emotions of sadness—wondering when you're going to see the other person again. But the farewell hits different when you're in love. Instead of an emotion, there's a physical component. Emptiness. Hollowness. The sense that you're leaving a part of you behind and you can only wish you'll find it again to become complete.

I had no idea I was in love with Sophie until we said goodbye.

"Hi," Sophie said.

The strangeness of seeing her in the reality of normal life jarred me. She'd been a tanned, otherworldly siren in the Bahamas—a figment of my dreams. But in the mundane setting of Ron's living room, she was even more stunning because she was real.

"Hi," I said.

I had experienced three magical days with her that had lived rent free in my mind every single day since, and all I could do was stare.

"It's good to see you." Sophie's tone was all business. It should have hurt me, but it couldn't when I saw the way her eyes searched mine. It gave me hope that there was still a spark in her heart for me, despite how things had ended back then.

"Thanks for offering to give me a ride," Sophie said as she headed past me toward the hallway leading to the bedrooms. "I'll just throw on my dress. It won't take long."

She darted away to get ready.

* * *

Ten minutes and we were out the door. She swept past me in a long, formfitting silver dress. It wasn't nearly as revealing as what she'd worn in the Bahamas, but she was beautiful just the same.

We got into my car. Aside from a thank-you when I opened the door for her, silence pervaded. It was more heavy than awkward. Everything left unspoken and unresolved between us weighed it down.

I switched on the music on a low volume to help out a little bit.

"How does it feel to be back?" I asked.

"It's nice," she said. "I had a chance to visit my mom and dad right when I got back. I saw Lola the day I flew in, and also a few of my other relatives."

"How is your grandma?" I asked.

"She's great." Sophie's voice took on a warm, joyful tone, and it filled me with light. "She's a bit forgetful, and she doesn't walk as much as she used to, but she's good."

Silence descended again. I glanced at her. She took on a pensive mood, her gaze turning to some far-off distance. I wanted to reach for her hand and stroke her skin with my fingers…ask her what was going on behind those beautiful eyes. Instead, I gripped the steering wheel and tried not to think about how many times I'd dreamed about us falling asleep in each other's' arms.

"I guess I should have come home more often," she said. "I don't know, it's just…never mind. It sounds like I'm making excuses."

"I'm sure that's not the case," I said.

"Okay. Well, here's the truth, then. When my career took off, I didn't know what direction it was going. It sounds naive, but it's true. I wanted to be some kind of social media influencer giving advice to other young women about dating and life and self-love. But then things kind of snowballed, and I ended up with *She Vibes*. It turned out the listeners loved the raunchy content, so I ran with it.

And you know my family. Even though my mom is one of Lola's youngest, she's pretty conservative. My dad too. When they found out what I did, they tried to be supportive, but I knew that some of their friends and relatives didn't approve. As I got busier, it just became easier and easier to find excuses to not come home. I know. It sounds horrible. I feel bad, and I really want to make it up to my family."

"From what Ron tells me, they're just glad you're home," I said. "They missed you a lot."

I missed you a lot.

There was one split second I pondered saying those words out loud. Luckily, Sophie received a call just then.

I heaved a sigh of relief. I always heard in romances that two lovers who haven't seen each other in a while easily take up again where they left off. It was like no time had passed. But with me and Sophie…even though it was like fireworks between us, I didn't know if she still felt the same. Five years was a long time, and we'd both changed a lot.

But the one thing that hadn't changed? My feelings for her. The years had passed, and the fire in my heart hadn't waned. I'd left that trip with the intention of picking up where we'd left off, except there was one problem.

I didn't think she felt the same way about me.

CHAPTER SIX

Sophie

I knew I'd hurt Travis. Deeply.

I thought I'd been in denial over so many things, like how much I really cared for him. How much I wanted him in my life. How much he affected me and had helped unlock the hidden confidence I'd always had to make my dreams come true.

We pulled up to the valet at Hacienda Luz—the gorgeous, stately old hotel that my grandfather's Irish American family had owned for generations. Travis came around to open my door before the valet got the chance. Our hands touched for the briefest moment when he helped me out of the car, but it was enough to set my heart on fire.

"Thank you," I said, resisting the urge to fan myself.

I knew Travis was a big-shot lawyer in San Francisco. From the intel I'd gathered here and there from Ron, he was a partner at a large firm. Something to do with corporate litigation.

Travis was a successful lawyer, but he still dripped with humility. He was the same quiet, sweet, broody boy I knew, except he had a shit ton more money. But even then, the money never changed him. He still visited his family practically every weekend in Napa. As a matter of fact, he'd actually seen my own family more than I had over the past three years.

But one of the worst things I'd done, just as bad as not coming home—ghosting him.

The light touch of Travis's warm hand at the small of my back sent invisible shivers through me as we walked into the hotel. My jaw dropped at the sight before me. A giant, beautifully decorated Christmas tree stood in the middle of the space, twinkling and sparkling with enough holiday cheer to last another hundred years. That was the moment I switched into full-on "Christmas feeling" mode.

When we entered the beautifully decked-out ballroom, the relatives I hadn't seen in years descended. There were shouts of surprise, yelps of delight, cries of happiness. Hugs and kisses assaulted me and made me realize how much I'd missed home ... and how much everyone had missed me.

The sight of my cousins, Laceley and Cindy, filled me with joy beyond compare. We all shrieked like banshees and enclosed each other in vice grips as if a tornado was going to pull us apart at any moment. Out of all the cousins, I was closest to Laceley and Cindy because we were among the youngest of the grandkids.

I was also very close to my cousin Ruby, too, but I didn't see her around. She was probably busy doing her catering business, but I made it a point to look for her at an opportune time.

The only other cousin who was older than me but I had a special connection to was Oliver ... but he wasn't here. My stomach did a painful little flip at his absence. There'd been some kind of big blowout between him and Ate Vida and the older cousins. I didn't know the details, but I secretly hoped he would make an appearance somehow.

Somewhere in the whirlwind of relatives, one of the aunties had placed a drink in my hand and swept me away to a corner of the room. It was Tita Nancy, the mother of Laceley, Cindy, and my older cousin Drew.

"I'm so glad I got a chance to talk to you," Tita Nancy whispered. "I've been listening to your podcast. It is so good."

"You like it?" I asked, my heart bouncing with amusement. "I'm so glad."

Her gaze darted around the room as if she was looking for eavesdroppers. Then she leaned in closer.

"I tried that move you were talking about in one of your episodes," she whispered. "The Tongue Twister 3000. Oh my god. I thought your uncle's soul left his body when I did it."

I gaped at her. Heat rushed to my cheeks, and all I could do for the next five seconds was sputter and blink uncontrollably.

"I—well— Um…I'm so glad you found my advice helpful," I finally said.

Thankfully, her husband (the one who benefited from the Tongue Twister 3000), politely interrupted and spirited her away to talk to some other party guests.

Even though my aunt had caught me totally off guard, I didn't mind in the least. It was clear that everyone had nothing but love to give. Overall, it was nice being back home. Despite my absence, everyone's love made me feel like I still belonged.

My gaze strayed to Travis. He also greeted my relatives and gave hugs and kisses. But even more notable was that he stayed within a comfortable distance to me, almost like a bodyguard giving his charge a wide, respectful berth.

His protective streak sparked something warm and potent in me.

"Thanks for staying close by," I said. "That was very sweet of you."

He smiled back. My knees threatened to turn to jelly.

"You think I'm sweet?" he asked, taking a step back. "Show me you mean it."

I scrunched my brow in confusion. He pointed above his head. He was standing under a sprig of mistletoe tied to one of the potted trees in the ballroom. I narrowed my eyes at him.

"That's underhanded," I said. "I had no idea you had an ulterior motive."

His smile faded a bit, but before it could disappear completely, I swept in and planted a swift kiss on his lips. I had no clue what came over me. If Ron had been close by, he would have seen me. Of course, I wanted to do more than just give Travis a quick kiss, but instead, I made the most of the small moment between us. His eyes widened a brief second, but I turned away with a smile before I could see the rest of his reaction.

We walked into the ballroom. It really shouldn't have surprised me to see so many people, but for some reason, it still shocked me. My Lola was a first-generation immigrant from the Philippines. Right before the start of World War II, she'd met my grandfather, a white American teacher who'd gone to the Philippines to teach English to the children in poor neighborhoods. They'd fallen in love and were able to get married right when the war ended. After the miscegenation laws ended in America, they'd moved to Napa with their three kids and ended up having three more. While in America, my grandmother had petitioned others to come here from the Philippines. She and my grandfather had opened their home and hearts to help other Filipinos get settled in the country.

"Sophie."

I recognized the voice. It was my older cousin Vida, who was Lola's self-appointed caregiver. She was retired already, and Lola lived with her.

"Hi, Ate Vida," I said, leaning in for a kiss. My eyes widened as I took a step back, gawking at her beautiful purple-patterned terno dress. The short, prominent sleeves and the colors flattered her to no end. "You look stunning! I love your dress. Super sexy."

Ate Vida grinned, and the most adorable flush stole into her cheeks.

"Thank you," she said. "Lola wants to see you. Do you have time to chat with her for a bit?"

"Of course, I do," I said. I made a move to follow but stopped abruptly. I turned back to Travis. "Can Travis come along too?" I asked.

"Yes," she said. "This way."

She led us out of the ballroom and an into a large private room that looked like a lounge. Lola was sitting in her wheelchair, looking gorgeous in her barong dress. Her favorite crocheted blanket, the one with turtles stitched into the corners, was draped over her lap. She even had on a tiara that bore the number 100 in fancy rhinestones.

"Stay with Lola for a minute," Ate Vida said. "I'll be right back."

I nodded, and Vida left the room.

"Hi, Lola." I spoke as loudly as I could without shouting. My grandmother was very hard of hearing and almost blind. She was forgetful but still as sweet as could be. I bent down and grasped her hand. I bussed her cheek, and she smiled.

"Oh, who's that?" she asked.

"It's Sophie. Ate Vida said you wanted to see me. Can I help you with anything?"

"Sophie," she repeated. "Oh, you're back already?"

"Yes, Lola. You look so beautiful in your dress. Where did you get it?"

She chuckled.

"I don't know." She gestured in Vida's general direction. "She got it for me."

"I think it's time for your party to start," I said. "Do you want me to bring you out to the ballroom?"

Lola paused for a few seconds, as though pondering my words.

"No," she finally decided. "They can wait. You should come home. Your mommy misses you."

"I know," I said. "I will come visit more often. I promise."

"Oh, who's that?" She looked over my shoulder at Travis. Despite Lola's severe vision impairment, there were some things she could still see.

"That's Travis. Do you remember Travis? He's Ron's best friend. He's here to wish you a happy birthday too."

I stepped back to give Lola a better view of Travis. He came forward.

"Happy birthday, Lola," he said.

"Oh. Pogi naman," Lola said. She extended her arms and flexed her biceps. "Like Burt Lancaster, di ba?"

I stared at Travis, my eyes wide with delight. I wasn't really sure who Burt Lancaster was, but I would have bet everything I had that Travis looked nothing like him.

"Yes, Lola Naty," Travis answered. "Thank you."

"He's a good boyfriend?" Lola asked. "I remember at the wedding. You were together back then."

Travis and I exchanged puzzled looks. It sounded like Lola was talking about Ron's wedding in the Bahamas. Her short-term memory was shot, but long-term was mostly intact. Travis and I thought we'd been careful when we'd snuck around together, but maybe Lola had seen something.

"Be happy together," Lola said. "Kindness and respect. That is the secret to a loving relationship."

I should have corrected Lola, but I didn't have the heart to do it. Travis wasn't my boyfriend, but I found myself yearning for so much more. Did I want to be with Travis? My heart said yes, but my head told me the odds were against me.

I glanced at Travis, nervous about his reaction to Lola's misunderstanding. All I saw was a sweet, handsome man gazing back at me with a gleam of amusement in his eyes…and maybe something secret meant only for me?

"Okay. I think it's getting close to party time," I said, snapping out of the trance before my imagination got too carried away. "It was nice chatting with you Lola. Happy birthday."

"Did you get me a gift?" she asked.

I froze as dread squeezed my heart. I considered telling her a little white lie—that I had forgotten her gift at home—but I couldn't bear it. Better to tell the truth than let my conscience die a slow, torturous death.

"Oh," I said, my hands fidgeting. "Well…"

"Actually, it's in my room," Travis replied. "Do you want to get it now, Sophie?"

I paused. I had no clue what Travis was up to, but for the sake of saving my ass, I went along with it.

"Yes," I said. "We'll see you at the party, okay, Lola?"

"Where is Ron?" she asked. "You go get your kuya. I want to talk to him."

"You already talked to him, Lola." Vida strode back into the room and approached our grandmother. "He was with his wife and baby. Remember?"

Lola nodded even though she didn't look convinced.

"Okay. Did I talk to Andrew?"

I smiled at the way she said my cousin's name, as if the very mention of him was reason for celebration. She'd never hide her pride for having a grandson who was a senator.

"You did after the mass. Do you want to talk to him again?" Vida said.

"Maybe later," Lola said. "How about Eden?"

Travis and I slipped away to let Vida arrange for the one-to-one encounters Lola wanted to have with her many descendants. I pulled Travis aside.

"Thanks for bailing me out," I said. My heart felt light and warm as I stared up at Travis. "I appreciate it."

"I really do have a gift for your grandmother," Travis said. "I left it in my room when I checked in earlier. Come up and take a look at it."

"Why?" I asked. Heat rushed to my face. Was this some sort of ploy to get me alone in his room? "What's so special about it?"

"It's a turtle."

I laughed.

"You're joking," I said.

"Come with me and find out."

I threw him a suspicious look. Everything Travis did delighted me to no end. I had no reason to believe Travis would be lying or exaggerating, but I had to see it with my own eyes.

"Okay," I said. "Lead the way."

* * *

Travis's room was on the second floor on a terrace overlooking a grand view of the lobby and giant Christmas tree below. He opened the door and walked in.

The first thing I noticed? He'd left the lights on.

"Is there someone else in here?" I asked, my stomach sinking.

"There is." He gestured to the desk near the window. On top of the desk was a plastic terrarium with a handle on top.

"Meet Jeremy," Travis said. "Jeremy, this is Sophie."

My jaw dropped. I slowly approached the terrarium and peered inside. And what do you know? There was a damn turtle inside. A part of me was a little disappointed that "gift" hadn't been a code word for something dirty he wanted to do to me in his hotel room. It served me right for letting my head drag through the gutter every time I laid eyes on this man.

"Oh my god," I said. "You bought a turtle for my grandmother? A real turtle?"

"It's actually a tortoise," Travis replied. "You told me Lola is obsessed with turtles. I don't think she'll mind the difference. And Jeremy is about as old as she is."

That warm feeling hit me again. I looked at Travis, my heart melting into a puddle.

"I can't believe you remembered," I said. "I told you that a long time ago."

Silence stretched between us. Something felt strange and wonderful about this moment. Did I dare to believe that Travis had it in his heart to forgive me and that he still had feelings for me? Or was it idealistic? This was the one man who had my heart. If he didn't return the sentiment, I didn't think I'd be able to handle it.

Travis's gaze grew more intense. He took a small step toward me.

"Sophie," he said. "I—"

My phone rang, interrupting Travis. I wanted to let it keep ringing, but I recognized the tone. It was my mother.

"I'm so sorry," I whispered as I answered the phone. "Hello, Mom?"

"Sophie, the party's started already," Mom said. "Where are you?"

"I'm already here. I'm on my way right now." I hung up and gave a look of apology to Travis.

"The party's starting," I said. "We should go downstairs."

The tiniest flash of disappointment colored Travis's gaze, but it vanished in an instant.

"Okay, let's go," he said.

Right before we left, he draped a cloth over the terrarium and fastened a big golden satin bow on it. As he led the way out of the room, I couldn't help wondering what Travis wanted to say. Whatever it was, it sounded important. Or maybe I was just making a big deal out of nothing.

In any case, I crossed my fingers in hopes I would find out what he wanted to say very soon.

CHAPTER SEVEN

Travis

Lola's birthday was similar to a wedding. There was a slideshow with amazing photographs of her long and meaningful life. The entire room was overcome with emotion during the parts showcasing the love story between her and her husband, who had died about fifteen years ago.

There were performers singing her favorite Tagalog and English songs. I'd grown up with parents who'd never taught me Tagalog. Despite that, I loved the songs. The one that moved me the most was "Pasko Na, Sinta Ko." It was so beautiful. I didn't understand the words, but it resonated with me because it somehow reminded me of how things had ended with Sophie.

Lola also loved dancers, because there was an hour-long set featuring a bunch of different dance numbers. There were traditional Filipino dancers doing the tinikling and the Maria Clara Suite. A professional ballroom dancing couple performed the salsa, tango, and several other impressive routines I wasn't familiar with.

Next up, several relatives and guests recited speeches of gratitude toward Lola, expressing their appreciation for her generosity and her support of the Filipino immigrants she'd helped petition over the years. It turned out Lola was a human rights activist as well, having fought for civil rights during times in the past when segregation and racism had reigned in the political landscape of America.

I'd had no idea how rich of a life Sophie's grandmother had lived. All I remembered from when I was a child was a quirky, cheek-pinching old lady who'd always tried giving me strawberry candies whenever she saw me.

She was remarkable.

Lola had blazed a trail for her family and inspired them in so many ways. I saw so much of her in Sophie. I knew that Sophie looked up to her grandmother and that Lola had helped give Sophie the courage she'd needed to blaze her own path. Granted, it was worlds different from Lola's own path, but Sophie had accomplished something amazing in her own right.

Sophie and I were seated at the same table along with Ron, his family, and some other cousins. We didn't get a chance to sit right next to each other because we were still playing that game of hiding the truth from Ron.

Ron and I had played baseball together since we were five. We'd played all the way to high school, but I'd continued during my time at Stanford while Ron had stopped when he was accepted at USC.

We had mostly nothing but love for each other. Several times during our lives, we'd gotten into physical altercations. Full disclosure: Ron was a hothead. He'd matured quite a bit as an adult, but the foundation was still there. In other words, if he knew what had happened between me and Sophie—and that I still wanted her—I'd probably end up with a black eye.

But of course, I deserved it. I could have been responsible. I could have exercised self-control and not had sex with Sophie multiple times.

When it came to Sophie, all bets were off.

She was a force of nature. There were so many reasons to fall in love with her it was hard to pick just one. She could be goofy and irreverent during times she was vulnerable. But at her core, Sophie was whip-smart and wise beyond her years. Her business savvy and marketing ability were unparalleled. She had taken an unknown podcast and catapulted it to fame. Her content was controversial, and her mouth was filthy.

Yet it was all calculated. Nothing that came out of her mouth—nothing she did—was without considerable thought. It was no accident that she'd been able to take *She Vibes* to a level that no other female podcaster could…and she'd done it by herself.

And on top of it all…she was full of love. Yes, she'd made mistakes, but she regretted them deeply. I could see in her eyes and her actions that her family meant everything to her. She was passionate and loyal and generous…and off-limits. But I couldn't help wanting her still.

I stood beside the bar, sipping my old-fashioned. I would have downed several drinks by now while in party mode, but I was too preoccupied with Sophie around. I watched as she danced with wild abandon with the very young relatives on the dance floor. Her face was the picture of pure bliss as she twirled her niece, Kali, around in her arms and returned back to the crowd of small children to twirl them around as well.

She looked up and caught my eye. Pure amusement flashed in them as she beckoned me onto the dance floor. I took the last sip of my drink and joined her. She handed Kali over to me, and I was all too happy to take the little girl for a spin. I lost myself in the fun, but all the while, I smiled because I felt Sophie's eyes on me.

* * *

Somewhere in the midst of the revelry, Lola Naty decided to scare everyone half to death by getting up out of her wheelchair and doing a choreographed dance to one of her favorite Bruno Mars songs. The whole room roared with joy. Everyone got up and danced alongside her, cheering and clapping and celebrating this amazing moment. Apparently, everyone assumed she couldn't move very well anymore because of her old age. Well, she proved them all wrong tonight. Sophie told me she'd used to dance a lot in her younger years but everyone underestimated her now. It turned out she could still groove … in her own cute way.

Sophie's long black hair was mussed and cheeks rosy after the evening ended. Once again, she devastated me with her beauty, but I had to pretend she didn't wreck me every time I looked at her.

"Sophie," Vida said, touching her arm. "Lola wants to see you again. Do you have a minute?"

Sophie nodded. She was about to follow, but she hesitated and looked up at me.

"Do you mind coming with me?" she asked.

"Not at all."

I didn't mind accompanying Sophie. Not only had Ron left early due to an overly fussy Kali, but he'd seemed to not pick up on the vibes between me and Sophie at all.

We found Lola stationed beside the massive tree in the lobby, saying goodbye to the guests. She looked a little tired, but she was still smiling from ear to ear.

"Hi, Lola," Sophie said, kneeling beside her wheelchair. "I cannot believe what you did tonight! How did you learn that dance?"

"Did you like it?" Lola asked.

"Of course! Everyone loved it."

"I'm still good, you know," Lola said with a wink. "Just because I'm old doesn't mean I can't dance anymore."

Sophie laughed and gave her grandma a big hug. "You're absolutely right," she said.

"Did you get me a gift?" Lola asked.

Vida bent down toward Lola's ear. "Yes, Lola. Sophie's the one who got you the turtle," she said.

Lola smiled. "That was so nice," she said.

"Actually, it was all Travis's idea," Sophie said, looking up at me. "He remembered that you love turtles."

"Who's that?" Lola asked.

"I think he's Sophie's boyfriend," Vida said, grinning at me.

"Oh. Burt Lancaster," Lola said, flexing her arms again.

"What?" Vida said, her brow creasing in confusion.

Sophie laughed. She leaned down and gave Lola another kiss. We were about to leave, but Sophie stopped abruptly and gave her cousin Vida a hug. "Happy birthday to you too, Ate Vida," she said. "I hope your birthday wishes come true."

A lovely smile touched Vida's lips at her cousin's warm words. "I do too," Vida said.

I also wished Vida a happy birthday before we left. Despite the little interlude, it didn't escape my notice that

Sophie hadn't corrected her cousin about me being her boyfriend. I was thirty-five years old, but that tiny moment made me feel like skipping all the way to my car.

I headed off down the road. Sophie let out a contented sigh and sat back in the seat.

"That was so much fun." There was a dazed, dreamy quality in her voice that stole my breath. "Can I be honest? I was terrified of showing up today. I didn't know how my family would feel seeing me for the first time in three years."

"Really?" I asked. "What were you expecting?"

"I don't know exactly. I guess…maybe they would have made some mean-spirited or disapproving comments. Told me I was vulgar or shameful."

"Has your family listened to your podcast?"

"Umm…I know most of my older cousins and some aunties have," Sophie replied. "Ron listened to a few episodes in the first season, but then he had to stop. He said he didn't feel comfortable listening anymore. And…my parents listened to a few. Overall, I don't really know. I haven't asked, and I don't think I want to know."

"Does your grandma know about your podcast?" I asked.

"She understands that I have an important role in entertainment," Sophie said. "But she doesn't really understand the podcast aspect. To her, I'm 'famous on the radio.'"

"I'm glad she liked Jeremy," I said. "Did you see her face when your aunt put him in her lap?"

"Yes! She was so happy," Sophie said. "Ate Vida didn't look too thrilled, but at least Lola was happy. It was so cute. She didn't want Jeremy to leave her side."

"So you approve of my gift-giving talents?" I asked. "Are you still thinking about your volcano eruption survival kit?"

Sophie's jaw dropped. Even though it was dark in the car, I could have sworn I saw a flash of embarrassment color her cheeks.

"Oh my god, I can't believe you remembered that." She buried her face in her hands. "Seriously. Don't hold that against me. It was a long time ago, and I was wasted. I can't be held accountable for anything I said."

The rest of the car ride was one of the best moments of my trip back home. We just shot the breeze and talked about what we were up to—mostly information about our general day-to-day lives in our respective cities, and the ins and outs of our careers. When I rolled up to Ron's house, a deep sense of sadness hit me. The night was over, and I really wasn't sure if I was going to get the chance to see her again. We hadn't broached the topic of the elephant in the room. I didn't know why. Maybe it was because we'd both spent the last five years trying to get over what had happened. Maybe it was too awkward on her part, and she was trying to let me down easy. Besides, she had a big, glamorous life in LA.

The truth was I'd listened to her podcast. Every single episode. She had a lot of experience in the dating field, but that wasn't even close to an issue for me. She was waiting for someone named Magic Mike to come back and sweep her off her feet. A part of me wanted to believe she was talking about me, but whenever I had that notion, I ended up feeling ridiculous for daring to even entertain that thought. Of all the athletes and famous influencers she'd dated, why would she want to settle for a lawyer approaching his forties?

Sophie glanced at me. An awkward smile touched her lips.

"Well. Maybe I'll see you soon?" she said as she opened the door.

"Yeah," I said.

She got out of the car. I felt her slipping away, and it broke my heart. She closed the door, and it literally felt like she was closing the door on my hopes and dreams.

"Wait," she said, knocking on the window.

I rolled it down, my heart lodged in my throat.

"We forgot to exchange information," she said. "You know. Just in case we want to stay in contact?"

"Of course." She took my phone number down and sent me a text. "Anyway. Thanks for the ride."

I smiled and waved at her, trying to ignore the sadness filling my chest.

"Anytime," I said.

Then I drove off down the road. I didn't turn my head to look back, but I gazed at her in the rearview mirror until I couldn't see her anymore.

When she disappeared from view, a painful hole opened in my heart. It was like losing her all over again. The pain was cruel and unfathomable. I gripped the steering wheel harder as I drove down the streets that led nowhere except to a bleak future without her.

* * *

Through the haze of my sorrow, I somehow got back to Hacienda Luz safe and sound. I headed straight for the bar instead of returning to my room. I ordered a whiskey on the rocks even though I had no desire to drink it. I chose to watch the ice swirl, tracking the condensation as it trickled down the side of the glass.

I'll admit it. I was feeling sorry for myself. It made me frustrated. I wasn't used to feeling this way, but Sophie brought out all these unfamiliar emotions within me. I'd already made my peace that my opportunity had passed and resigned myself to living off those memories in the Bahamas for the rest of my lonely days.

I hated thinking about those days of torment after the wedding when Sophie hadn't responded to any of my attempts to contact her. In an effort to ease the pain of our lost relationship, I had reached out to women from my past, or anyone who'd shown interest in me. I'd gone barhopping every night, partied with my friends, allowed myself to get physical with others…but it wasn't good enough. Nothing was ever good enough…not when my heart knew it belonged to Sophie and no one else.

I'd succumbed to drowning in my very own pit of sorrow right when I got a text.

The text. It said:

Can you please come over?

It was from Sophie.

Five simple words, but they had the most complex effect on my heart.

After wasting two precious seconds rereading it to make sure I wasn't hallucinating, I threw a few bills on the bar to more than cover my tab and booked it out of there.

The adrenaline pumping through my veins brought me surging back to life. The pain that had once swallowed my heart seemed to disappear. Hope dawned again. The excitement overshadowed all sense and reason to the point that I'd almost forgotten how late it was. Just about three in the morning. Hmm. It would be poor form to knock on their door. Just then, Sophie shot me another text:

> The gate is unlocked. My room is through
> the glass door by the pool.

So we were like two high schoolers sneaking around. I was down with that.

With as much care as a CIA agent infiltrating the inner sanctum of Al-Qaeda, I got out of my car and snuck to the side gate. The groan of the gate's old hinges shook the entire night. The stakes were high. I knew what would happen to me if Ron caught me.

Fortunately, nothing happened when I let myself into the side yard. No dogs barked. No motion sensor lights flooded the area. Instead, I saw the sliding glass door Sophie referred to. I rapped it gently with my knuckle.

"Sophie?" I whispered. Through the glass door, I saw her turn around. She was standing in the middle of the room. Right when she saw me, she rushed over and slid the door open. With my heart hammering in my chest, I stepped inside and let her slide the door closed behind me.

"We have to be very, very quiet," she said. "Grumpy sleeps all the way down the hall in Ron and Aditi's room, but he has good ears."

"Grumpy or Ron?" I asked.

"Both."

She gestured for me to sit on the floor, and she sat cross-legged in front of me, looking beautiful in her long nightgown. She hugged a cushion to her midsection as she looked at me.

"This is so weird—asking you to come over in the middle of the night. But I couldn't just walk away from you," she whispered. "I treated you so horribly, and I couldn't bear doing it to you again."

These were the words I'd been waiting five years for. I'd wanted an explanation. It had left me angry and frustrated a long time ago, but I'd come to realize it would do no good holding a grudge. Especially since we'd never really been together.

"I want to tell you I'm so sorry for ghosting you," she said. "It's…there's no excuse for it. What I did was awful, and I don't blame you if you…if you hate me."

She filled her lungs with a shaky breath before going on.

"When I saw you today, I was so afraid you would hate me. But then I realized I deserve it. You've been nothing but kind and respectful. You even did the sweetest thing in the world—you not only got my grandmother an amazing gift, but you saved me from looking like the world's worst granddaughter. You've been nothing but amazing and thoughtful and wonderful. I don't know what I've done to deserve your kindness because I don't deserve it. At all.

"If I weren't a coward who chose her career over love, I would have called you back," she went on, her words freezing like blocks of ice in my chest. "I would have chosen to be with you. But instead, I was selfish. And I'm so sorry for hurting you. I'm so sorry, Travis."

She turned her gaze to the ground. Her silence squeezed me into a pile of nerves until I realized she was crying.

"You probably don't even really care," she murmured. "You're this big-shot lawyer in the city. You were a baseball player at Stanford. You can have any woman in the world, and here I am thinking I have any effect on you at all. God, this is embarrassing."

"Stop, Sophie."

The sound of my voice made her look up at me.

"Listen. The way you treated me…I'll admit. It was shitty, and it hurt. Especially after everything that happened between us in the Bahamas." I let out a rueful chuckle. "I thought we could be something more. I didn't understand what was going on with your career at the time. I didn't know the amazing things you were trying to accomplish. Instead, I thought I was at fault somehow. But of course, looking back, I can understand why you did what you did. I can only imagine how hard of a decision it was to make. Just know that I don't begrudge you for choosing your career, especially based on how amazingly successful you've been."

There was so much pain in her eyes, pain I'd underestimated. It spurred me to go on.

"Here's the truth, Sophie. It's been five years since we last said goodbye in the Bahamas after that amazing weekend. But in my heart, not one day has passed…because I'm still every bit in love with you as I was back then."

Her glistening eyes widened as her breath seemed to catch in her throat.

"I don't hate you," I said. "I feel the opposite even though it's strange. I shouldn't feel so strongly after all the time that's passed, but I do."

Sophie clutched her pillow, and silent tears trickled down her cheeks. She was so lovely I wanted to capture her in my arms and never let go.

"I'm still so in love with you, Travis," she whispered. "You're the one I've been waiting for. It feels like I've waited for this moment forever. You see…I had this vision of us together on repeat since the Bahamas: us lying in each other's arms, watching the sunset. I was so blissfully happy with you. That's why I called you Magic Mike. You'll never know how sorry I am—"

The admission took just a second on her part, but it reverberated in my head a million times. *I was Magic Mike?* I couldn't believe it. In the space of a second, I relived as much of her podcast as I could that had to do with Magic Mike.

He was the best sex of my life.

He made me feel things I only thought existed in fantasies.

He's my real Prince Charming.

He is literally one of the hottest guys I have ever seen.

No one compares.

And now I knew the truth of it all.

I closed in.

Our mouths were a breath apart.

"I've been waiting five years to kiss you," I murmured. "You have nothing to be sorry for."

She closed the space between us and pressed her lips to mine. The salt and sweet of her came through and made every sense, even the ones that had lain dormant, come blazing back to life.

Our mouths clashed as we drank and tasted each other, eager to make up for the years lost. I eased her to the ground but not as gently as I'd hoped. The desire in me seemed to destroy any finesse. She grunted when she thumped against the rug. Her eyes widened in surprise for a moment.

"I'm so sorry," I breathed, gently smoothing my hands under her head. "Are you o—"

She crashed her lips back against mine, silencing my apology.

Her body was so soft and pliant under me…perfect in every way. I tried so hard to control myself, but it was no use, especially when she wrapped her legs around my waist and pressed herself against me.

Suddenly we were back in the Bahamas. There were no inhibitions, no thoughts to the consequences. We were blowing the rules to smithereens and letting the pressure of our hidden desires explode forth, like a bottle of champagne in an earthquake.

Her hands…good god, her hands. That was what I'd remembered, and what I'd missed so much. Her hands were so eager…exploring every part of me she could reach. She was bold and curious. She wasn't shy…not in the least. When her hand skimmed down my abs and grasped me through my pants, I almost lost it.

"I want you, Travis," she whispered against my lips as she tore at my clothes. "I want to feel you inside me again."

My mind was a mess. The part that was Ron's friend screamed at me to stop, get my hands off her, and run away like the devil was on my heels. But then I remembered what had happened the last time I'd listened to reason:

I'd lost her.

Five years ago, I'd let her silence dictate our destiny. Instead of persistence, I'd chosen complacency. I asked myself, *Why didn't you reach out to her again? Why did you give up so easily?*

I had no good answer for it. Maybe my wounded pride had won out. Or maybe I'd been scared that all she'd wanted was a one-night stand and that my heart wouldn't recover if I found out she wanted nothing more from me.

But now I knew the truth. She wanted me as much as I wanted her. All these years, she'd felt the same exact way I did, but we'd had to wait for the right time.

And the right time was now.

I hauled her against me until there was not one inch of space between our bodies. I slid my lips down her jaw and nipped at the tender skin of her throat. She gasped and held me tighter as I ran my hand up her nightgown and gripped the soft curve of her ass.

I wanted to get even closer. I wanted to consume and be consumed by every beautiful part of her. I gathered the hem of her nightgown in my hands and eased down her body, but something went wrong. As I was positioning myself to pleasure her, my foot caught the leg of the bedside table. It tipped over and hit the tiled floor with a crash.

The barking started. My life flashed before my eyes.

"Sophie? Are you okay?"

I had no idea how fast Ron got his ass down to Sophie's room. But when he knocked and threw open the door, I did have an idea of what he would do to me.

Sophie and I scrambled to our feet. She tugged her nightgown back into place as I did my best to hide my erection.

But there was no fooling Ron.

"Ron, what is going on—" A bleary-eyed Aditi showed up in the doorway. Her eyes widened when she realized what was going on. "Oh my."

"What are you doing in here?" Ron demanded, pointing a finger at me. "Are you…are you messing around with Sophie?"

"No, it's not that," I said. "It's—"

"Dude, how could you do this?" Ron said, his face twisted in shock. "How long has this been going on? Behind my back? This is…gross. You've known her since she was a kid."

"Ron, please stop," Sophie said. "Can you give us a moment?"

"Like hell I'm gonna give you a moment," Ron said. "This is my house."

"Ron." Aditi gave him an imploring look. "Come back to bed, babe. Sophie's a grown woman. I think she's got the situation under control."

Ron's temper visibly eased with his wife's words. His eyes were still full of murder, but he unclenched his fists.

"Goddamn it," he muttered, rubbing his eyelids as if to scrub away any images of me and Sophie together. "I can't look at you guys."

"Ron—" I said.

He didn't even acknowledge me. He turned and left. A big knot formed in my gut at the disappointment in his voice. I made a move to follow him, but Aditi stopped me.

"It's okay, Travis." Aditi grasped the knob and started closing the door. "He's your best friend and Sophie's kuya. He'll get over it."

With a final wink and smile, Aditi closed the door all the way.

You would have thought this interruption ruined our moment.

It didn't.

Determination filled Sophie's beautiful face. It was out in the open now. I felt bad for traumatizing Ron, but the burden of hiding my feelings for so long had lifted and liberated me. She rushed at me and jumped into my arms, wrapping her legs around my waist.

"Let's go to your hotel room," she said.

She didn't have to tell me twice.

EPILOGUE

Sophie

Saint Vincent and the Grenadines, Bahamas

One year later

My scream ripped through the jungle, scattering the birds and sending monkeys fleeing through the treetops.

I sailed down the zip line at an alarming speed. The wind whipped my hair into my face as I held on for dear life to the harness.

The zip line trip couldn't have taken more than thirty seconds, but it felt like my entire lifetime. My feet hit the platform, and the tour guide unsnapped my harness once I regained my balance. My eyes landed on Travis, who was doing a poor job of hiding his amusement. I swatted his arm as I gave him a death stare. Then I stormed off.

"Babe, don't be mad," he said. "You did it. You conquered one of your fears. I'm so proud of you."

"Yeah, but you're laughing at me." I could feel him keeping pace beside me through the sandy jungle, but I kept my nose turned up in the air.

"I'm not laughing at you. I'm laughing with you."

I yelped as Travis swept me off my feet and over his shoulder.

"Ahh! Who the hell do you think you are? Tarzan?" I cried.

"Yes. Me love Jane," he said, giving my bottom a hearty smack.

* * *

Right about now, I knew it had been a horrible mistake to involve Travis in my new podcast segment, "Conquering My Fears." So far in the past few weeks, I'd let a tarantula crawl on my face, eaten two mouthfuls of a raw onion, given one of my friends a pedicure, and sung karaoke in front of total strangers. And now I'd faced my fear of heights with this zip-lining atrocity. The segment was a hit with my listeners. I didn't know how they would take the news that I was officially off the market. I was afraid it would be the death of my podcast, but instead...

It was a hit.

When my listeners finally found out the identity of Magic Mike and learned about the true story behind us, they went wild. Not only did I gain a stronger following, but my listeners proved how loyal they were. It turned out they loved a story of evolution and growth. And how better to show the development of a serial dater than seeing her settle down with her one true love?

But back to the fear conquering. I'd asked Travis for help in developing this segment, and he'd eaten it up. He'd strategized the content and made it his mission to help me curate a series of the highest-rated episodes in my career.

We'd decided to celebrate our "hookup" anniversary back at the scene of the crime in the Bahamas—on the same island where my brother had gotten married. After the zip-lining fiasco, Travis had another surprise fear session for me. He wouldn't divulge the secret no matter how much I cajoled him.

So here I was, riding in the back seat of a Jeep as it rocked wildly back and forth up rocky terrain. I was blindfolded and crawling out of my skin.

"Are we almost there?" I demanded, grasping the knot of my blindfold. "I can't stand this thing anymore."

"No, babe. Not yet," he said, brushing my hand away. "Almost."

Lucky for me, "soon" meant about five minutes. The moment the car door opened, I was hit with a curtain of heat.

"What in the world is going on?" I asked as Travis untied my blindfold. "Where are we?"

I felt Travis's hand supporting my back as I looked down. We were standing at the edge of a huge crater, looking down into a vast valley of steaming rock. Bright-red cracks of angry magma surged down below. I let out a scream and stumbled back.

"You brought me to a volcano?" I shouted. "You're telling me there's an active volcano on this island? Hell no. I want off!"

I tried to run. Travis caught me and held me in a big bear hug, gripping my wrists.

"Ha! I knew you were afraid of volcanoes," he said. "You wouldn't admit it, but you really are."

"You know all about me and my irrational fears already," I cried. "Does me being afraid of volcanoes actually surprise you?"

He held me for a few seconds. The tension melted from my muscles when his lips pressed against my temple, and his thumbs caressed my wrists.

"Shh," he crooned. "The geothermal energy from the volcano can have some positive effects on anxiety. Just stand here for a minute and watch the lava flow down below. It's really satisfying."

If there was anything that could trump my irrational fear of volcanoes, it was videos of satisfying stimuli. I gazed down and fixed my eyes on a rolling clump of magma flowing out of a fissure. I became transfixed. Travis was right. It really was satisfying.

"Sophie," Travis said.

"Hmm?"

"Sophie. Look at me."

I looked at Travis. He'd released me. He was down on one knee, with a small velvet box in his hand. My world burst into disbelief, then melted into pure joy.

"You're the best thing that's ever happened to me, Sophie," he said. "You make life better in every way. Anywhere you want to go, I'll follow you. And for your information, I got the blessing from Ron, your dad, and Lola Naty. Sophie Natividad Palacio, will you marry me?"

He opened the box and slipped the emerald cut diamond ring on my finger. Two bright red rubies framed the brilliant center stone.

I'd be lying if I said I'd never dreamed about this moment: my knight in shining armor, Magic Mike himself, down on one knee, asking me to be his forever. It wasn't a happily ever after just because I'd loved him since I was a child. It was my happily ever after because Travis was the one meant for me. Not once had he ever tried to change who I was. He was proud of me—with my raunchy podcast, filthy mouth, and all. Fierce devotion shone in his gorgeous eyes every time he looked at me. He made me feel loved and treasured, the way I deserved.

It was the epic love story I'd written for myself that had come true.

"Yes," I said as the tears started to flow. I flung myself to my knees and hugged Travis with all my strength. "Yes, I will."

THE END

ABOUT ELLE CRUZ

Elle Cruz is an author of contemporary romance. She has a bachelor's degree in English and a doctoral degree in nursing. By day, she works in the medical field, but at night, she writes swoon-worthy stories perfect for all the hopeless romantics out there. In addition to being an author, Elle is active in the writing community and loves to mentor and give advice to new authors. She has a supportive husband and two amazing children.

Booklist

How to Survive a Modern Fairytale

Catching Feelings

Pasko Na, My Love

Forevermore

Love at the Fiesta

Social Media:

@ElleCruzAuthor – Facebook and Instagram

The Deal

TIF MARCELO

The Deal

TIF MARCELO

Blurb:

Prodigal cousin Oliver Moore returns to Hacienda Luz to attend Lola Naty's hundredth year birthday party only to find out that he's not on the guest list from divorcée event planner Norah Sha. In catching him as he tries to break in, she feels sorry for him and makes a deal to sneak him in, both discovering Christmas can still bring forgiveness and new love.

Content Note:

Profanity

CHAPTER ONE

Ollie

Oliver Moore's heart thrummed in his chest, and it had less to do with the hollow drumbeats coming from Hacienda Luz's ballroom and the giant Christmas tree in the middle of the lobby blinking multicolored lights. It was the fact he had yet to steel himself to walk into the party in said ballroom.

A line had formed at the podium situated in front of the ballroom's double doors, manned by hotel workers wearing black polo shirts and Santa hats. The doors were open, and beyond the threshold was a brightly lit room with people walking past. He caught sight of barongs, tuxedos, and long flowing dresses made of silk and lace.

Then he looked down at himself, wearing dark jeans, a Henley, and a puffer vest.

"Shit," he said.

The couple in front of him turned. Ollie didn't recognize them, though he smiled back.

He didn't know what was worse, being completely underdressed or not recognizing the people attending his grandmother's hundredth birthday party.

Both.

All of it at the same time.

The line shuffled forward, though he didn't follow suit. His feet refused to move, and his nerves had balled up and nestled themselves at the base of his throat.

Gah. He should've tried to call one of his cousins sooner than tonight to let them know he was coming. He would have known about the dress code then. But his phone call earlier to Ruby, the baby cousin of the family, though in her late twenties, hadn't gone exactly as he'd planned. She'd literally hung up on him.

Insecurity bloomed in his belly, and it triggered the runner side of him (literally and figuratively), to get the hell out of there. It was rude to show up underdressed. It was obvious he wasn't needed here—the fact that the party had gone off without a hitch was proof of it. His cousins were probably still pissed at him.

Correction: they *definitely* were, seeing as he hadn't spoken to them in months. To boot, he hadn't come home for a year.

His heart and head continued to jostle for dominance as he stood there seconds longer. And just before his head won out, the musician in the ballroom started to sing. The song: "Pasko Na, Sinta Ko."

At the tune, his heart grew twice its size and crowded out the rest of his thoughts. "Pasko Na, Sinta Ko" was his grandmother, Lola Naty's, favorite song, though, truth be told, Ollie never had understood why because it wasn't a happy song at all, despite the hopeful instrumental. He and Lola Naty had debated the lyrics time and again when he was younger, and the fact that it was being sung at this very moment meant that it had to be a sign.

He couldn't phone it in. He'd come too far and practiced this moment too often for him to turn around now with his tail between his legs.

He had prepared himself for the criticism from his cousins that he'd done little to help coordinate the party.

He'd pumped himself up for the questions that always seemed to come his way, like *"When are you finally going to get a real job?"*

And, he'd readied himself for the hug from his grandmother, because that was going to make everything worth it.

So, with the two meticulously wrapped presents in his hand—thank goodness for gift-wrapping services this time of year—he strode forward to the podium when his turn came, and walked right on by.

"I'm a Moore," Ollie said flippantly as he passed one of the hotel workers, catching sight of one of his nephews singing alongside the musician. It made him grin; memories of him and his cousins taking their turn at the mic rushed back.

They were a close bunch despite their large span of ages, since Lola Naty had six children, and by God, he missed them.

He stepped across the threshold of the ballroom...

Only to be stopped by somebody.

More specifically, a gorgeous woman with dark hair draped over her right shoulder. She was of Asian descent and had brown eyes, golden-brown skin, and plump kissable lips. Though that was neither here nor there, because those lips were pressed into a line of pure disapproval.

"I'm sorry, you can't just enter," the lips said. They were painted a berry color, more cherry than strawberry. His mind went straight to wanting to see if she tasted like either.

"Sir?" the lips said, and this time, their stern tone reached his conscious mind.

His eyes darted upward to her eyes. "Excuse me?"

With a hand, she gestured to the podium, shaking her head. "Please return to the podium."

He didn't understand what was going on. Was he a kindergartener waiting his turn on the monkey bars? And yet, he shuffled back to the podium, shrugging at the people waiting in line. They were dressed to the nines and were clearly not impressed with his Lands' End ensemble.

Too bad for them because he was family.

The hotel worker—Norah, as labeled on the tag pinned on her shirt—thumbed a tablet on and asked, "Your name, please."

"I said who I was. I'm a Moore."

She swiped up on the tablet's screen. There was a hell of a lot of names on this list. Soon, she got to the letter M. "Your first name?"

"Oliver."

Behind her, a glob of young teens passed by the doorway. Ollie raised a hand to get their attention, though they paid him no mind. Squinting at the crowd, he tried to find someone he knew. The family was extensive. Surely a cousin or an aunt or uncle would pass.

A sliver of guilt ran through him. He should know everyone on this guest list. How did it get this bad?

"I'm sorry, but I don't have your name here."

His vision swept down to Norah. "That's impossible. There must be a mistake." Except, inside, his initial foreboding had begun to bloom.

They wouldn't have cut him out of the guest list, would they?

He knew his reputation was shot with the family—he'd never been able to overcome this image they had of him as the lackadaisical, unserious, playboy cousin. Who even said playboy these days?

They did.

He also knew that he'd ditched in the middle of planning this party, even after committing to it, and he owed them an explanation.

But surely, *surely*, his cousins weren't vindictive.

Or were they?

He shook his head and said, "Can you check again? There are a lot of people with my last name. That must be at least half the list. But I'm on there."

Norah's face was impassive, and after a beat, she scanned the list again. "I…I apologize, but your name isn't on the list, and I have strict instructions for entry."

"Can you get someone in there? They'll tell you. My family owns this hotel!" He pointed over her shoulder and spotted his cousin Drew Hizon, looking down at Gel, his ex-girlfriend, who was wearing a fancy gown. They were standing so close that he could feel the intimacy from here.

But Drew and Gel had broken up years ago.

When in the hell did they get back together? Why didn't Drew tell me?

"Next," Norah prompted, gesturing a set of guests forward, waking Ollie from his runaway thoughts.

"Wait!" Ollie waved to the double doors. "There's one of my cousins. Drew! Andrew!"

Faces in the foyer turned toward him, but he didn't have a lick of care. He was a Moore, dammit. "Don't you have something with all the photos of the family members? Having to prove who I am is ridiculous. Drew!"

Except Drew didn't hear him, and he and Gel disappeared deeper into the room.

Then the double doors shut in front of him.

He looked to Norah, who had a hand against the closed door. "Why'd you do that?"

"As I said, this is by invitation only, and I have strict instructions for entry. Perhaps you can call someone inside the event and they can come and check you in?"

"I tried." Ollie said, though as the words left his mouth, panic rose within him. Because he'd changed his phone number recently—a consequence of a toxic relationship gone awry, and hence his disappearing act until he could get himself together—and he only had one number memorized. It was his baby cousin Ruby's, who had the easiest number to memorize: 415-222-1212.

And she'd hung up on him earlier.

But the bottom line was as clear as the lyrics of "Pasko Na, Sinta Ko." echoing through the closed double doors.

Ollie had been shut out.

He backed up from the podium now, face hot with embarrassment, and watched as more people were admitted. People who were strangers, allowed into his family's inner sanctum. And yet he hadn't been.

He deserved this, right? It was his fault. He hadn't fulfilled what he'd promised to do. Every Moore cousin had made a commitment in both dollars and time to this party, but he'd simply been unable to. He just didn't have the finances for it. He'd been stuck in a relationship that had taken him away from the family. A relationship that had taken every bit of him to escape from.

Ollie had been ready for some pushback today, just not as drastic as this.

How many times had his cousins, his parents, his Lola Naty told him how family was forever? That forgiveness and understanding were paramount? That in this world, the only people one truly had were their family, blood or found. He'd certainly done his share of meeting people halfway. Each one of the Moore cousins was stubborn and headstrong and individualistic, and growing up with them had taken all kinds of patience.

And yet, underneath the excuses that threatened to bubble over, the truth burned bright.

He could have done better.

Hell, he was trying to do better now.

As he clutched the gifts, irritation wormed through him. He was going to get in there, come hell or high water.

It was at that moment that a woman accidentally dropped the contents of her purse on the ground next to the podium, and Norah bent down to help retrieve them. It was as if a spotlight had beamed his answer, and the double doors became a target. Ollie's legs propelled him forward, with thoughts of his family as his motivation.

Until he was dragged back by a strong hand on his shoulder.

"Whoa there," a deep voice cautioned.

Looking up, Ollie was met with the snarl of a man twice his girth and a head taller. This person did not have the hotel's logo on his shirt, but a singular stitched word in all caps: SECURITY.

His body slackened.

Oh my God, he was getting kicked out. He was *really* getting kicked out of a family party. "This isn't right." He was in full begging mode now. "I should be in there. This is a misunderstanding. I'm Ollie Moore. Ask someone."

"That's something you'll have to take up another way," the security person said, gripping Oliver by the elbow. He felt like a rag doll being dragged out of Hacienda Luz—the hotel he'd all but grown up in.

All the while in a state of shock.

CHAPTER TWO

Norah

Norah Sha limped down the employee hallway with her jingle-bell Santa hat in hand as soon as she was relieved by another hostess, eager for space and to put her feet up. A blister on the back of her right heel was screaming at her, all from today's preparations for Naty Moore's hundredth birthday and Christmas Eve celebration.

This is what you wanted, her conscience reminded her.

I wanted the promotion, not the searing pain, she countered.

Still, she was mollified by the reminder. It was her first big function after being promoted as Hacienda Luz's event supervisor, and perhaps she had been too eager to run around everywhere instead of delegating as she knew she should have. But she'd wanted to make sure that her boss saw how appreciative she was of the opportunity. And, at the very end of it, she wanted Mrs. Moore's event to go off without a hitch.

Norah heaved a breath just as the party event planner, Eden Rosales passed her, and plastered a smile on her face. They'd worked closely together on this event, with Eden taking on all the details of the actual events and Norah supervising the hotel staff and equipment in support of it.

Eden was organized and on point and, most of all, calm. The opposite of what Norah was feeling. But she was a sight for sore eyes after the commotion she'd left upstairs. "Hey! Everything good?" Norah asked.

Eden held up an iPad. "Backup device. Had to charge the other one. But everything is good. No sign of the party winding down."

Norah laughed. "No kidding. I think the older ones are going to outdo the teenagers."

"Well, last on the list is Santa's visit, and that's sure to wake up anyone who's fading away." She frowned, eyes dragging downward. "Are you…okay?"

"Uh-huh." Norah only then realized she wasn't putting pressure on her right foot. She shifted and straightened, wincing on the inside. Though fibbing was not her MO, last thing she wanted was to give the impression that she wasn't keeping up. So, she waved a hand in the air, all nonchalant. "Darn no-show socks. The right sock's at my toes. It's why I'm headed to the break room. I have an extra pair in my locker. Maybe I'll have more luck with it."

"Believe me, that's happened to me more times that I can count."

"For real." And yet, when Norah looked down, she noticed that Eden was wearing heels. *Heels*, whereas Norah was wearing black no-slip walking shoes.

Norah needed to step it up.

Thank goodness for their phones buzzing at the same time. It was their shared calendar—also Eden's idea— which told them that there were thirty minutes until the Santa event. It reset the moment, and they bid goodbye with the decision to meet again at entrance B of the ballroom to help usher in Santa and his elves.

Relief was only a few feet away, with the break room door in sight, and Norah beelined toward it. She pushed down on the bar handle, though as she took a step through the heavy door, she heard her name. The voice that said it, though an alto, worked on her like nails on a chalkboard.

And yet, she had no choice but to turn around.

The hotel general manager, Mr. Kawolski, strode toward her in his penguin suit. He was a white man, balding, with a gaunt expression. Like most everyone who worked at Hacienda Luz, he was competent and professional, but unlike most, Mr. Kawolski seemed to carry the world's worries on his thick black eyebrows. As usual, they plunged downward in suspicion, and he had his own iPad in his hand. The Santa hat on his head didn't soften his demeanor one iota, even if every step toward her was punctuated by a soothing jingle-bell sound. Without preamble, he said, "It's not time for your break yet."

"I need to change my socks." Norah's answer came out with more bite than she'd intended, but he was still speaking to her as if she were a newbie and had to be managed. "I've been here all day, and I skipped my two breaks." *Not to mention all the breaks I missed with other events*, she added mentally. But Norah wrangled her tongue to keep from spilling forth the rest of her complaints.

Her employment at Hacienda Luz began a couple of years ago, when she and her then-husband officially separated. She'd intended for it to be a side job, but the perks had her asking for more and more shifts. She loved prepping and sometimes giving input about the events. Through them, she had been able to escape her sometimes chaotic life of co-parenting a teenager with a man who thought being a father required only a once-a-month appearance.

Now that she was divorced, this position was the stepping stone for a better life. And she didn't take a single thing for granted.

She added, to soften the moment, "Is there anything I can help you with, Mr. Kawolski?"

"Please make sure that there's another person staffed at that podium. I've a feeling that event crasher won't be the last one. I want everything up to code."

Norah wanted to raise a finger to tell him that *up to code* wasn't quite the idiom to use—it was his favorite thing to say, about everything—but refrained. "Already done. I left two at the podium just now, as well as security."

Truth be told that situation with Ollie Moore—if that was even his real name—had shaken Norah up a little. In the two years she'd worked at the hotel, she'd never seen security do their duty, and part of her had felt pity for the guy.

Because if he really was Ollie—and if she remembered the family tree, it would make him the son of the Mrs. Moore's third child—then the drama must have been bad for him not to have made the guest list. Every Moore was on that list, as well as friends of friends of the Moores.

"Good. Security and privacy have to be our utmost priorities after that fiasco," Mr. Kawolski said, nudging Norah out of her thoughts.

"Understood."

"And you're okay?"

The man's concern surprised her, and she said, "Yes, I'm fine."

Finally, Mr. Kawolski nodded, releasing her from his proverbial grip, and she entered the break room. She grabbed the first aid kit from on top of the lockers and flopped down on the couch. Peeling off her right shoe and sock, she spied the open pink blister, hissing at the sight.

Maybe it hadn't been a good idea to break in her new shoes during this event. Or grabbing a size that wasn't quite right. But the shoes were on sale. And one did what they had to do.

The wound needed to be aired out for a few minutes, so she crossed her right ankle over her left knee. As she fanned the blister with an open palm, she checked her phone for texts. None were from her son, Braeden, who was spending Christmas Eve with his dad.

Braeden had a tendency to clam up on these visits. She texted him:

Norah

Happy Christmas Eve!

Proof of life pls!

Miss you

Braeden

Things are good

Dad and Lisa have been ok

I'll send pics

I hope you have fun at that party at least

Norah set her phone face up on the arm of the sofa and leaned back, relieved that Braeden was in somewhat good spirits. Her gaze wandered to the ceiling. Her body sank into the cushions, though her mind churned. While she'd told Mr. Kawolski that she was fine, the Ollie Moore situation had bothered her for another reason. Norah had detected the pain in Ollie's expression when he'd realized he hadn't been included on the guest list.

Norah knew that pain down to her bones, the pain of being turned away. Of being rejected. Of realizing that what one thought was real and unflappable was actually fragile and vulnerable. She hadn't been able to make it through her divorce, through that phase of crushing low esteem, without the kindness of friends.

Of strangers.

Once, in the middle of being in debt to her eyeballs with her family lawyer, her debit card was declined at the grocery store. The person behind her had simply slipped past her to pay for the groceries, in cash.

Part of her wished that she could have done more, maybe to help Ollie Moore. If nothing else, let him know that whatever he was going through, it would get better.

The second break room door, the one that led to the outside, opened with a bang, and a figure stumbled forward with a grunt. Norah sat up on the couch, stunned at the sight of the man who had earlier been thrown out, all but executing a judo roll. Sweeping back the hair that had fallen over his forehead with his fingers, he stood to his full height and stiffened when he saw her.

Oliver Moore.

"Oh, hi," he said.

"Hi." For a beat, Norah was stunned, not only with surprise, but with how she'd apparently conjured him. Okay, so maybe she was also staring at him because of how goddamned good-looking he was. Though sorely underdressed, he was easily the handsomest man of the evening. His features were those she'd become familiar with while working with the Moore family: light brown skin, high cheekbones, brown hair with streaks of light in between, and a distinctive sharp jawline.

He was so handsome that had she not been on the clock, and if he wasn't a Moore, she might have offered to buy him a drink at the bar. Sadly, it had been *years*. This black hole of celibacy had not been her choice. For so long, she just hadn't been in the mood, caught up with starting her life over with Braeden.

This man could fill that black hole.

As if he heard her thoughts, an eyebrow shot up. Then he said, "You're from upstairs."

"Yes." She was still breathless. Then she remembered that in order to access that secondary door, he would have needed a key. She grabbed her phone from the couch. Her thumbs clicked through to her recent calls. Her thumb hovered over the name Up To Code, aka Mr. Kawolski.

He raised a palm. "Wait. N…no…don't call anyone. I'll just be on my way." He pointed to the door across from them. The one that would lead him to the employee hallway, and then to all the internal doors of Hacienda Luz.

"How did you get in?"

He lifted a hand. From his finger hung a clump of keys on a ring.

"Where did you get that?" A decision tree appeared in Norah's head. Maybe dialing 9-1-1 was better. But were the police necessary, and would calling them create a bigger commotion? It was Christmas Eve. And the party, it would be ruined.

"I can't tell you." A sheepish smile appeared on his face.

"Well, it doesn't matter." *Mr. Kawolski it is.* Apparently, the staff had been breached. "I'm calling my manager."

"No, please. Hear me out," he said, inching sideways toward the door, like a small child trying to fool his parent. "I tried to call my cousins, like you guys told me to, and it's probably so damn loud in there that no once's seeing my texts and calls. And I changed my number recently. I bet that's the reason why all of them, a hundred percent of them, didn't answer." His Adam's apple bobbed in what she could detect was disappointment and even sadness. His eyes were glassy. His cheeks were red.

"So, no one answered? Or texted back?"

"No. And I can't not be there tonight. It's my Lola Naty's birthday, you know."

"Yes, I know." This event was the largest and most important of the season. Everyone at the hotel was on call tonight because the ballroom was filled with VIPs, from government officials to tech CEOs. In turn, every valet was here and all the parking spaces were packed. There were no vacancies on the property or in local partnered hotels.

"And I am the favorite grandson."

Norah's stance went from guarded to relaxed because this she found funny. She cackled, crossing her arms. "And that's why you aren't on the guest list?"

"I didn't say I was everyone else's favorite." His lips pressed into a line, and what looked like regret passed across his features. "But I'm still family. I'll show you Ate Vida's Facebook page. Hold up, let me show you." Seconds passed as he plucked his phone from his puffer vest and swiped up with a thumb. "See?"

The screen was presented to her, and sure enough, his face was there among Vida's and the other cousins' faces Norah recognized. "Okay, so I believe you, but it still doesn't change that fact that not only are you not on the guest list, but you somehow bribed or maybe stole keys into the building. Which is highly illegal."

"I mean, if this building belongs to my family, wouldn't this make this my key? And for the record, I didn't steal it. It was within my reach, and I simply fingered it off the security guy's belt. It was helpful that all the keys are labeled."

That earlier pity she felt for this man? It left the building. It left the county of Napa. Because this guy? He was slick.

"And you can simply turn your head, like you didn't see me," he continued. "I'm not trying to do anything illegal. Or, not really. I just want to make sure I can see my Lola and give her a birthday present. Ate Vida too, because it's also her birthday. Then I can be on my merry way."

"I…can't allow that. The event is closed, and it's for good reason. There are too many people in there who are important. Even if you did get back up the stairs, you can't simply walk in. There's extra security inside, and all staff are walking in through one specific door. The others are blocked by security."

His eyes flashed with excitement. "So, you know exactly how to get in?"

She winced at her mistake at showing her cards. "I do."

He rushed at her, stopping short at a few feet away, eyes blazing. "Will you help me? Please."

"Absofreakinglutely not." The idea was preposterous. "I could get fired. And unlike most of those folks up there, and you, for that matter, nothing has been handed to me on a silver platter. I need this job."

His eyebrows lifted into his forehead. "Wow."

She clamped her mouth shut at her judgment. She was just tired. Tired doing everything right and perfect so she could barely get by in her life, while he flippantly asked for a favor that could obviously change it for the worse. "Sorry. I didn't mean—"

"No, you're right. *I'm* sorry for suggesting it. I put myself in this situation and I need to take myself out of it. But I need to think. Can I sit?"

The sag in his shoulders softened Norah, and she nodded. When he came round to the couch, he said, "What's up with your foot?"

Her face flamed hot and bright. "It's nothing."

Stepping forward, he bent down. "Ouch. That looks painful."

She tried to hide her right foot behind her left, but as she did so, her balance betrayed her. So instead, she stood as proudly as she could. "It isn't a big deal. I'm just about to put a Band-Aid on it."

"Hmmm." His eyes wandered to the first aid kit on the couch. He sifted through its contents with a finger. "Have you ever taken care of a blister before?"

"I mean, yeah. What person hasn't?"

Norah thought twice. In truth, she'd taken care of blisters by staying off her feet, but in this case, she would need to get back into her same ill-fitting shoes from earlier, and just the idea of it made her grimace.

"Then you know that you have to build some cushion around blister."

"I was planning on doing that."

Not really—she'd been planning to suck it up until she got home.

He pointed to the couch. "Sit."

"What?"

"Sit, please."

"I can take care of my own blister."

"Yes, but you don't understand that this is something I'm good at. I'm a long-distance runner, and I went through a hiking phase recently, and I can do this pretty quickly." Ollie took his place on one side of the couch. "And though your predicament could really allow for me to escape, I can't leave knowing I could have helped."

Norah did what she was told. In truth, it would probably take her twice as long to fix her wound. And though this Ollie was a stranger, he was indeed a Moore, and that had to count for something.

He patted his knee like she was supposed to put her foot on it. A giggle escaped her lips.

"What's so funny?"

"This is way too intimate. I don't let anyone just touch my feet."

"I helped a ton of people on the trail with their blisters. Once, I even pulled a tick off someone's back." He grinned.

"A tick? Gross." She shivered, and it was enough to dash away her initial hesitance. She settled her ankle on his knee, and he donned the disposable gloves from the first aid kit. He turned her ankle gently to get a good look.

His hold on her foot was confident and yet gentle, and immediately, Norah felt comforted. She committed the moment to memory, because this was the strangest way to spend her Christmas Eve.

"It looks like it may ooze. So, after I create the cushion, I'll put a layer of gauze on top. That okay?"

"Sure."

He got to work, cutting a hole in the moleskin. His expression turned serious, and the quiet was almost unbearable to Norah. It was the hardest part of being single and an empty-nester—that the house was still. These days, the TV was turned on to the cooking channel twenty-four seven.

"What do you mean on the trail? What trail?" she burst out to fill the silence.

"The Pacific Crest Trail. Or PCT for short."

"Wow." She straightened. "I know what the PCT is. You hiked the whole thing? That's like a thousand miles."

"Over twenty-six hundred miles." He halted, looking up for a beat. "Though there was a section of the trail that was blocked, so I hitched a ride around it. Other than that, though, yep."

"Why would you do something like that? I can barely go through a shift without a blister." She half laughed.

He shrugged. "I guess it's for the same reason as with many who have done the PCT. Looking for something."

"Did you find whatever you were looking for?"

"Yeah." He peeled the backing from the moleskin and pressed it against her heel. Lifting her foot, he inspected it. "It's why I'm here, I guess. I have a lot to be thankful for, and I wanted to make up for some things. Except, it's not quite turning out as expected. Hmm, you need another layer of moleskin."

"Thank you." She inspected his profile, thinking about how to approach her next question. This Ollie was a nice guy. What on earth had he done to not be invited to his grandmother's party? "Why aren't you on the guest list?"

He was back to cutting moleskin. "Let's just say that I'm not great at keeping in touch. I…missed all the planning for this. Though I had a good reason. But more time passed, and there was my pride…"

What he was saying was vague, but Norah didn't push. She knew what it was like to be in strife with family. It was only now, years later, that she was starting to heal with hers after having been isolated by her ex. So much misunderstanding had built up over time, though it all boiled down to the fact that she and her family hadn't talked enough. Being with a man who was domineering eventually had stopped her from reaching out to people.

Ollie pressed another layer of moleskin over the first and covered the whole area with a large Band-Aid. "Voila!"

"Wow. This is…great." She turned over her foot to view his handiwork. Definitely better than what she could have done.

"Not a problem. It will be slightly uncomfortable when you put on your shoes, but it will buy you some time until your shift is over. As soon as you get home, air it out, and hopefully you'll be on the mend tomorrow." He took her foot off his lap, and when he let go, she missed the contact immediately. It had been nice to have been taken care of. It had been nice to be reminded that someone else could take charge.

"I don't know how to thank you," she said.

"I know exactly how you could help me," he said with a heart-stopping grin.

The truth dawned like sunrise over the Pacific Ocean, and she gasped. "I can't believe I fell for that. Here I was, thinking you were helping me out of the goodness of your heart." She tugged her sock on, feeling foolish. After steeling herself, she placed her foot into her shoe. To her surprise, she wasn't met with pain.

But she wasn't going to fall for him. No, she wasn't!

"I didn't help you just so you'd let me go," he said.

She shook her head. "Uh-huh. And that sob story about finding yourself on the PCT and why you weren't on the guest list? And hoping to make up with your family?" She tied her shoelaces. "And here I was, actually feeling sorry for you."

"Look, none of that was a lie either. I'll prove it to you." He stuck his hand in his pocket and took out a piece of paper. He unfolded it. "See?"

Norah peered at it from a distance. Was that... "It's a paper napkin."

"It's my speech. Sort of." His gaze dropped to the floor. "It's what I'm going to say when I saw my cousins." The napkin fluttered as he shook it. "Go on, read it."

~*~*~*~

CHAPTER THREE

Ollie

Ollie rubbed his hands together and paced as Norah read his apology speech scrawled on the paper napkin. He'd written it on the plane en route to Oakland Airport in a sudden burst of inspiration, and after some liquid courage.

Though now, he wasn't sure if it was as good a speech as he thought when he'd written it, considering how Norah's face had turned to stone. It was a far cry from how she'd looked on the couch, which was vulnerable.

Vulnerable and beautiful if he was telling the truth.

He wasn't sure what had come over him to help Norah with her blister, except that she'd looked exasperated when he'd busted into the room. Add her refusal for any kind of help, and well, it was all he wanted to give her. And she had been right, it was an intimate gesture to tend to her heel, and the experience had been very much unlike when he'd helped others on the trail.

Those thru-hikers had nothing over Norah though, who had something about her, something he couldn't put a finger on. Normally, he'd go for the flashy, the outspoken, the heart-on-your-sleeve kind of person, and Norah was as closed and as private as a person could get. And yet, she'd been able to draw his worry out of him, so much so that he was now trusting her with his apology note.

It made him want to get to know her. And find out whatever was going on in her head.

Norah set the napkin on the couch and met his gaze.

"So?" He bit the inside of his right cheek as he waited, though she remained silent. "Is it that bad? Oh God. It's bad, isn't it?"

"No, it's not bad. Not bad at all."

Except, her expression was not encouraging. In fact, it was *dis*couraging. "But…"

She heaved a breath. "But now, I don't know what to do."

He was confused. "About what?"

"About how I'm supposed to allow you into the ballroom."

He was hearing things. His expectation was that he'd eventually have to muscle his way through to the ballroom. But this… "Are you serious?"

"I am. And I might regret it. But I can't not let you apologize to your cousins. And your grandmother is turning a hundred only once in her life, and I know that Mrs. Moore would love to see you. She loves all of you."

"This is…this is amazing!" He leapt to her as she got to her feet. Out of instinct, he opened his arms, stopping short of making his mistake. "Oh, sorry. I was just about to hug you." He stepped back.

Color rose to her cheeks, "It's fine, Ollie. Anyway." She heaved a breath. "I will help you, but we have to do it my way. Because I can't lose my job."

"Yes, sure! I'm down for whatever way."

"Here are the rules," she said. "I'm going to let you into the anteroom to the ballroom. Once you're in the anteroom,

I'll leave. It will be up to you to head in and find the first person you know who's in charge to vouch for you. Got it?"

He nodded fervently. The plan was good. Better than good. "Yes, okay, agreed. Thank you."

"You understand that I will fully deny knowing you. I will deny helping you. If you're caught by security, that's your problem, not mine." To his surprise, she closed the space between them. Heat sparked in his belly as he noticed the slight wrinkles around her eyes and mouth. He wasn't great at telling ages, but she seemed to be his age, in her midforties, and in her features he read experience and thoughtfulness. The initial attraction he'd felt meeting her for the first time deepened with gratitude. She was risking her job to help him.

"Yes, of course." What she'd said earlier came back, about him being privileged. And while he'd always been portrayed—and yes, okay, acted many times—like a spoiled rich kid, he didn't want to be that person.

He stuck out his hand. "Maybe we should start over. I'm Oliver Moore."

Her lips quirked into a smile, sort of. "Norah. Norah Sha." Her handshake was firm and confident, and her gaze trailed down his body. And it wasn't in an ogling way, more that it was interrogative.

"Yep. I think you're the same size," she said.

His smile slipped. "For what?"

"The uniform." She dropped his hand, then made her way to the other side of the break room, where a wardrobe stood. She opened the door with a squeak and rifled through it. "The only way this will work is if you look like one of us"—her head tilted up to the clock on the wall—"and it just so happens that the Santa event is beginning soon.

So…" She hummed, then whipped out a hanger with a squeal. She peeled off the black polo and tossed it to him. "Here. Put this on."

He lifted the shirt. On the left-side lapel was an embroidered name. *Kyle.* The size: small.

Ollie groaned inwardly. He was a medium. He rubbed the fabric between his hands. The fabric wasn't cotton, but polyesterish with very little give. "If it even fits."

From the hallway came the sound of voices. Norah's eyes rounded into panic. "Put it on now. It's my boss."

He didn't think twice after hearing the urgency in her voice. He peeled off his puffer vest and long-sleeved shirt, then lifted his T-shirt over his head.

"Oh my God, lemme turn around," he heard through the fabric of the shirt. When he lowered his arms, Norah's back was to him.

He slipped the black polo over his head and tucked in the shirt in time for the door to open. Three people stepped in. One was unlike all of them, an older gentleman wearing a tux.

"Mr. Kawolski," Norah said, though her voice sounded more like a squeak. She gestured to Ollie. "This is … Kyle."

"Are you new … Kyle?" Mr. Kawolski's beady eyes slid from him, then toward Norah.

Her cheeks were flushed, though she'd plastered on a smile. "He is one of the temps I hired for the party. Cleanup and such."

"Well, you're late. Not up to code." He was all but spitting. "We needed you hours ago during dinnertime."

"I apologize," Oliver stuttered out.

"We're headed up to the ballroom to assist for when Santa makes his entrance," Norah said.

"Nope, not so fast." He held a hand up. "It's exactly why I'm here. Santa and his elves need help in conference room C. Looks like their agent has turned up drunk, and well, if we can't wrangle them, they won't make it to the anteroom at all. Surely the both of you can handle that?"

"Not a problem," Nora said. She went to the door and gestured Ollie over with her chin. "We'll head that direction."

"Good. I'll send security to the anteroom to help when you arrive."

To his relief, Norah's boss brushed past them and headed down the hall, in the other direction.

"That was close." Ollie pulled at the neckline of the shirt. He felt like sausage stuffed in casing.

"Too close."

"So, off we go to the anteroom?"

"No, we can't."

"Why not? It's so close."

"And then what? You're just going to walk in? Did you hear what Mr. Kawolski said? He's sending security to the anteroom. The same security that threw you out earlier. And if I'm seen with you, that will be the end of me. The best thing is to head to Conference Room C, and maybe we can walk in with Santa and the elves, and you'll go unnoticed with all the commotion."

Oliver mulled over his choices, realizing he really didn't have any. But for the first time since arriving in Napa, he was filled with hope that things were going to work out. And it was all because of Norah. "Okay, then. Let's go."

CHAPTER FOUR

Norah

To get to Conference Room C, one had to exit a side door and walk about a hundred meters on a stone pathway to another, smaller, building. Norah was glad for the sound of crickets when they reached the outside, to drown out the competing thoughts in her head.

Because this Oliver? He was hot. She'd been unprepared for him to slip off that shirt—which he had done so with such ease, which meant he was comfortable in his own skin—and she all but melted on the spot. He had that mix of muscle and mass, of hard and soft. And her eyes... they'd started to follow that trail of hair from his belly button to...well...

And then that apology letter. Oliver's scribbles were illegible in some areas, but she had gotten the gist of what he was trying to say. He was sorry for what he'd done. So sorry and so nervous about apologizing correctly that he'd written it on a paper napkin.

So caught up was she with these two things—and the fact that she didn't notice even a twinge of pain on the back of her heel because he'd been an angel for fixing her up— that she'd decided to help him.

Which might be detrimental to her in the end.

Why did she do this?

She had been like this with her ex—so eager to please. So eager to fix, to take charge, so eager to risk. What if this was the wrong decision?

Her thoughts stuttered to a stop when she felt a hand on her elbow. She turned to Ollie. "Yes?"

"I just wanted to say … that I know that you can lose your job by helping me. That you could have made one phone call and had me thrown out right on my butt. I really do appreciate your help. Honestly, seeing my family will make my Christmas. It will make my year."

Him reflecting back the risk she was taking made her heart skip a beat in worry, but she waved it away. "Well, Christmas is a good time to start over, I guess."

"Are you starting over too?"

"I have been." And with that thought, she smiled. For all the complaints she'd had, especially today, everything she was doing at this very second was her choice, and that was something to celebrate. Two years ago, it hadn't been so. She'd felt suffocated under her ex's thumb. "It took me a long time to figure out what I wanted, and while I haven't realized all my dreams just yet, I know I can take my time to do so, and I can enjoy what I've made for myself."

Still, something nagged at her. "Can I ask you something?"

"Sure."

"As much as that apology letter told me a lot of what you're feeling, you haven't really said what happened between you and your cousins. Was it just because you didn't help out with the party? It seems … drastic to disinvite you because of that."

He tugged on the shirt, clearly uncomfortable. "It's complicated."

"Is it really complicated?" She shrugged. "Because everyone's got something going on."

After a few steps, he finally said, "I am … what some would call a flake."

"That's … harsh."

"It's the truth." Again with the tugging. "They really wanted me to step up to help make this party happen. It's a big affair."

"I can see."

"And … in the beginning, there were meetings. Where we divvied up duties, when we discussed costs. I went all in and gave them a commitment that I would contribute equally."

"You mentioned that."

"But there's more. I agreed to all those things knowing I didn't have the money, but I didn't have the courage to tell them. You see"—he cleared his throat— "I had the tendency to get into relationships where I was taken care of. It was all fun and games that way, I guess, until my last relationship, when it went sour. And toxic. I was planning my exit from the relationship at the beginning of the party planning. When I finally stepped away, there went all the money, I guess." His voice had dipped to a whisper. "And how was I supposed to explain how I'd gotten so dependent on a person? I was ashamed."

"Hence why you went on the PCT?"

"Yep. It was my escape. Literally. It was a good thing to hike the trail—it kept me from going back to that relationship. It also kept her from finding me. But it also kept me from calling the family. At a certain point, I thought showing up would be more meaningful."

They had gotten to the double doors of the next building, and Norah used her badge to scan them in. Inside, a myriad of voices bounced against the walls, in addition to blaring Christmas music. But before they could move forward, she had to know his status now, because she felt for him. She felt akin to him and his journey.

"So, you came here after hiking the trail?" she asked.

"Detoured a bit. I moved myself to a new place, landed on a startup who didn't mind a rusty coder. But in terms of my family? I'm realizing that I'm almost a little too late." Ollie's voice cracked, and he stepped ahead of her, as if ditching his admission by the sidelines. Norah felt the weight of his regret from the isolation, from this loneliness.

She reached out to him, against her better judgment. She understood this feeling, just from another point of view.

Her fingers brushed against his arm, and he turned. "Miscommunication can break families apart. We think we're all alone in our pain, but everyone, at their core, really wants to talk to one another, wants to be able to understand. But somehow, it feels easier to think that we're alone with this. I don't know why we do that to one another.

"And though I don't know you all that well, I've worked enough with the Moore family to know that the love is big among you all. If your apology is real, and if you can explain and reflect back on what you're apologizing for, then you might find some peace with them."

"It's not that easy to open up."

She half laughed. "You're preaching to the choir. But I know it's in you."

His expression softened. "Thank you."

"Of course."

The moment between them was heavy with more. Norah had the need to tell him her story. That at times, all she'd wanted was a real apology, and how that would have gone so far in her marriage.

It wasn't about wanting to be right in a marriage. It was about finding what was right between her and her ex—the nuance of forgiveness even if at the outset, right and wrong should be black-and-white.

But the door slammed open, causing her and Oliver to jump back in surprise. A person clad in green stepped out, huffing and with a sour expression. "That's it! I'm done. This place is out of control!" He spun around.

At the same moment, she and Ollie burst out laughing because the person standing in front of them was an elf. Mariah Carey's *All I Want for Christmas* blared from the conference room.

It was surreal.

"Great." The elf swiped his pointed hat off his head. "You're laughing. Another thing I didn't sign up for."

"Okay, okay. Sorry." Norah attempted to stifle her giggles, and after one last snort in which she took a big breath, she gestured with her arms. "Calm. So, what's happening?"

"That! *That* is happening." He waved toward the open doorway. "He does this. He does this *all* the time."

"He?"

"Santa. Why does he get to choose the pre-party music? And Larry is blitzed, and Santa is too by the way, in addition to being a jerk every day of the year."

"Who's Larry?" she asked.

"Our agent."

"Right …" Norah started, though she was stumped. It was clear that nothing was going to be solved, nor would Santa and his elves would be at the party if she and Ollie didn't deal with this elf. "Show me."

As they followed the elf into the conference room chaos, it became very clear that it would be all hands on deck. Santa was drunk, half dressed in his costume, dancing on one of the tables along with who she presumed was Larry, a slim man with his Oxford shirt unbuttoned to the middle of his chest. The rest of the elves were running amok.

"Now *this* is something I never thought I'd see," Oliver whispered.

"Same," she said through gritted teeth. "Thank goodness you're here with me."

And with a blip of a thought, she realized that she meant it.

~*~*~*~

CHAPTER FIVE

Ollie

It took the two of them to corral all the elves together and their combined effort to herd the entire group to the threshold of the double doors that would lead to Lola Naty's birthday party.

Oliver was sweating, and it wasn't in a sexy way. It was the shirt, which he realized was currently covered in bits of tinsel and fuzz. But looking at the group now, at how somewhat decent they all seemed to be despite what had transpired in Conference Room C, he couldn't help but laugh.

What a difference a few minutes made. And for that matter, what a difference a night made. None of it would have happened without Norah. Next to him, she was beaming, and it was quite possibly the best thing he'd witnessed all night.

"My cheeks hurt," she commented. "I've never been part of anything so funny."

"Same," he said, and realized that it was true for him too. He'd been on a mission to get to this party. It was the carrot that kept him going on the trail and through this unbelievable night. But Norah was the surprise.

Oliver let his shoulders relax and said, "Honestly, I thought you were going to knock Santa out."

"I almost did. Then I remembered that there are four hundred people waiting for him in there." She shifted on her feet, though she didn't meet his eyes.

It gave Oliver pause. Norah had been so straightforward with him. It was what made her so compelling. For her to not look at him now meant there was something more. And perhaps, as usual, he had been only thinking of himself. "Norah."

"Yeah?"

"Back there, before we had to deal with Santa, you had more to say."

"Oh, nah." She waved his thought away like it had been a fly. "It's nothing."

And yet, he couldn't let it go. Despite the commotion around them, all he could feel was what was unsaid. If his instincts were right, she understood him somehow, even in the short time they'd spent together. "Look, we just cajoled Santa from going rogue. If that wasn't a bonding experience, I don't know what is." he said, voice softening. "You don't owe me an explanation, so you don't have to tell me a thing, but if and when you're ready to, I'm listening."

She lifted her eyes to him then, as if making a decision. "I was just going to say that an apology isn't enough if there isn't a commitment for change. In my marriage, I would have done anything, worked even harder at it, had my ex's apology been real. I would have bent truths and moved mountains had my feelings been acknowledged. I would have lived in the gray if I had known he was trying to be better."

Her firm declaration stunned him into silence. His respect for her doubled, tripled. How honest she was being, after overcoming so much.

He'd been raised and surrounded by strong women in his life, though he never fully understood until now.

It was probably because the romantic relationships he'd had had been less than stellar.

Or perhaps he never really gave people a chance.

Or maybe he hadn't been completely honest with what he wanted and needed for himself.

But right now, he was seeing Norah in a completely different light, despite the dim hallway.

"Two minutes to showtime." Mr. Kawolski's voice interrupted his thoughts. Down the hallway he stalked, followed by others wearing the Hacienda Luz uniform, including the security person who'd kicked him out earlier. He was obviously not in the Christmas spirit, face scrunched into a frown. Quite the opposite of Santa, who had begun to hum another Christmas carol and was still three sheets to the wind.

"Oh no. Hide." Next to him, Norah stiffened. Her hands gripped his forearm. "Go, closer to the front of the elves. I'll try to keep everyone in the back."

"Okay, but …" Ollie's belly turned at how quickly things were happening. He was being shoved to the front. The colors of everyone's costumes, the myriad voices. The triumph that finally, finally, he was going in. He was going to see his family. He was going to make things better between them. "Thank you."

"We're even. A fixed foot for a foot in the door."

"Totally even." He opened his arms instinctively once more, but this time, she stepped into his embrace. She wrapped her arms around his neck, and he breathed her in, in gratitude. "Hopefully, this doesn't come off as too cheesy, but you're my Christmas gift."

Falling back on her heels, she looked up at him. "My son wanted me to have a good time tonight, and I did. So, I guess you were mine too."

He bent down and leaned in, testing their closeness. He didn't want to overstep. Still, an overwhelming urge surged through him to show her, somehow, how much she meant to him.

It was she who made up for the distance and pressed a kiss against his lips. It was brief, chaste, but said it all. That this time together had been meaningful for her too.

Then the ballroom doors opened, and he was scooped up by the crowd.

Norah fell farther behind him. They both raised their hands in farewell.

He pulled the paper napkin from his pocket. It was indeed showtime.

When he saw his Ate Vida, the eldest of the Moore cousins, sitting to the right of Lola Naty's wheelchair at the head table, he rushed to them. When Vida saw him, confusion, anger, and remorse flashed through her eyes. As he neared, Lola Naty's gaze was bright, and an arm rose to beckon him in.

Oliver's heart grew to the size of the ballroom. He stuffed the paper napkin back into his pocket. He wouldn't need it.

~*~*~*~

CHAPTER SIX

Norah

Norah watched Oliver from afar, though the warmth of their kiss had remained. She pressed her fingers against her lips.

She couldn't believe she kissed him. But she harbored not a single ounce of regret. Tonight was confusing and dreamy and exactly what she'd needed. She'd meant it when she said that Ollie was a gift. That Christmas spirit? She was feeling it. She was living it, finally.

Beyond the elves, Santa, and the festivities, Ollie stood among a small group of people, a few of whom she recognized, including Vida Moore, the eldest of the cousins, and of course Mrs. Naty Moore, the guest of honor. And though Norah couldn't hear what Ollie was saying, she knew that he was speaking from his heart. Then came a round of hugs, the sight a gift she hadn't known to ask for.

"Why is Kyle speaking to the Moores? Is something going on?" Mr. Kawolski sneered.

"That guy looks familiar. But it's not Kyle," Justin, lead security, said. "Wait. He was the guy trying to crash the party. Oliver Moore."

"So why is he wearing our uniform?" Mr. Kawolski stepped in front of Norah, blocking her view, properly snatching her attention. "Norah? Something is definitely not up to code." The lines on his face deepened with his frown.

Norah took deep breaths. She hadn't quite thought of how she was going to explain herself if she got caught.

So she would need to accept it. Accept that she'd made another decision out of haste. And now she would have to face the consequences.

But the strange thing about it was, she wasn't afraid.

"Norah, let's head down to my office. Now," Mr. Kawolski directed.

She nodded, turning to follow him to the anteroom.

"Wait! Wait. Mr. Kawolski. Ms. Sha." A woman's voice cut through the Christmas music.

Mr. Kawolski snapped to, a smile appearing on his face. Walking toward them was Vida Moore, wearing a traditional Filipiniana dress with butterfly sleeves. With Oliver. Norah froze.

"Why, hello, Ms. Moore," he said.

"This is my cousin Oliver. I apologize for the commotion earlier. It was an … oversight that he wasn't on the guest list."

"Ms. Sha went above and beyond to make sure this reunion happened," Oliver added. "And I commend her for it."

Mr. Kawolski's expression stiffened. "That's splendid, Mr. Moore. I'm glad that she could help."

"Yes, and I expect that she won't be feeling any repercussions for her help. Not only was she instrumental in coordinating this event, but this party wouldn't have been complete without Oliver. Had she not stepped in, it would have been a very big mistake." Her expression fell for a beat before she recovered, and the smile reappeared.

"Of course, ma'am."

"Good." Ms. Moore nodded, then stepped away. After a huff, Mr. Kawolski mumbled instructions on when to usher Santa out of the room.

The entire situation left Norah dumbfounded and beaming, looking up at Ollie. "Thank you for that."

"I wasn't going to leave you hanging. Besides, I figured that now you owe me again."

Norah laughed. Inside, she was giddy and light. It was Christmas Eve, and the man she'd taken a risk in helping, in kissing, was still standing in front of her. "And what did you want in return?"

"For me to help you the rest of your shift and—"

"But you can't be working."

"Aren't I already wearing the T-shirt? And you didn't let me finish."

Norah couldn't keep herself from smiling. "Okay…go on, then."

"That after your shift" —he took both hands into hers— "we could have Christmas breakfast together. I know of this hotel that serves breakfast from the hours of six through nine."

She reveled in their interlaced fingers, in the way he gazed upon her. "And what will we do in the time after the party ends until six?"

"I'm sure we can think of something." He flashed her a wicked grin.

Warmth flushed through Norah. If this had been any other man she'd met a short two hours prior, she would have had a mind to deck him. But not this man. This man, she already felt comfortable with. She could trust. "I don't have any doubt."

With her insides coiling with need, she pulled him down by the shoulders. He kissed her once more. She savored it this time, anticipation rising for what could come later.

"Party time!" Santa yelled, interrupting Norah and Oliver's kiss.

Santa had peeled off his hat. He'd begun to swing it around, to the horror of the elves.

"Until then, I think we have our work cut out for us." Oliver laughed. "But Merry Christmas, Norah."

She tucked herself into him. "Merry Christmas, Ollie."

THE END

ABOUT TIF MARCELO

Tif Marcelo is a veteran US Army nurse and holds a BS in Nursing and a Master's in Public Administration. She believes and writes about the strength of families, the endurance of friendship, heartfelt romances, and is inspired daily by her own military hero husband and four children. She hosts The Stories to Love Podcast and is the *USA Today* bestselling author of *In a Book Club Far Away*, *Once Upon a Sunset*, *The Key to Happily Ever After (a Target Diverse Book Club pick)*, *The Holiday Switch,* and the Heart Resort and Journey to the Heart series. She and her books have been featured in The Today Show, *Shondaland, Real Simple Magazine, The Asian Journal,* and more!

Booklist:

tifmarcelo.com/books/

Social Media

@TifMarcelo on Facebook, Instagram, Twitter

Illicit

MIA HOPKINS

Illicit

MIA HOPKINS

Blurb:

Event planner Eden Rosales and Catholic priest Nick Salgado reunite at Hacienda Luz and settle a score fourteen years in the making.

Content Notes:

Mentions of child abuse

Explicit language

Explicit sex

CHAPTER ONE

Hiccup

Pinky is livid.

I put her on the speakerphone of my car to get the full effect of her anger. "A disaster," she says for the third time. "A complete disaster, Eden. I'm popping Nexiums like Altoids."

"Put down the prescription medication," I say calmly, "and tell me what you're dealing with."

"Okay. The bride was running an hour late to the hotel." I picture Pinky waving her hands dramatically the way she always does when she tells a story. "Fine, no problem, our schedule can handle that. I directed her bridesmaids to the bridal suite. And that's when everything started to go horribly wrong."

"What do you mean?"

"Signs, Eden. Signs. All over the room. Big red stickers. *Contact with fire sprinklers will cause flooding. Do not touch sprinkler heads.*"

"Oh, no."

"Oh, yes! The mother of one of the flower girls hung a dress on a sprinkler head to steam it. And guess what?"

I allow her the sick joy of telling me. "What?"

"Flooding!" Pinky shrieks. "The sprinklers went off in the bridal suite. The fire alarms were going *woop-woop-woop*! Lights were flashing. Pandemonium. The whole hotel had to evacuate, including the staff and vendors. We all stood waiting in the parking lot until the maintenance team figured out what happened. The bridal suite was under an inch of water. Furniture, carpet, drapes. Everything ruined."

"And the bridesmaids?"

Pinky sighs. "Except for that poor little girl's dress, they got out of there just fine. Someone's aunt drove two blocks to Target and picked up a new dress for her. I found the bridal party another room in the hotel and they're all getting ready now. The bride arrived ten minutes ago. She's finishing hair and makeup now too."

"Was she around for Noah's Ark?"

"No. She didn't see any of it."

"Well done, Pink. You handled that beautifully."

"And we're still on schedule, miracle of miracles."

"So not really a disaster, then, was it?"

A sigh. "I suppose not. Just an epic…hiccup."

Pinky is my strongest team member. She gets spun up sometimes, but who wouldn't? The event planning business is all about managing frustration. If you can do that, you're golden.

"Thanks for letting me vent," she says.

"Of course."

"I should go. The flowers arrived just before I called you. Three plastic buckets of uncut red hypericum berries and a flat of glass bud vases."

I pause. "No florist?"

"No. The family told me to arrange the vases and put them on the tables."

I stifle a groan. "Pinky, do not touch those flowers."

"What do you mean?"

"You are the DOC. A day-of coordinator, not a florist. If you arrange those flowers, I will have to retroactively charge the family for additional services, and those bills never get paid."

A touch of panic reappears in her voice. "What should I tell them?"

"Easy. The father of the groom signed the contract with me and pays the bills. Go to him discreetly and say, 'I'm so sorry about this. My company doesn't arrange or place any florals, but since there is a need, we're happy to accommodate you for an additional two hundred dollars.' If he agrees, go ahead and do the flowers. If he doesn't agree, I guarantee you he will find someone else to do it. Text me when you get his answer."

"Okay," she says, and hangs up.

I turn the music back up in my car—my relaxing piano playlist, although I feel far from relaxed. I cross the bridge into Vallejo and pass the old C&H sugar factory. Below, under the overcast sky, the deep water is blue and green. Not quite a river, not quite the ocean.

I grip the steering wheel a teensy bit tighter. My shoulders ache. My neck is rigid.

Why? Why do I feel so tense? For months, I've been working on this birthday party with what I thought was cool, professional detachment. I've gone over the details again and again with hotel staff, dozens of my cousins and Tita Vida. My team has prepared schematics, flow charts, diagrams and endless lists.

I've overseen hundreds of parties much more complicated than this one. Ugh. Why do I feel like a rookie at bat for the first time?

Of course, I know why.

Because this is not a strangers' wedding or another soulless corporate wine retreat.

This is a party for Grandlola Naty. And after fourteen years of avoiding my past, I'm finally returning to Hacienda Luz, the heartbreakingly beautiful place that, for a short time at least, was my only real home.

That is, until I met Nicholas Salgado.

My phone buzzes with a text, breaking me out of the firm gut-grip of regret.

It's Pinky again.

> The father of the bride says yes to the 200. Good call, boss.

I clear my throat and recite a text reply.

> See? No problem. You've got this.

I send Pinky the message and realize I'm completely unable to send the same message to myself.

~*~*~*~

CHAPTER TWO

A Well-Behaved Child

My biological mother was a Moore. When I was three, she died in her sleep from a fatal heart arrhythmia. My only real memory of her is her skin—light brown with freckles, just like mine.

Trying to outrun his pain, my father remarried quickly and moved us all to Los Angeles to be with his new wife, a pious but distant woman who dutifully took us to church every Sunday but resented the family that God sent her— six wild children and a man gone numb from grief.

Years passed. Money was always tight. Often, my parents' unspoken disappointments would explode into rage—at each other, at us. Out came the slipper, which was funny. Out came the belt, which was not.

I was the youngest. My brothers and sisters left home as soon as they could. Found jobs far away, got married young, joined the military, took whatever express train they could out of that house.

At eighteen, I was the last one standing, the final focus of my father and stepmother's frustrations.

And me? Mousy and obedient? A quiet, God-fearing honor student?

Nope.

I was an insufferable little shit. A wannabe punk who pretended not to care about school. Boys were my only hobby. One of them, a much-older drummer in a local band, took me to prom and, drunk and high, crashed his car on campus. I was in the front seat cradling an open forty. After the tow truck and a team of specialists unwrapped the 1986 Oldsmobile station wagon from the giant fig tree on the quad, I was promptly expelled. I was three weeks shy of graduating.

Furious, my father threw me in the family minivan and drove me nonstop to Napa. He didn't talk to me the entire drive. Seven hours later, when we arrived in front of Hacienda Luz, I was sober and catatonic with regret.

"We don't know what to do with you," my father said at last, dropping my duffel bag in the empty parking lot. "You have forgotten how to respect us. Maybe you will respect your grandlola Naty."

Cold realization hit me. "Dad," I said, "are you leaving me here?"

"Pray to God, Eden. Ask Him for help."

I tried to grab his arm. "Who are these people? Dad, no."

A Filipino woman in her thirties walked out of the front door of the hacienda.

"Daddy, please don't leave me here! Please!" Hot tears. I never cried in front of him.

"Pray to God," my dad said again. "Just pray to God." With eyes flat and black as highway asphalt, he pulled his arm out of my grasp, got into the minivan and drove away without saying goodbye.

I don't remember too much else about that evening.

The woman wiped away my tears with a handkerchief that smelled like flowers. Later, I would learn that the flowers were sampaguita—a very sweet jasmine, the national flower of the Philippines. And later I would learn that the woman was my Tita Vida, a cousin of my mother's.

As the sun went down, Tita Vida led me through the grounds of the hacienda, a sprawling Spanish-style hotel with red clay roof tiles. Behind the building, we entered a small cottage. There, she said little but fed me rice and vegetable soup, then let me take a bath in a big clawfoot bathtub. I changed into a clean T-shirt and gym shorts, and she led me to a little bedroom. Across the hall, an old lady slept soundly in a big four-poster bed.

"Don't wake her," whispered Tita Vida. "She's your great-grandmother. You can call her Grandlola Naty."

Tita Vida didn't ask me any questions. Instead, she tucked me into the twin-sized bed and smoothed my hair like I was a small child.

"You're safe here," she said. "Sleep now."

I had been in trouble before with my parents, but not like this. This was capital-I, capital-T, In Trouble.

I had heard gossip about girls in our church parish being sent back to live with family in Mexico or the Philippines because they had gotten pregnant and their families wanted them to have their babies in secret. I wasn't pregnant—I was fanatically careful about that—and this wasn't the Philippines. It was a luxurious wine country hotel in Northern California. I was confused, to say the least.

The next day, Tita Vida laid it out for me: I was to finish my high school coursework, get my diploma and enroll in the local community college. I would work at the hacienda for wages, but Tita Vida and her family would provide my room and board for free.

"Why?" I asked.

"Because we take care of our own. And you are one of our own."

We forged an agreement. I would complete my studies during the week and work Friday nights, Saturdays, and Sundays as a banquet server. I would remove my piercings (boo), dye my hair back to its natural black (boo) and be a good employee.

In return, I'd get my own room and freedom to do as I pleased as long as I didn't bother any of the guests. Tita Vida also gave me access to a groovy powder blue '74 Dodge Dart for errands—my first car.

"For errands, like getting started on your community college paperwork, right?" Tita Vida said, raising an eyebrow at me.

"Right," I said, and I meant it.

"Right." Her smile was gentle. "Now we understand each other."

What was it about Tita Vida that made me want to be good? She wasn't much older than me. I rebelled against all other authority figures. In hindsight, I suppose she could see I was lost and, above all, lonely. She gave me safety, space, and the freedom to make the right choices. I was a bonehead, but even I understood this was a tremendous chance.

And so, with her in mind, I spent the first weeks of summer being a completely different person. I put my boy-craziness on hold. I contacted my high school and an annoyed guidance counselor explained how to get my GED. I enrolled in college classes.

A seemingly endless supply of cousins who also worked at the hacienda welcomed me into the family. I listened to my supervisors and became a pretty decent banquet server. The work was physically demanding but not hard to understand, and I slept soundly at night.

Mabait na bata, Tita Vida cheerfully called me when she introduced me to other staff or family members. A well-behaved child—and I was.

But then Nick arrived, and everything changed.

CHAPTER THREE

Lovesick

It's winter in Napa, starkly beautiful and quiet. A light rain is falling as I pull up to the hacienda. Heavy clouds tease a storm, but for now, sunlight spills through cloud breaks and falls on the dark, naked grapevines.

A valet opens the door of my Audi SUV. A bellhop takes my garment bag out of the trunk. I step out of the car, and my heels click on the tiles leading up to the entrance.

Anxiety bubbles up, and I beat it back. I remind myself of two things.

First, I'm not scared little Eden, the bad-girl charity case from LA.

Second, I am Eden Rosales, owner and founder of Garden of Eden Events.

I have worked with wealthy bridezillas, with corporate royalty like Google and Apple, with law firms and annoying YouTube stars and every fire-breathing dragon who wants to throw a big party in the Bay Area. I'm not afraid of anything.

I push my anxiety way down deep, as deep as it can go, and stand up straight. For the first time in fourteen years, I walk into Hacienda Luz.

The hotel staff has decorated the lobby of the hacienda. Late afternoon sunlight pours through the windows, but the interior is dim enough to showcase the twinkling lights and fake garlands strung on the rafters and columns. An enormous, bedecked Christmas tree stands guard in the center of the room.

A sharp-looking woman with long, dark hair stands at the front desk. Her nametag catches the light. She's Norah Sha, the hotel's event supervisor. We greet each other warmly. We've been working together for months on this project but we've never met in person. Her poised professionalism increases my sense of calm. We chat as a front desk clerk checks me in and hands me my keycard. Norah directs the bellhop to my room.

"Have the guests begun arriving for tomorrow's party?" I ask Norah.

"A few. Senator Hizon and his party checked in an hour ago. We're expecting a van from Napa airport in half an hour." She studies her computer screen. "And a number of international guests will be arriving from SFO this evening, Ms. Rosales."

"Please, call me Eden."

Norah gives me a friendly smile. "And please call me Norah." She takes out her iPad. With well-manicured fingers, she taps and swipes. "Let's see. Most guests are arriving tomorrow. I'm sending you an updated list of guests who are staying at the hotel. There is a note about the groups that are arriving together by bus or van. The VIPs are in the suites."

My devices chime merrily as she sends me the document. I like Norah a lot. "Perfect," I say. "Also, can you please tell me where I can find Tita Vida—I mean, Vida Moore?"

"Certainly. Right this way."

* * *

Summer—it was another blazing hot day in Napa. The only scheduled event at the hacienda was a small morning wedding followed by a brunch buffet. After cleaning up, my manager told us to go home. A free Saturday afternoon was a rare treat, and I was happy.

At the cottage, I stripped off my black work pants and starchy white shirt. I took a quick shower and changed into a white tank top, jean cut-offs and my tattered Converse low-tops. I had extra money for gas and use of the Dodge Dart, which I'd nicknamed Lovesick on account of her being blue.

As I headed out the front door, Tita Vida called me from the kitchen.

"Eden, is that you? Come in here. Come meet our guests from the Philippines."

I suppressed a sigh and quickly brushed my damp hair forward over my chest. I wasn't wearing a bra. I closed the door.

"Hi, Tita Vida," I said in my sunniest voice.

She was sitting at the kitchen table with a serious gray-haired older man in a short-sleeved shirt with a priest's collar. Next to him was a smiling young guy in a Disneyland shirt and jeans. They had the same haircut, which looked okay on the old man but pretty awful on the young one.

"Eden," said Tita Vida, "this is Monsignor Ledesma from the Mater Dei Seminary in Manila, and this is his student, Nicky Salgado. They are making their first visit to California. Nicky is the grandson of your grandlola Naty's neighbors back in the Philippines."

Monsignor Ledesma frowned with disapproval at me. Behind his glasses, I caught his eyes roving over my outfit.

Tita Vida saw this too. "Mabait na bata, Monsignor," she said, loud and proud. "Eden is a good worker and very polite. She has a bright future."

"Nice to meet you, po." Dutifully, I shook their hands and touched my forehead lightly to the older man's proffered hand—mano po, the sign of respect my father taught me to perform a long time ago. But my feet were itching in my shoes. My whole body was pointed toward the front door, aching to escape.

"Where are you going?" Tita Vida asked.

"Into town," I said, which wasn't a total lie. "I need to buy a few things from the drugstore." That *was* a total lie. "Do you need me to pick up anything, Tita?"

"No, Eden, thank you, I don't need anything," Tita Vida said, "but I think Nicky needs a break from the hacienda. Could you please take him on a tour of the town? Maybe have something cold to drink at Starbucks, my treat?" She stood up and grabbed her purse from the kitchen counter. Now both the old and the young man at the table were frowning.

"There's not much to see—" I started to say.

"What? There's a lot to see. The movie theater? Maybe the bowling alley?" Tita Vida said cheerfully. In a remarkably smooth move, she grabbed my wrist, pushed some cash in my hand, pulled Nicky to his feet and ushered us to the back door. "Take your time. Call us if you won't be back for dinner."

Dinner? That was in hours. "What?" I said, confused.

"Have a good time!" She opened the door and gently shoved us outside. The door lock clicked behind us.

For a moment, we stood on the back step looking at each other, blinking.

"Your name is … Nicky?" I asked.

"Nick," he said. His voice was deeper than I'd thought. He looked down at me—he was a little taller than I'd thought too. "And you are Eden, correct?" He had a Filipino accent—of course—but his English was precise and formal. He sounded like a fobby schoolteacher.

Frustrated, I finally sighed the sigh I was holding back. Goodbye, free afternoon.

"Come on." I tucked Tita Vida's money into my back pocket and started down the back steps. "Lovesick is this way."

"Lovesick?"

"Yeah," I said. "Let's go."

CHAPTER FOUR

It's Not A Jungle

I tore out of the long driveway, hit the asphalt, and punched the gas for absolutely no reason. Even though none of this was Nick's fault, the latent asshole lurking inside me wanted to take my frustration out on someone. Sitting in the passenger seat, he was the only target within snapping distance.

"Are you a priest or something?" I asked.

"No, not yet," he said, "but I'm entering the seminary in September."

"So you'll be a priest in September?"

"No, it takes many years to become a priest."

"Why would you want to do that anyway?" Before he could answer, I cut off a tractor-trailer. When Nick gripped the armrest, I felt a pang of satisfaction. I wanted to be the worst tour guide he'd ever had. I wasn't going to suffer through this alone.

"I did not think a car this old could accelerate like that," he said in his perfect grammar.

Hoping to come across as stuck-up, I said, "Why would they call it a Dodge Dart if they didn't make it fast?"

Spewing carbon monoxide, I zoomed through some lazy Saturday afternoon traffic until we reached downtown Napa. At an intersection, we idled in the heat, sweating without air-conditioning.

Nick bounced his knee and looked around. "Where are you taking me?"

Instead of answering, I followed Tita Vida's advice and drove to the supermarket. I pulled into a space by the door, and Nick followed me in. At the Starbucks counter, we got in line behind some wealthy-looking tourists on their weekend wine trips.

Nick and I didn't talk, but out of the corner of my eye, I could see him sizing me up. I folded my arms over my tank top, regretting for the second time not wearing a bra in the frigid air-conditioning.

"What do you usually order?" Nick asked suddenly, and I jumped a little.

"Coffee. Black." To impress the wannabe writers and artists I dated, I'd trained myself to drink black coffee and pretend I liked it. I narrowed my eyes at Nick. "Let me guess. You like sweet stuff."

The line moved, and we automatically took a step together, moving closer. At my eye level, Nick's half smile made a shallow dimple in his left cheek.

"Not that sweet," he said, and a glimmer of handsomeness twinkled behind the nerdy exterior. He smelled faintly like laundry detergent—the cheap kind my stepmother used back home. Clean and familiar.

Then someone said something to me.

I blinked. "Sorry, what?"

We were at the front of the line. The bored-looking barista repeated, "Um, what can I get for you today?"

"Oh." I cleared my throat. "I'll have a medium drip coffee and he'll have…?" I raised my eyebrows at Nick.

"An iced grande Americano with half-and-half, no sugar, please."

I must have looked confused because he turned to me and said, "What? We have Starbucks in Manila." His eyes twinkled. "It's not a jungle."

As we waited for our order, the cashier in the checkout line closest to us suddenly raised her voice.

"No, no, no. Flip it around. I told you, that's the wrong way."

Nick and I turned to see an older Filipino woman trying to buy groceries but struggling with her debit card. The impatient cashier was being short with her. The long line of customers behind her began to grumble.

"Hold on," Nick said to me.

I watched as Nick approached the Filipino woman. When he greeted her in Tagalog, the worried expression disappeared from her face. After a quick exchange, Nick helped the woman handle the card, keypad, and payment. He flashed a smile at the cashier, who instantly softened. To expedite things, Nick bagged the woman's purchases and placed them carefully in her shopping cart before pushing it toward the door for her.

In Tagalog, Nick asked her, "May I help you to your car?"

"No, thank you, young man," she replied in Tagalog, patting his arm. She glanced at me then looked back at him. In English, she exclaimed loudly, "Where were you fifty years ago?"

The customers in the store tittered as she left.

When Nick returned, I handed him his drink. He took a big slurp and grinned at me, his hero complex glowing around his head like a halo.

"So," he said.

"So."

"We are stuck with each other this afternoon, Eden, but it doesn't have to be terrible. I know you're annoyed with me. I just want you to relax."

"Relax?" I marched to refrigerators near the cash registers and Nick followed me like a puppy. "I just met you, and now I have to spend my only free afternoon playing tour guide. Wouldn't you be annoyed?" I opened the refrigerator door. Nick held it as I took out two large bottles of water.

"Okay," he said, the way Filipinos say it, deeper in the throat. "Then tell me. What were you going to do right before your tita called you into the kitchen? Besides going to the drugstore?"

He remembered my lie. "Nothing exciting." I paid for the water bottles. I handed him one and he took it. "Something extremely boring, as a matter of fact."

"What?" Nick looked at me expectantly. "Tell me."

"You don't want to know."

"I do."

I studied his face. "I was going to throw rocks."

"At people?"

"No!" I snorted. "I was going to drive to the creek and throw rocks there."

He said nothing.

"I told you it was boring." I sighed.

"Is it nice there?"

"It's quiet."

Silent, Nick took another sip. We lingered at the front of the supermarket by the ice freezers, neither of us eager to go back out into the afternoon heat.

"Hey, Eden," he said.

"What?"

"If I'm very quiet, will you take me to the creek to throw rocks with you?"

I considered it for a moment.

"We have rocks too." He smirked again. "In the Philippines."

Oh no—he was handsome.

"Rocks and Starbucks," I said. "Practically a civilized nation."

"Practically." He smiled and touched the cold plastic bottle to his forehead. A tiny drop of condensation rolled down his sharp cheekbone like a tear. "Tayo na."

CHAPTER FIVE

Saint Nick

Lake Berryessa was an hour away. Nick and I rolled down all the windows. There was a single speaker in the car that still worked, and the old radio could get only one radio station, KVYN, the Vine. We listened to that forty-year-old speaker burp out Blues Traveler and The Doobie Brothers. Add the wind ripping through the car on the highway, and it was hard to have any conversation at all.

Nick looked out the window, bopping his head to the music, perfectly content. I wondered what he was thinking about the things he saw. The sunbaked landscape, rocky and golden. A few oak trees. Burn scars from old brush fires. An ancient barn, falling down in very slow motion.

As we approached the lake, I bypassed the busy campgrounds and boat launches clogged with families and drunk weekenders. I exited the highway, taking a dusty turnoff partially hidden from the main road by a rocky outcrop. The air cooled and the brush got thicker as we followed switchbacks down to the water. The dirt road ended at a stand of trees. I parked the car. We got out, stretched and yawned. The air smelled like rosemary and sagebrush. A welcome breeze cooled our skin.

"Come on," I said.

Nick followed me down the narrow trail hidden in the thick trees. I moved branches out of the way, and dry leaves crunched under our feet. After a short while, the trail broadened into a rocky clearing at the edge of a wide, fast-moving creek. The water was clean and a strange bright blue, almost completely clear. There was no one to be seen, either on this side of the creek or the other.

"My cousin Sophie told me about this place," I explained. "She grew up in Napa. Apparently, this is where locals come to escape the tourists."

Quietly, Nick and I made a pile of pebbles on a flat rock by the water's edge. When we'd built up enough, I began to throw them into the burbling water, one at a time, skipping the flat ones across the water's surface and hurling the jagged ones as far as I could into the deep. Nick joined me. As promised, we didn't talk for a long time.

When the pebbles were almost gone, we took off our shoes and cooled our feet. The cold water made us gasp. Nick stuck our water bottles in the creek to cool them down. Together we listened to the rushing water, the birds and the rustle of wind in the trees.

After a long time, I asked, "Are you related to the Moores?"

Nick shook his head. "Not by blood. My mom's family were your Grandlola Naty's neighbors in the Philippines a long time ago. My dad died in a motorcycle accident when I was six. That year, Mom came to the States to work."

"How about you? Where did you live?"

"Different places," he said cheerfully. "I stayed with relatives at first. After that, I went to the convent."

"Like an orphanage?"

"No, it was a school. I lived and worked there."

"Worked? What did you do?"

"Cleaning, gardening. Sometimes kitchen work."

He must have been very young. This sounded horrible to me, but I didn't comment. "And now you're going to the seminary?"

"Yes. It's my calling," he said. "Your Grandlola Naty is helping to pay for my education, so Monsignor Ledesma and I made a trip to meet her in person and say thank you."

"How about your mom? Where does she live now?"

"In San Diego. She's a housekeeper and nanny. I went to see her last week." He smiled. "We went to the zoo."

I wiggled my toes in the cold water. "How often did you see her growing up?"

Nick thought about this. "She came back to the Philippines for my first communion."

I waited for more, but he didn't say anything else.

"That's it?" I asked.

"That's it." He studied what must have been my puzzled expression. "But we have a good relationship. We Skype every day. We pray together. We confide in each other. She tells me what is happening in her life, and I do the same thing. There isn't anything my mom doesn't know about me. We're close, even though we're far." He nodded to himself at this paradox. "We love each other, even though to other people our relationship probably seems strange."

The pebble in my hand suddenly felt cold and heavy. I threw it into the water and tried to deny the sharp spike of jealousy I felt. I grew up in my parents' house and yet we could never manage to be close like Nick and his mother, thousands of miles apart. My heart started to feel the way it did late at night in the cottage when I was the only one awake and the loneliness was so strong, I couldn't bear it.

"Are you okay?" he asked.

"I'm fine." I picked up another pebble but put it down abruptly. "Hey, I have an idea."

"What?"

"Let's go swimming."

He looked around. "Now? Here?"

"Sure."

A worried look shadowed his face. "I don't have-"

"Neither do I. Who cares? There's no one else around. Come on." I turned slightly away from him and took off my shirt. I unbuttoned my shorts and wiggled out of them along with my undies. I laid my clothes out on the rock where they would stay dry.

Nick turned his head to be polite, but I could see that his shoulders were tense.

"Saint Nick," I teased him. "It's just swimming."

He sighed.

"Is swimming a sin?" I asked. "If it is, you can confess to your monsignor later. He'll make you say ten Hail Marys and everything will be fine."

When Nick didn't budge, loneliness stabbed again at my chest.

"Fine," I murmured. "Be holy, then."

Annoyed, I turned and ran into the water, stumbling on the slick stones at the bottom of the creek. The water was frigid and I screamed, shocking myself out of feeling these terrible feelings I didn't want to face. My shrieks and deranged laughter echoed along the canyon.

Taking a deep breath, I closed my eyes and dunked my head under the surface. Cold water filled my ears. I let myself go limp for a moment, surrendering to the pure sensation of the current. I drifted a little. No thoughts allowed. No feelings allowed.

Soon, my lungs grew tight and hot. I kicked upward and broke the surface. I brushed the wet curtain of hair out of my face and gasped for air.

When I opened my eyes, Nick was right next to me, treading water. All of his clothes were laid carefully next to mine on the rocks.

"I just consulted with Jesus," he said, breathless and shaky from the cold. "He told me you were right. Swimming isn't a sin."

I put my hands on Nick's broad shoulders and dunked him, laughing, underwater.

~*~*~*~

CHAPTER SIX

Just You, Me, and Jesus

Nick was a gentleman.

I didn't know anything about gentlemen.

At the time, I only went out with guys in their early twenties who had no problem sleeping with a barely legal high-schooler. Looking back, that's fucking disgusting. Why didn't I run away from guys like that?

Lots of reasons, I guess.

I mean, I didn't have good supervision or guidance. My stepmother never, ever talked to us about sex—never even acknowledged its existence. My older sisters had moved out of the house by then. So, to fill the void, I suppose older guys taught me about sex. I can see why I let them—they had a little more money. They could score alcohol and weed without any trouble. They had cars that could take me far away from my lonely, messed-up family life. They could make me feel, if not older exactly, at least like someone else. Someone cooler, freer and happier than Eden Rosales.

But Nick? He made me feel more like Eden Rosales than anyone else.

The endless summer day lingered on. Nick and I splashed in the creek and crossed it back and forth, racing each other until we were panting. We drank cold water from our water bottles. We sank down to the bottom of the creek and popped back up, again and again. We talked and laughed. The whole time, Nick kept a respectful distance and didn't ogle me at all. The only time we touched was when I touched him, to hand him the water bottle, to grab his arm to keep from slipping on a rock, to get his attention to point out an interesting bird or insect.

Under the water, I caught glimpses of his body. Lean and strong. A runner's physique, so different from the pallid creeps I usually dated. With his dimples and sharp cheekbones, Nick was the hot nerd you daydreamed about during Bible study. And so, treading water in the middle of the creek while watching a turkey vulture circle lazily overhead, I asked the question I imagine lots of people asked themselves upon learning Nick wanted to join the priesthood.

"Are you sure being a priest is really your calling?"

Nick smiled again. That smile was deadly, and he knew it. "Ask me what you really want to ask me, Eden."

We locked eyes. In the cold water, my blood ran hot and icy. Instead of losing the staring match, I splashed him.

"Don't be rude," I said.

Defiant, he laughed and raised one eyebrow at me. "Come on. Ask me."

"It's not one question. It's a lot of questions."

"Just ask," he said again.

"Okay, fine." I sighed. "Are you a virgin?"

His smile wavered, as if he was nervous to admit it to me. "Yes."

My body started to do strange things. Why was my skin tingling? "How old are you?" I asked.

"Nineteen."

"And you're okay with remaining a virgin your whole life? Like, your whole life until you die?"

"If God is calling me to serve others, then I am more than okay with it. I want to be a good and faithful priest, and that means living according to the rules of the church. All of the rules, not just some."

"But aren't you curious about sex? Don't you want to know what it's like to have sex with…women? Men?"

He thought about this for a minute as the current rushed between us on its never-ending journey. "Yes, I am curious. But I'm curious about a lot of things. Like going to the moon, for example. What's that like? I won't make it there, but I can still live a full life without boarding a space shuttle and landing on the moon."

"I understand your analogy," I said, "but we're talking about the rocket in your pants, Nick."

This time he splashed me.

"What happens if you like someone?" I asked.

"Then I pray that she finds a good husband because it can't be me. If I'm a priest, I'll never get married," he explained, "and I don't believe in premarital sex."

"Ah." I waggled my eyebrows. "But can it really be called premarital sex if you're not planning on getting married?"

He smiled to himself and shook his head. "I feel sorry for your priest."

"Right now, you're the closest thing I've got to a priest, so go ahead and feel sorry for yourself." I floated on my back and Nick turned away immediately, averting his eyes yet again. I fired off what I hoped was another scandalizing question. "Will you be able to jack off?"

Unbothered, Nick said calmly, "It's not allowed."

"I think they're asking too much of you."

"Maybe," he said, "but celibacy takes discipline and understanding. I'm ready to practice all the disciplines required of me by the church. I'm ready to learn what life as a priest is really like. Day by day." He glanced at me and moved closer to me. Still averting his eyes, he said, "Here. Stretch out your arms."

Still floating on my back, I did it. He floated on his back and touched the tops of our heads together. He rested his forearms on mine. There, looking up at the sky, we were connected but still separate, naked but out of each other's lines of sight. The strange intimacy of the position made my heart beat faster.

"Ask me some questions now," I said.

He thought about it. "Is sex a big part of your life?"

"Yes."

"Does it make you happy?"

"Sometimes," I replied.

"Have you considered becoming a nun?"

I snorted.

"Okay, you don't have to answer that one. Let's just enjoy this moment," he said. "You, me and Jesus."

"Stop."

Now he was laughing softly. "Jesus is always watching. He sees you when you're sleeping. He knows when you're awake."

"You can't trick me. That's Santa Claus."

"Fine. You, me, Jesus, and Santa Claus."

CHAPTER SEVEN

The Glory Hole

Nick and I lay down side by side on the flat rock. We didn't have towels because I hadn't planned ahead, so we drowsed in the sun until we were dry. We didn't touch each other, but my eyes did all kinds of geometry to study him without being caught. Out of the dorky clothes, with his bad haircut mussed up and wet, he was ridiculously handsome. Dark brown skin. Fit. Comfortable in his body.

It seemed a waste to donate all of that to the church.

As the sun started to slip toward the horizon, we got dressed and headed back to the car, slapping at mosquitoes along the trail. I started the engine and drove back up the dirt road.

"Let me show you something," I said.

We drove up the highway to the dam and stopped at an overlook next to a chain-link fence. Late afternoon sun bathed the deep blue lake in golden light. We shaded our eyes and looked out at the narrow canyon walls, the drowned trees and the hilltops now turned into islands in the middle of the lake.

Across the water, on a tall outcropping, stood a huge concrete structure, round and open, like a drum without its skin.

I pointed it out. "Do you know what that is?"

Nick shook his head. "No."

"Technically, that is called the Morning Glory Spillway. But you can probably guess what everyone calls it."

"What?"

I giggled. "The Glory Hole."

"The Glory Hole." He looked at me blankly. "Why is that funny?"

I stopped laughing. "Seriously?"

"Is that a joke? I don't know that joke. What does Glory Hole mean?"

Nick looked so innocent in that moment, I couldn't handle corrupting him further. "Look it up online," I said, "but make sure you're alone."

He was still confused. "Okay."

"Pay attention," I said. "This is Monticello Dam. When they built it, they flooded farms, ranches, even a whole town." I pointed at the Glory Hole. "My cousin's friend Travis says that sometimes in winter, when there are rainstorms, the dam fills up to capacity. To keep the dam from breaking, they built that spillway to channel all the excess water. When the water reaches the edge, it just spills in and drains at the bottom of the dam. The hole relieves pressure on the dam, regulates the water level and keeps the dam from breaking."

Nick narrowed his eyes at the Glory Hole. "The water reaches that level? That's so high."

"Yes, sometimes. That's what Travis told me anyway."

A cool wind rushed across the surface of the lake and whipped at us. Almost casually, Nick reached over and brushed my damp hair back from my face, tucking it behind my ear.

"If only 1-life were like that," I babbled, my heart thumping wildly at his touch.

"Like what?"

"Like the spillway. If only there were a built-in way to relieve pressure, so we don't break when things get too difficult."

He said nothing, just looked into my eyes.

"Is that what God is for you?" I asked. "A relief?"

"No," he said softly. "For me, God is the rushing water. The rainstorm. How can I explain it?" He looked deeper into my eyes. "I want every barrier inside me broken. I want my heart to be flooded. With Him."

My back was to the chain-link fence, and Nick was so close I could feel the heat rising off his skin. My head was spinning with wanting him. His brown eyes had caught the sunset, and they glowed hazel with flecks of fire.

With a half-step, he closed the remaining space between us. I placed my hands lightly against his chest. I could feel the powerful beat of his heart, fluttering hard just like mine.

"Have you kissed a girl before?" I asked. My mind raced. What would have turned me on more, if he said yes or no?

Nick cradled my face in his achingly gentle hands. His answer was barely a whisper. "Yes."

When he kissed me, a thunderbolt seemed to shake me from the top of my head to the soles of my feet. I had been with lots of guys. Nick was the opposite of what I usually looked for in a partner. But this chemistry was unreal. Why did kissing him feel so good?

I wrapped my arms around him and held him closer. Nick pulled away a few millimeters and buried his gaze in mine. "Ang ganda mo talaga, Eden," he whispered against my lips.

I blinked, lightheaded. "What does that mean?"

"Kiss me again."

* * *

After an epic make-out session, we held hands on the drive home. The dark highway felt safe. We could pretend that no one knew where we were and no one cared.

A couple miles from the hacienda, Nick turned off the radio and rolled his window up.

"Can I ask you something?" he said.

"Anything."

"Do you want to stay up here? Or go back to Los Angeles?"

I'd been turning that question over in my mind for weeks. "I thought that Napa was my punishment. But Tita Vida and the Moores have made me feel more at home here than I ever felt in my parents' house. I'm enrolled in classes at the community college this fall. And I like working at the hacienda. My coworkers, my cousins, everyone is really cool."

"But don't you miss your family? Your friends?"

I thought hard about my answer. "Sometimes. But I'm in Napa now. And it actually feels good to be here, like this is where I am supposed to be." I paused. "I think I can really start my life here. What it is supposed to be."

He reached over and stroked the back of my neck with a touch that made me tingle all over again, and I felt a pang of selfish regret that we would never sleep together. Anyone who could touch me like that would be amazing in bed.

Maybe if I worked at convincing him, I could give him something really interesting to bring to his weekly confession.

"When are you leaving?" I asked.

"In three days." He looked at me sideways in the faint light of the dashboard and took my hand. "Whatever you're planning, it's not going to work."

"What?" I laughed. "I didn't say anything."

"No, but you were thinking it."

I squeezed his hand. "Don't worry about what I'm thinking, Saint Nick."

CHAPTER EIGHT

There's a Drought, You Know

We got back just as the kitchen was closing. Giggling, I led Nick in through the pantry and dug through one of the walk-ins for something to eat. I grabbed a large tub of chicken wings labeled *family meal*. Yet another one of my cousins was working in the kitchen that night. Bussing dishes, Ruby sized up Nick, winked at me and looked the other way. By the bar, I found a stash of leftover wine from the morning wedding brunch and grabbed a bottle and a corkscrew. There were always loads of booze left after events.

"Come with me," I whispered.

We tiptoed along the shadows to a dark corridor by the chapel cordoned off after hours by a velvet rope. We stepped over the rope, and I led Nick to the room at the end, the bridal suite. I turned on a lamp, shut the door and clicked the lock behind us.

In the dim lamplight, the bridal suite looked like the sitting room in a Victorian brothel—a thick oriental carpet, mirrors everywhere, gilded sconces and velvet drapes.

"Wow, so fancy," Nick said.

We took off our shoes, plopped down in the middle of the carpet and opened the wine. I took a drink from the bottle and read the label aloud. "Viognier." I exaggerated my French accent. "Vee-oh-NYAY. 'Hints of honeysuckle, mango and rose.'"

"Ooh-la-la."

I passed the bottle to Nick. He took a big swig, like a pirate. I popped open the container and we tore into the cold chicken wings like ravenous wolves. For napkins, we used a box of tissues meant for weeping members of the bridal party. Instead of tears, we dabbed buffalo sauce. Some dripped on Nick's shirt.

"Just take it off," I said casually.

Nick pulled the T-shirt over his head and treated me again to his bare chest. We feasted until all we had were a big pile of clean bones and an empty bottle. I was feeling warm and mellow and a little feral.

The bridal suite had a small bathroom.

"Take a shower with me," I said.

Nick was sitting cross-legged on the floor. Flushed from the wine, he turned even redder. "What?"

"Come take a shower with me."

He stared at me, and the hunger in his eyes made me blush too. But after a long time, he said, "That would be too much temptation even for me, Eden."

I smiled. "You sure?"

"I'll go after you."

"We'd save water. There's a drought, you know."

He stretched out on the floor, covered his eyes, and made a sound halfway between a sigh and a grunt. "Go. Take. Your. Shower," he growled. "Leave me in peace."

Laughing, I went into the bathroom and took a long hot shower by myself, washing off the creek water. I put on one of the fluffy white robes hanging in the closet and tiptoed back out into the suite. Nick was sleeping on the floor with one arm thrown over his eyes. His beautiful lips were parted softly. I settled down next to him and embraced him. Lazily, he gathered me against his chest and kissed my forehead as we lay side by side.

He brushed my hair back again, and I shivered with pleasure. But then he froze.

"What's wrong?" I asked.

"What's this?" He touched his thumb lightly to my hairline.

I often forgot it was there. "That's just a scar."

"How did you get it?"

I sighed. "My dad. We got into an argument about my grades last semester and he pushed me off the porch. I hit my head on the handrail before I fell."

His voice changed. Deepened. "What?"

"He didn't mean to do it," I said quickly. "It was an accident."

"He didn't mean to push you off the porch?"

I paused. "Well, no, he meant to do that. He didn't mean for me to hit my head." Gently, I removed Nick's hand from the scar. "It looks worse than it was. Luckily, it's in a spot that's not so obvious. I went to school the next day and no one knew. No biggie."

"Did he hit you a lot?"

"My stepmom and dad both did. But they did that to all of us, not just me." I shrugged. "It's not a big deal. Lots of people grow up that way."

"I didn't."

I stroked his chest with my fingertips, hoping he wouldn't say anything more. This moment was for us. Not for my messed-up family.

"I'm sorry that happened to you, Eden."

Only my immediate family knew about how we were treated at home, and we never talked about it with each other. It was normal for us. I was taught that was how all good children were raised. We were all taught the absence of corporal punishment led to spoiled, entitled children—not good guys who became priests.

No one had ever acknowledged my pain. Until Nick.

We lay still for a very long time.

I kissed the smooth, hard curve of his shoulder. "You want to know something?"

"What?"

"I was jealous of you today."

"Jealous? How?"

I remembered the sensation of jumping into the creek, the cold water shocking me out of all feelings, good and bad. "I felt jealous of you when you told me how close you were to your mom, even though you are physically so far apart."

"In love," he said slowly. "distance is nothing. If people love each other, they will always love each other, no matter how far apart they are." He stroked my cheek. "I think God wants a durable kind of love like that for you. For all of us."

Warm and drowsy, we held on to each other, our bodies effortlessly woven together. We kissed and kissed and kissed. Deep under his spell, I tried to persuade him to go further with me, but his hands stayed gentlemanly and his jeans stayed on, a modern-day denim chastity belt.

In the end, I decided to savor the moment. I realized we could be lovers, just like this. This was how we could be close without him ending up resenting me.

Sun-drunk, wine-drunk, and drunk on each other, we slid into a deep, sound sleep.

We were still asleep at ten o'clock the next day, when Tita Vida finally found the key that unlocked the bridal suite, and we woke up to her, Monsignor Ledesma, and my stepmother and father glaring down on us where we lay tangled and half-naked on the floor.

~*~*~*~

CHAPTER NINE

Order in the Chaos

It's Christmas Eve, the day of Grandlola Naty's birthday party, and I'm up and working by eight in the morning. I coordinate guest arrivals by bus, shuttle, van, and private cars. The front desk is hopping. Hair and makeup teams arrive for guests waiting to get dolled up in their hotel rooms.

I've made arrangements with all of my preferred vendors, and I greet them as they arrive at the hotel, one by one.

Tables and chairs for four hundred, along with a mighty setup crew.

Stage, sound and lighting.

Dance floor, durable enough to handle a family who loves to boogie.

Linen rentals.

Props, including a full-size sleigh and North Pole backdrop for the photo booth.

An ocean of gorgeous flowers, courtesy of my favorite Napa florist and her team.

Under my direction, the ballroom takes shape before our eyes. I've kept the budget under control for Tita Vida, but you would never know—I bibbidi-bobbidi-boo Hacienda Luz until it is a glittering Instagram-ready palace, worthy enough for the Moores. Worthy enough for Grandlola Naty.

After a quick afternoon coffee break, I head to my room to change into my evening outfit. I sweep my hair back into a sleek chignon and carefully apply my makeup. Last, I put on my tailored suit and sky-high heels and look in the mirror.

And there I am.

Eden Rosales, event planner, captain, orchestra conductor, family therapist, fire extinguisher. Order in the chaos.

I check my watch—it's almost six. Instead of holding Simbang Gabi at midnight, the Moores decided to celebrate the traditional Filipino Christmas Eve mass at five o'clock to accommodate their more distinguished guests who find it difficult to stay up late. I think it's a wise move. After a hundred years of living, Grandlola Naty should be able to go to bed whenever she damn well pleases.

Okay.

Let's rock and roll.

I leave my room, take the grand staircase, and find my way to the wedding chapel.

With each step, my body gets warmer and warmer. I'm tingling all over. There's still a chance—albeit a very remote one—that I can avoid Nick. I'm good at blending into the background. I'm an event planner, for God's sake. I can be invisible when I need to be.

As I approach the doors of the chapel, a light suddenly switches on. Above my head in the vestibule, a galaxy of parol light up, the star-shaped lanterns that symbolize Christmas in the Philippines.

The doors swing open, releasing the scent of just-extinguished candles and the tinny sound of prerecorded organ music.

And walking out, in all his fully enrobed glory, is Father Nicholas Salgado, youngest ever Vicar General of the Archdiocese of San Fernando and the second man, after my father, to truly break my heart.

I freeze.

Father Salgado and I exchange a glance. His smile turns to recognition and then, surprisingly, to sadness. Before we can speak to each other, everyone exits the chapel and engulfs us with chatter, hugs, and kisses. And we lose the moment—again.

* * *

I can't.

I can't think about him now.

Again, I put on my event planner mask and fasten it tight.

It's time to work. Orchestrate. Smooth over. Handle every last detail so that Grandlola Naty and her gigantic, beautiful family can enjoy this evening without worrying about the broken PA system or missing swag bags or that one valet who is clearly higher than a bat's ass.

As I listen to a burly security guard who's sprained his finger throwing out some weirdo who tried to crash the party, in the back of my mind, I wonder if I can jump into work the same way I used to jump into sex, the same way I jumped into that ice-cold creek fourteen years ago—to knock myself numb. To keep myself from feeling anything at all, good or bad.

After checking in with Ruby about a cake kerfuffle in the kitchen, I accidentally catch another glimpse of Father Salgado across the ballroom. He's tall and almost absurdly handsome in his black suit and collar. He's thirty-three now, good hair, dimple in place, cheekbones sharper than ever. He's talking to a small group of doting old ladies by the bar, but their twenty-something granddaughters are hovering on the perimeter, nodding, and hanging on his every word, the Christmas lights twinkling in their eyes like stars.

I wonder to myself how this ridiculous heartbreaker has affected churchgoing at his parishes. Record numbers of butts in pews. I'd bet big on that.

Out of the corner of my eye, I catch an elf scurrying across the lobby into the conference room. Over the headset of my walkie-talkie, I call Norah to confirm that Santa and his elves are in costume and ready for their appearance in the ballroom, but she isn't answering.

As discreetly as possible, I walk over to the conference room. Through a crack in the door, I see Norah and someone else—is that Ollie? —coaxing a drunken Santa off a table while "Little Saint Nick" by the Beach Boys blares on the sound system in the room. I'm about to go inside when I pause. Ollie and Norah look like they have this situation under control. I decide to leave them to it.

Back in the ballroom, the speeches continue, followed by dinner. I linger in the back, watching from the shadows. This family is beloved to me, but I don't belong among them. Not really. I settle for the next best thing—taking care of them from a distance.

The rest of the party goes relatively smoothly.

There's lively karaoke and impromptu toasts. Soon the dance floor is packed. To the extreme delight of her guests, even Grandlola Naty does a little shuffle. Cake is served. Birthday presents are opened.

Wait, is that a tortoise? Who is giving Grandlola Naty a tortoise?

After Grandlola Naty makes her speech, the family assembles for a million photos. When he's done, the exhausted photographer makes a beeline for the bar. I don't blame him.

Grandlola Naty is wheeled safely home to her cottage, and the party begins its final crescendo. Drinks flow freely. There's line dancing to "Electric Boogie" and "Todo, Todo, Todo." For hours, the band keeps rocking until even the hardiest revelers begin to fade out, one by one. At last, "Pasko Na, Sinta Ko" plays once more, its sweet melody echoing in the quiet ballroom.

I pay the bandleader. He has a question for Tita Vida, but I can't seem to find her anywhere. Where is she? I have no idea. I tell the man to call her in a couple of days.

Most of the guests have gone home or upstairs to bed. Some last inebriated hangers-on are lingering at the lobby bar talking about how to keep the party going. They're decorated with tinsel and bows from presents. I have just finished up with my last vendor when, at the quiet end of the lobby behind the Christmas tree, I spot a figure sitting by himself near the fire.

I smooth my hair and stand up straight.

He hears the click of my heels before he sees me. He gets to his feet, and as I approach, I see that in my Tom Ford stilettos I can finally look him in the eye.

"Father Salgado," I say, using the placating voice I reserve for clients who want the most I can give them for the least amount of money.

He takes my hand in both of his and shakes it warmly. "I was hoping to get the chance to see you. Tita Vida told me you were the event planner, and I didn't want to interrupt you as you worked. What a wonderful event. Absolutely beautiful."

"Thank you," I say genially, but I pull my hand back and hold my arms at my sides. When I do this, I see a small spark in his eyes. He purses his lips.

God—his lips. Still full and soft and mesmerizing. He is the best kisser I've ever kissed. No contest.

"I'm having a nightcap before I head back to my room." He gestures to the two large armchairs facing each other before the fire. An untouched glass of whiskey on the rocks sits on the side table. "Do you have a moment?"

~*~*~*~

CHAPTER TEN

No Thanks to You, Asshole

I take a tiny step back. "I…I just wanted to say hello. That's all."

Father Salgado looks me in the eye, and I see it again—sadness. "Of course," he says softly. "I don't want to keep you."

My heart aches at the word *keep*.

Tentatively, I rest my hand on the back of the chair. "You…flew in from the Philippines?" I ask.

"Yes." He doesn't sit back down, watching instead for my cues. "This morning. I'm hoping the drink will help me sleep tonight. Would you like one?"

I take a breath, step forward and take a seat. "Sure."

He brings me a whiskey from the bar, but when he comes back, he has a red bow stuck on his shoulder, a gift from the drunken partygoers. Smiling, I reach over, remove it for him and drop it on the table. Chemical reactions crackle between us as we clink glasses. I take an absurdly large swallow and the booze burns the back of my throat, but I hold back the wince.

He puts his glass down. "So how?" he asks. "How did you become an event planner?"

I clear my poor throat. "Well," I croak. "After…the incident…I was so embarrassed. I couldn't face Tita Vida or Grandlola Naty. I didn't want to go home with my parents. So, I left the hacienda and drove to San Francisco."

"You took Lovesick all the way to San Francisco?"

He remembers the stupid name I gave the car.

"Yes," I say, "and I slept in Lovesick until I got a job as a banquet server at one of the big hotels downtown. I worked at that hotel for two years. Then I got hired by an event planner. I worked for her for eight years. She taught me the ropes. When she retired, I inherited her employees, her vendors, and her client list. I renamed the business Garden of Eden Events and have been running it ever since."

Father Salgado listens to my story, rapt and grinning. "Remarkable. I knew you'd find a way."

No thanks to you, asshole, I think. But out loud I say, "I had some rocky years. My parents never spoke to me after that day, and I was so embarrassed I didn't want to accept any help from the Moores. I threw myself into work until a path to support myself became clear." I take another sip. I don't often tell my story aloud, or allow myself to realize that things could've gone very differently for me if I weren't lucky.

"I returned Lovesick to Tita Vida when I finally had money to buy my own car. Apparently, she sold it for scrap."

"Oh, no! Sayang naman. What a waste," he says. "But what do you drive now?"

I know he's giving me a chance to show off. "An Audi Q8," I say sheepishly.

He whistles quietly. "Nice."

"But I still miss that Dodge Dart sometimes. I really do."

We watch the fire burn, slowly nursing our whiskies and our wounds. I wonder what he's thinking. I wonder if he's hurting like me.

"Married?" he asks quietly. "Partner?"

"No, neither." I take another sip. The ice has melted and mellowed my drink. "I got close to getting married a few years ago, but we just didn't work out. Too different, in the end." I glance at him. "You? Married?"

He grins and lightly touches his collar. "In a way. He's really demanding, to be honest."

At last, I let myself smile, and something untangles in my chest.

We relax a little. He asks me questions about my life in San Francisco, about my friends (none really) and hobbies outside of work (same). He asks me if I talk to my family—every other year or so I receive birthday texts from my siblings, who are scattered to the four winds, but other than that, no. I don't. My parents cut off contact with me.

Unable to talk about family, he brings our conversation back to my work. "Do you enjoy event planning?" he asks.

I think about this. "I suppose I enjoy running a business, and I enjoy having a profession. Nothing really beats the satisfaction of a job well done," I say. "But sometimes my clients come to me for emotional support. I witness the cracks in their relationships with their loved ones and their colleagues. I see a lot of miscommunication and dissatisfaction, and I have to help everyone make peace in order to get the job done. It's a hidden aspect of my work."

"Do you feel any strain?"

"Yes, sometimes." I tap the rim of my glass with my finger. "To be honest, I feel like an emotional ATM. Like everyone is making withdrawals but no one cares to make a deposit."

"Then we have something in common," he says. "Professionally, at least."

Our conversation meanders on, and soon I notice we're sitting on the edges of our seats, leaning forward, relaxed in each other's confidence. The partygoers at the bar have all dispersed. The bartender closes down the bar and turns down the lights.

The glow of the Christmas tree illuminates Father Salgado's face—Nick's face, now a man. He's come into his own power, and this makes him so attractive to me; I feel high.

Which means there's only one thing I need to say.

"I should go." I put down my glass and stand up.

He stands up too. "Yes. I should, too. It's quite late."

When he embraces me goodbye, we hold each other tighter than we should. His body is broad and rigid against mine.

I think again about our perfect day by the creek. I think again about how terrible fate can be, and how sad it is when two paths that should run concurrently cross for only a minuscule amount of time.

Before I let go, he whispers in my ear, "For what it's worth, I'm sorry. I'm so sorry, Eden."

My name on his lips makes every nerve in my body ignite like a thousand candles. I freeze, caught in his arms, a sudden rush of pleasure cascading through me.

"I never thought I'd see you again." His top lip grazes the edge of my ear.

Shaking, I break away from him, turn around and head upstairs without another word.

~*~*~*~

CHAPTER ELEVEN

Truly Wicked

I shut my door and bolt it with a loud click.

Everything is in perfect order in my hotel room. My garment bag hangs in the open closet. The bedding is turned down. Soft jazz plays quietly on a Bluetooth speaker—nice touch. Some kind of aromatherapy is happening in here—I smell rosemary and sagebrush, a scent that reminds me of summertime in Napa.

A scent that reminds me of Nick.

My brain is frazzled. If I thought fourteen years was enough to dilute the chemistry I felt in the company of Nicholas Salgado, I was wrong. A hundred years, a thousand years would never be enough. Our bones could fall to pieces and there would still be sexual attraction between the grains of dust.

I'm flushed and giddy and so wired my hands are trembling.

"Get a grip," I say to myself. But it's no use.

The idea of Nick becoming a priest was sexy enough, but now that he's all grown up and actually a priest, I might just spontaneously combust right here. Housekeeping will find a pile of ashes and a pair of scorched stilettos that smell like burnt hair and sexual frustration.

My phone dings. I look at the screen. It's a friendly check-in text from Pinky.

Hope the big party went well, boss! See
you Monday.

What happens Monday?

More planning. More meetings. More contracts. More
phone calls. More weddings, more birthdays, more
fundraisers, more corporate events.

And the Monday after that?

The same. Again and again, an endless line of Mondays,
my life eaten by this business I've built.

But what else do I have besides that?

I look at myself in the mirror. Even after a long night of
running around, I have to admit, I still look impeccable. It's
taken a lot of practice to become this version of Eden
Rosales, down to knowing which kind of primer will make
my lipstick stay on for hours and hours and which kind of
styling wax will keep my flyaways in strict submission.
From my grooming to my car to the business degree I put
myself through night school to get, everything I've done I
did to distance myself from that messed-up, humiliated girl
who woke up on the floor of the bridal suite fourteen years
ago.

And just like that, the memory comes rushing back to
stab me in the heart.

* * *

They stood in a circle around us, looking down.

"How dare you corrupt this boy," Monsignor Ledesma said sternly to me. To Nick, he said, full of pity, "Nicky, get up and get dressed at once. Let's go."

Always one for religious melodrama, my stepmother started weeping and wailing. "What did I tell you, Monsignor? This girl has been possessed by the devil."

My father pulled me up by my arm and shook me hard. "What is the matter with you? We come here to finally take you home, and this is how you behave? You humiliate us?"

Tita Vida stood between my father and me and pulled us apart. "Stop that now," she said sharply. "Let her go."

My father released his grip.

"But nothing happened," I tried to explain over my stepmother's howling. "We didn't—we didn't sleep together. We didn't."

Monsignor Ledesma looked at Nick with gentle concern. "Is this true?"

Nick looked at their faces—my parents, gripped as always by tragic emotion. Tita Vida, confused. The sanctimonious priest, already ready to forgive his young protege, fallen prey to the wiles of an evil young Jezebel.

Then Nick did something that surprised me completely.

"Monsignor Ledesma, sir," he said softly. "I am sorry to say this was all Eden's idea. I just went along with her, sir."

"What do you mean, Nicky?" said the priest.

"Eden stole a bottle of wine and made me drink it."

"What?" I said.

"Go on, my son."

"I am weak, and the wine made me weaker." Nick cleared his throat and looked Monsignor Ledesma in the eye. "She was very persuasive. We had sexual intercourse. I know it was wrong. I am so sorry, sir. I know I don't deserve anyone's forgiveness."

My stepmother let out a long, wild animal howl.

My father walked out into the hallway, cursing to himself.

For a moment, I was speechless.

Then I grew hot with rage. I turned away from Nick and faced the adults. "You're all going to believe him? Over me? I'm telling you the truth. Nothing happened. We did not have sex. We kissed, we talked and we fell asleep. That's it."

"Enough!" Monsignor Ledesma barked at me. "You must stay away from this boy. Pray to the Lord for mercy and forgiveness because what you have done is truly wicked."

Her face dark with rage, Tita Vida opened her mouth to respond to him, but I couldn't bear another second.

I ran out of the room.

I kept running, and I didn't come back.

* * *

For years, I was angry at Nick.

My anger was a steady hum, a constant reminder to be on the alert. Nick's actions had taught me not to trust anyone, no matter how kind and friendly they appeared. Even though I tried to move past it, for a long time, my anger kept me from forming close relationships with anyone, romantic or otherwise.

Am I still angry with him?

Yes and no.

I try to see the situation from his point of view. He was only nineteen years old. The stakes were high. He had the favor of a powerful clergyman and a clear path to his dream of becoming a priest. Grandlola Naty and his mother were cheering him on and funding his education. Of course he would protect himself by blaming me. But why say that we had sex when we didn't? What was that all about? I am still baffled.

Fourteen years later, what were the results of his actions?

For him, phenomenal.

Out of a mixture of spite and curiosity, I've followed his career, periodically searching for him online to see what he has accomplished. The list is long. Charismatic and approachable, he has worked in a number of parishes and traveled around the country speaking and teaching. He's earned multiple advanced degrees and written articles on faith and immigration for magazines and academic journals. He's appeared on TV shows, radio shows and podcasts as an authoritative new voice of the church. In short, he is a rising star. Some believe he'll become bishop before too long.

I look at the sad face in the mirror. I take off my necklace and my watch. Gently, I begin to remove my earrings. My fingertip brushes the edge of my ear, and suddenly, I remember the sensation of Nick whispering to me. "I'm sorry. I'm so sorry, Eden."

I frown. Something sharpens inside me.

Sorry.

Sorry?

You know what?

Father Salgado can take his holy sorries and go fuck himself.

That conversation by the fire was far too polite. I may be out of practice letting myself feel emotions, but I can identify every single one coming to a head inside me right now. Anger, absolutely. Sadness, yes. A deep desire for closure, if not outright revenge. And, if I'm being honest, horniness—but the horniness sharpens the other emotions like a whetstone. He needs to know how much he hurt me. He needs to know what he took from me.

Time to settle this score.

Before I can change my mind, I pick up the phone in my room and dial the front desk. I tell the clerk I'm the event planner and I need to return something to Father Salgado. The clerk tells me his room number. Simple as that. Heart beating wildly, I slip my shoes back on, grab my keycard and rush out the door.

But Nick is standing in the hallway right in front of my room.

We lock eyes. I notice we're wearing the same wild, desperate expression of people about to do something they are afraid they will regret.

"I'm so sorry, Eden," he says again. His voice is raspy. "I had to come find you."

"But why—"

At once, his lips are on mine.

And … sweet, merciful God.

I forget what I was going to do. I forget my anger, my desire to fight. I forget it all—I think I even forget my name.

Locked in a raging kiss, we grab at each other and stumble blindly back into my room, slamming the door behind us.

CHAPTER TWELVE

Breathe

Fourteen years is a long time to wait.

I'm out of practice, and I have no idea what kind of sexual experience Nick has, if any. Caught in the whirlwind, we kiss and pull clumsily at each other's clothes. His suit jacket falls to the floor, followed by my blouse. I unbuckle his belt and unfasten his pants. And now we're on the bed. I'm straddling him, trying to undo the collar around his neck, but the adrenaline surging through me makes me jumpy.

"Wait," he whispers.

Gently, he moves my hands away. With deft fingers, he removes a small silver stud and carefully slides the rigid piece of plastic from his black shirt. He puts the clerical collar on the nightstand.

There's a faint line around his neck where the stiff material has pressed into his flesh. I run my fingertip over the mark with the barest touch. He closes his eyes and takes a deep breath.

"Doesn't it hurt?" I whisper.

"No, not really. It is supposed to be a constant reminder of my commitment to the Lord."

Nick sits up and gently touches his forehead to mine. Blood is pounding in my ears but I force myself to hold still. In the quiet, a sudden bad feeling wells up in me. Against my will, I have a flashback to the bridal suite and Nick's accusatory face.

"I—I don't want to be something you regret," I stammer.

"I would never regret this." He cradles my face in his hands and runs his thumb across my cheek. "If you want to be here with me, I want to be here with you, Eden. More than anything." He pauses. "But I have to tell you something. Something important."

He's breaking his vows for me. I would never sleep with a married man, but a man who's pledged his life to God? A hundred questions rush through my head, but my heart refuses to listen. All I know is that I want him, and if we complicate this, we will never have another chance.

"Whatever it is, don't tell me now," I say. "Tell me tomorrow."

"Are you sure?"

"Yes."

He purses his lips, thinking. When he speaks, the rasp is back in his voice. "All right."

We undress each other completely. Off come the carefully pressed clothes, the carefully polished shoes, all of the armor. In the soft lamplight, we study each other's bodies and the way time has changed us. Nick looks at me with wonder, as if I were a precious jewel he's found, and my heart aches. He's still lean and fit, but his body is thicker and stronger all over. When I stroke his chest, he groans deep in his throat.

"Does that hurt?" I ask, confused.

"No, not at all. The opposite. Please understand," he says, "no one touches me."

Quietly, I ask, "Do you touch yourself?"

"It's been a long time. Years."

"Would you like to show me how you like it?"

"Really?"

"Yes," I say.

We lie down together. He takes my hand, and together we stroke him. He leans back on the pillows and shuts his eyes. His chest rises and falls with each deep breath. After just a couple minutes, his grip tightens on mine. When he comes with a loud gasp, I am mesmerized.

When he catches his breath, his eyes are glassy and his beautiful dark skin is covered in a sheen of sweat.

"I'm sorry," he says, yet again.

"Sorry for what?" I say. "I've never seen anything so sexy in my entire life."

We go to the bathroom and take a long hot shower together. We make out in the steam, and I'm so raw that I suspect the water dripping on my skin could make me come. Nick carries me back to the bed and drops me on the rumpled sheets. He kisses me until our lips are swollen and flushed. He kisses my neck and strokes my breasts. I show him how to use his hands on me. Studious and gentle, he brings me to the brink with his fingertips. Then he does the same, surprisingly well, with his tongue. My body feels incandescent, vibrating with unreleased pleasure.

"Have you done this before?" I ask. What would turn me on more, yes or no?

When he says nothing, I kiss him again. Then he looks me in the eye and gives his head the slightest shake. "No."

A shiver runs through me.

"Are you ready?" I whisper.

"Yes, I think so."

There are condoms in my garment bag. I walk over to the closet and pull one out. Nick watches me carefully and silently as I put one on him. We lie down together, and I hold on to him tightly, looking deep into his dark, glittering eyes as I guide him inside me. We go slow, both of us concentrating hard on holding back.

I whisper in his ear, "Breathe."

He takes a breath and thrusts. I am so close, but I hold on to his hips, helping him find his rhythm. It takes all of my strength to restrain the raging flood inside me. But the dam begins to give way.

"Nick," I gasp.

He catches my moan with a deep kiss, and I taste myself in his mouth. I hold him tight, breaking. When the wall hits us both, we're lost, drowning in the dark, together at last.

~*~*~*~

CHAPTER THIRTEEN

Illicit

In the morning, we make love twice more.

First in bed, before dawn, tangled in the bedsheets. Then after sunrise, in the armchair by the window, pale sunlight illuminating Nick's dark brown skin just like it did by the water all those years ago.

After round two, I sit on his lap and he gathers me close. I snuggle up against his chest and listen to his breathing.

"Is this how you thought it would be?" I ask.

"No," he says. "It is a million times better." He kisses the top of my head. "Merry Christmas, Eden."

"Merry Christmas."

Mellow, with messy hair and five o'clock shadow, he is a different person from the starched and authoritative Father Nicholas Salgado I met yesterday. With a sad sigh, I realize that Nick will have to become that man again soon, and this, like everything wonderful between us, will just be another memory. So it's now or never if I want to find out why he did what he did to me.

"Can I ask you a question?"

"Anything," he says.

"I have to know. Do you regret what happened?"

He stops stroking my hair. "What do you mean?"

"I mean, do you ever think about how your life would've turned out if you hadn't pinned the blame on me when we were young?"

He sits up straighter and looks me in the eyes. "Yes, I've thought about that. But in the end, I know I did the right thing."

"The right thing?" Annoyed, I slip out of his arms, stand up and walk to the window. I peek out the sheer curtains. The bare grapevines are unsettling, almost like skeletons.

"It's in the past," Nick says. "We don't have to talk about this if it hurts you."

"Yes, we do." Anger is rising inside me again, bubbling up low and slow. "You said what you said and went on your way. But you took so much from me, do you understand?" Suddenly realizing I'm naked, I grab a white robe hanging in the closet and put it on. It's identical to the one I wore in the bridal suite when I was eighteen. "Tita Vida was so kind to me. I had a home and freedom and a future here. And because of your lie, I had to leave. I lost all of it."

"That was never my intention, Eden. I didn't know you would run away." He stands up and puts his hands on my shoulders. "You know Monsignor Ledesma and I went to San Diego before we came to Napa, right?"

"Yes, to see your mother."

"That's right. But after San Diego, we had another stop before Napa. For a high school graduation gift, your Grandlola Naty gave me a ticket to Disneyland. I didn't have money for a trip to the States, much less money to visit a theme park. She thought I should see it just once." He pauses. "We stayed with your parents in Los Angeles."

I turn around. "What?"

"Yes. I met them in person before they came to Napa. In Los Angeles, they painted a very different picture of you from the Eden I met here. They said you were unhappy in Napa, but that they were willing to give you another chance if you were truly sorry for the bad things you had done. They told me they were coming to pick you up and bring you back to Los Angeles."

I'm stunned by this hidden chapter of the story, but the pieces fit—he wore a Disneyland T-shirt. He smelled like the laundry detergent my stepmother used because she was the one who'd washed the shirt.

"After we talked, and after I saw the scar you had, I realized they were all wrong about you. Napa was the right place for you, not Los Angeles." Very gently, he kisses the faded scar at my hairline. "You needed to be around your Tita Vida and family who loved and understood you, not parents who abused you."

I can't help it. Tears begin to form in my eyes.

"So when they found us together that morning," Nick continues, "I made up a story about how you seduced me. I knew they would be so angry they'd leave you here in Napa, where you belonged. After you were safe, I would tell you the truth. But then you ran. I tried to contact you, but no one knew where you were."

Outside, the gray clouds rip apart like wet paper, and bright yellow sunlight shines through. My whole understanding of this man flips, twists and turns upside down.

"I regret that I was so full of myself I thought I could protect you when I had just met you. I was so stupid. But please understand, I was not trying to hurt you," he says. "I was trying to save you."

* * *

Together, we drive back to Lake Berryessa. The noonday sky is clear and the highway is empty.

I park my Audi, and together, Nick and I walk to the chain-link fence at the edge of the overlook. The air is cold and crisp. In Nikes, joggers and a warm Patagonia jacket, Nick looks like just another Bay Area guy, albeit one who is excessively and unnecessarily handsome. In another life, we could be together. In another life, I could let my ridiculous heart fall in love with him.

"Look," I say. "There it is."

After the winter rainstorms, the dam is filled to capacity. The surface of the lake is three feet above the Glory Hole, and water falls steadily into the perfectly round spillway, pouring smoothly over the rim in a loud rush. It is mesmerizing. Nick and I look at the hole, at the lake, at the canyon walls. Then we turn and look at each other.

I hate feeling this sad. If there were a way to unzip my chest, remove my heart and throw it into the Glory Hole, I would do it, just to avoid the pain I know is coming.

"When are you flying back?" I ask.

"Flying back?"

"Yes. To the Philippines."

He smiles. "I'm not flying back to the Philippines. Not anytime soon."

I'm confused. "What do you mean? Why not?"

"I'm leaving my archdiocese," he says. "I've been offered a position as a lay professor of divinity at the University of San Francisco."

I freeze. "You're staying here?"

He nods.

For a moment, I think I've misheard him. "Did you just say *lay* professor?"

He nods again. "Yes."

As hard as I tried not to learn anything in Catholic school, I inadvertently did learn the meaning of that word. "You're leaving the priesthood?" I ask incredulously.

"Technically, I've already left. But your Tita Vida wanted your Grandlola Naty to see me in my vestments at least one time, so I put everything on yesterday and celebrated mass. Church officials would call that an illicit ceremony since I'm no longer an ordained priest." He smirks, giving me that dimple once again. "Shh. Don't tell the pope, please. I could get in big trouble."

If you add it up, I have spent two full days with Nicholas Salgado, but no one has changed my life as dramatically as he has. If not for him, I would have taken a very different path. I would be a very different person. And I wouldn't be standing here with a man whose smirking face I simultaneously want to slap, kiss and ride for as long as he lets me.

"You're an ass," I say. "Why didn't you tell me?"

"I tried to."

Shit. He did. "But...what about...?"

"My calling?" he says. "To be honest, during the last five years or so, I've struggled to understand my place in the church. I sought counsel from all kinds of people, religious and non-religious, Catholic and non-Catholic. Of course, I talked to my mom. And I prayed—I prayed a lot." He pauses, studying my face. "Long story short, I believe God has a new calling for me. It's to teach. My field of study is the intersection of immigration, identity, and religion. USF offered me a place to continue my research, and after much discussion, my superiors and I agreed it was time for me to leave the priesthood and follow this path instead."

I'm afraid to ask, but I do it anyway. "Does this path include following your heart, Nick?"

He smiles. "Yes, it does. Wherever it leads."

We look at each other, and a new world opens up in front of us, ready to explore.

"And you're not a priest," I say.

He embraces me tightly and rests his chin on the top of my head. "No, I'm not. Not anymore," he says.

Together, we listen to the rushing water, endlessly flowing, endlessly renewed.

After a long time, Nick says, "Can I ask you a favor?"

"What?"

"Can I hitch a ride with you to San Francisco? The university is providing me with faculty housing and I'd like to check in today."

"Of course."

Later that day, we say goodbye to Grandlola Naty, who gives us each a smile and a soft pat on our faces. We say goodbye to the Moore family and the staff of the hacienda, and I feel my connection to this place renewed and rekindled. This is home again—it always was, even when I wasn't ready to return to it.

Nick and I get into the same car. Through my open window, Tita Vida takes my hand and squeezes it. "He has always wanted to protect you," she whispers to me. "Just as I have. You have always deserved love, Eden, and lots of it."

"Happy birthday, Tita. Merry Christmas," I say. "I love you."

"Maligayang Pasko. I love you too." Her smiling face is luminous. "Come back to us. Soon. Often."

I'm crying as we drive away from Hacienda Luz.

Nick puts his hand on mine and keeps it there all the way back to the city.

THE END

ABOUT MIA HOPKINS

Mia Hopkins writes lush romances starring fun, sexy characters who love to get down and dirty. Her award-winning books have been featured in many publications, including The New York Times, The Washington Post, USA Today, and *Entertainment Weekly*. She lives in Los Angeles with her family. For more information, please visit www.miahopkinsauthor.com or connect with her on social media @miahopkinsxoxo.

So It's You

MAIDA MALBY

So It's You

MAIDA MALBY

Blurb:

Vida and her maternal grandmother, Naty Moore, share a special bond—the same birthday on Christmas Eve, fifty years apart. This year, Lola Naty will celebrate her 100th birthday, and Vida plans to do everything to make sure her grand party goes off without a hitch. Even if that includes hiding the identity of the man she's dating.

Rafa Balmaseda fell for Vida long before he became her grandmother's physician. Ten years younger than her, he chafes at being kept a secret. When he pushes for a deeper commitment, will Vida continue to deny his role in her life? Or will she finally admit that they belong together?

Content Note:

Profanity

CHAPTER ONE

Vida

Vida's heart thumped wildly inside her chest as she flung open the front door of Bahay ni Lola, the owner's cottage of their family-owned hotel, Hacienda Luz. The door closed behind her with a thud, rattling the parol—the Filipino Christmas lantern made of capiz shells—that decorated it. She dropped her purse on the floor, neglecting to take off her coat or her boots. There wasn't time. She had to get to Lola Naty before—

No. She shook her head, blinking to clear the onset of tears. *Lola is fine. She's strong. She's going to make it.* Praying under her breath, she ran through the living room, past the adjoining kitchen, veered left towards the master suite, and slammed right into a wall. A moving green wall.

"Umph!" Stunned, Vida lost her balance and began to fall. She brought her hands to her head and curled forward so she'd land on her butt. Braced for impact, she closed her eyes. And promptly opened them when her back came in contact with muscles and bone instead of hardwood floor.

An olive-green Henley with the top two buttons unfastened filled her vision. A fine dusting of brown hair covered the brown skin that peeked from the open vee. Stubbles darkened a square jaw. Literally a five o'clock shadow, for it was that time of the day now.

Vida's pulse thrummed a much different beat than when she came through the door. She knew who held her in his arms. That earthy, outdoorsy scent of bespoke soap similar to the fragrant, freshly cut Douglas fir tree in the living room, mixed with the sharp hint of antiseptic could only belong to one person.

Raising her eyes to meet her rescuer's, she whispered, "Rafa."

"Hello, Vida." Brown eyes so light they were almost amber twinkled at her. Full, symmetrical lips smiled as he pulled her gently to her feet.

A flush rose up Vida's neck, warming her cheeks. He'd been holding her in a dip while she gawked at him like a swooning teenage girl at the sight of her first crush. She was too old to still be blushing when she came into contact with an attractive man. Yet she always did for this man. "Thank you for catching me."

"No thanks necessary," he said. "It was my fault you almost fell. I wasn't looking where I was going."

Too flustered to look him in the eye, she focused her gaze on his cotton-covered broad chest. The "wall" she'd bumped into. Her hand lifted of its own volition. "I—"

"Doc, you're still— Tita Vida, you're home early."

Vida startled and would have fallen again if not for Rafa's steadying hand on her arm.

"I thought you were going straight to your weekend date after your errands," her nephew Carlo said. "Didn't you get my text that Grandlola is fine?"

Lola Naty! How could she have forgotten about her grandmother? Facing her nephew, she said, "You also texted me that Lola took a spill. Of course, I had to drop everything and come home. How is she now?"

The fact that both her grandmother's physician and her caregiver were outside her room meant Lola Naty was probably okay. Vida's fears wouldn't be allayed, though, until she'd seen her grandmother's condition for herself.

Watching over the matriarch of the Moore clan was her full-time job. She hadn't retired from the day-to-day running of Hacienda Luz Hotel and Vineyard only to fall short on performing her duties to her grandmother.

"Like I said, she's all right. Promise to God. Let's go to the kitchen. I'll tell you what happened while I prepare dinner," Carlo said.

"Your lola is resting," Rafa assured her, pronouncing the Filipino word for grandmother the same way she did— *loh-lah*. "I gave her a light dose of ibuprofen. She's probably sleeping right now."

Vida stepped away from Rafa. "I want to see her," she told both men and turned towards her grandmother's bedroom before they could offer more assurances. Lola Naty was *her* responsibility, *her* priority. Only *she* got to decide if Lola was fine or not.

Before entering her grandmother's bedroom, Vida took off her boots. If she were awake, Lola would scold her for wearing shoes inside the house. She nudged open the door that Carlo had left ajar and slipped quietly inside, her footfalls muffled by the thick carpet. Dimmed soft light from a floor lamp festooned with sparkling tinsel bathed the room in a warm golden glow. Outside the bay window, the sun had disappeared behind near-dormant grapevines, leaving a purplish hue on the horizon.

Lola Naty lay on her back, chest rising and falling evenly beneath a crocheted blanket stitched with turtles at the corners. Her left arm was encased in a sling but there was no IV drip or respirator attached to her. No bulky bandages, no bruises visible.

Vida gripped the bar on the foot of the hospital bed and sagged in relief. *Lola is okay.*

She reached for the tablet, lowered herself to the sleeper sofa, and read today's chart that detailed the small accident. Carlo's report was short and factual, Rafa's diagnosis and treatment plan even more so. Both eased Vida's mind tremendously.

Rising to her feet, she took in the entire suite: the portable x-ray machine, the oxygen concentrator, the wheelchair, and all the high-tech medical equipment. She uttered a short prayer of thanks for having the resources to afford the best of what money could buy to care for her grandmother in her own home.

If only money could buy time. Gazing at her grandmother's frail form in repose, Vida felt her heart clench. With her thinning white hair and slack, transparent skin exposing veins and brittle bones, Lola looked every day of her soon-to-be one hundred years.

I'm being selfish, she admitted. Maria Natividad Moore had been blessing the world with her presence for more than ninety-nine years and eleven months. Vida had been lucky to spend nearly fifty of those years living with her lola. How much more time could she ask for? A year? Two? Not if it meant Lola would be in more pain. Not if she lost more of her memories, more of her pride and dignity.

Until Christmas Eve. That was all Vida could ask for. Until Lola's one hundredth birthday. Her own fiftieth. The only birthday and Christmas gift she wanted was for her grandmother to live to see her family all together on Christmas Eve. That wasn't too much to ask. Only one more week.

After checking that the monitor was turned on and a glass of water was within her grandmother's reach, Vida left the room. In the hallway, she paused and listened to the two voices that rose above the Christmas carols playing on the smart speaker. One was the animated high-pitched chatter of Carlo. The other, the rich timbre of Rafa Balmaseda's baritone.

Blasted by a sudden wave of heat, Vida shrugged off her coat. Must be the perimenopause. A hot flash, nothing else. No tall, handsome man with tiger eyes and a crooner's voice could affect her that much. Could he?

She poked her head around the corner and had to hold on to the wall, her knees weak. Rafa was standing in front of the stove tending a pot of boiling water. *Dang, yes, he could.*

Gathering herself, Vida rolled her shoulders and strolled forward with as much nonchalance as she could muster. "Hmm, arroz caldo," she said, nose in the air. Her mouth watered at the fragrant scent of ginger and garlic. There was no better Filipino comfort food than the chicken and rice porridge her nephew was cooking, especially on a cold day out in Napa Valley and after a scare like the one she'd had.

She draped her coat on the back of a chair and sat in front of the large island separating the kitchen from the living room.

"It's Tita Baby's recipe," Carlo said, ladling a huge serving of the porridge into a bowl.

"You told me your Aunt Ruby was the chef who taught you how to make arroz caldo. Who is Tita Baby?" Rafa asked. He turned off the stove and transferred the eggs into a strainer to run them under cold water.

"They're the same person. Ruby is my dad's and Tita Vida's first cousin, Grandlola Naty's youngest granddaughter. The baby of the family until recently. She's twenty-eight," Carlo explained.

"Hold on. You call her tita even though she's three years younger than you?" Rafa asked, his face a mask of confusion.

Carlo shrugged. "That's the Filipino way."

Rafa looked at Vida as if asking for confirmation.

She nodded. "It's this particular family's way based on what Lola Naty taught us about Filipino kinship and honorifics. We don't do the 'once or twice removed' thing. That's why even though Carlo is my cousin's offspring, not my non-existent sibling's, he's considered my nephew."

Rafa nodded. "It must be fun growing up in a big family." His voice held a wistful note.

Vida's heart went out to him. She knew his remaining family was only an older brother who lived in Florida with his wife and two children. "It was," she said simply. Especially for an only child like her with absentee parents who were dedicated to their political causes in their birth country, the Philippines. She was grateful that she had numerous younger cousins.

Shaking off the suddenly somber direction of her thoughts, she turned to her nephew and asked brightly, "Is one of those for me?"

Carlo was garnishing two large bowls of congee with chopped scallion, saffron threads, and crispy fried garlic bits. "You can have this as soon as Doctor Bal is ready with the hard-boiled eggs."

Vida watched Rafa peel an egg with surgical precision, tapping it with the back of a tablespoon to break the shell on both ends and removing the hard outer layer starting from the wide end where there was an air bubble.

He looked at home here. After nearly one year as Lola's physician, he had a right to feel comfortable. Between her, Lola, and Carlo, they'd made sure to include him whenever his visits coincided with lunch or dinner. Over time he'd progressed from being a mere guest to assisting in meal preparations.

Vida accepted the bowl Rafa handed her as he sat beside her. She turned her attention back to her younger relative who gave her a glass of water. "Carlo, you're not eating?"

"I'll join Grandlola when she wakes up." He began washing utensils while he talked. "Speaking of … I guess you read the chart." At her nod, he continued. "Before I explain, I want to remind you that you approved of us doing a surprise dance number for the party, and Dr. Bal cleared it."

Rafa chimed in. "As long as your grandmother doesn't overdo it, she'll be fine."

"Ugh," Vida said. "I'm beginning to regret giving in to the three of you."

"Well, after you left this morning, I taught Grandlola the steps the cousins and I choreographed to the tune of her favorite Bruno Mars song. It's just the basic Electric Slide, which she already knows." Carlo demonstrated as he talked. Grapevine right, grapevine left, rock forward and back with a toe touch, quarter turn left. "As you might expect, she learned quickly and we were done after a couple of rounds."

"But …" Vida said. She already knew what her nephew was going to say, but she wanted to hear it anyway. Her grandmother might be hard of hearing, couldn't see very well, and had occasional memory lapses, but she was still a perfectionist, even at her advanced age.

"I left her sitting in her chair while I prepared her bath. Apparently, she decided to practice on her own and lost her balance when she crossed her right foot over the left on the grapevine step. She banged her left arm against the metal frame of her wheelchair before she was able to right herself. When I came back, she was back in her seat, face pale, and cradling her aching arm," Carlo explained. "I didn't think she'd broken it, but I called Doc Bal to confirm."

"Thankfully I was passing by on my way home and was able to do an x-ray. Her wrist was only swollen, not dislocated. I put her arm in a sling so she wouldn't move it. She should be able to take it off in a few days. Well before the party next Saturday," Rafa added.

Praise God, Vida thought. "Thank you," she said. Rafa acknowledged her gratitude with a smile.

"I'm sorry, Tita. I made Grandlola swear on Greatda's memory that she wouldn't practice without me again." Carlo's contrite voice stopped her from staring too long at the handsome man beside her.

"I'm not blaming you. Much," she said to both men's laughter. "It was an accident. We all know Lola Naty. She can be stubborn and too independent at times." Relieved that her worst fears hadn't happened, Vida started to eat the tasty porridge in front of her.

"Your grandma is strong in will and spirit. Body and mind too, for a centenarian. She told me she plans to be in the *Guinness World Records*," Rafa said, amused.

Carlo laughed. "Lola Iska, the world's oldest Filipino, died in 2021 at 124 years old. Grandlola Naty might outlive us all."

Vida nearly choked on a bite of chicken. She took a sip of water and said, "Let's just make sure we keep her alive until her centennial party, or the clan will kill us."

"It's going to be so much fun!" Carlo punctuated his enthusiasm with a clap. "Our first family reunion in a decade. How's the party planning coming along?"

"We're still waiting for more parol to be delivered, but it's going well," she said. Lola wanted all the windows and doors of the hacienda decorated with the colorful star-shaped lanterns. "I've delegated as much as I can to the other cousins and to the Hacienda Luz staff—Eden has ordered everything and Norah will handle them when they arrive—so I can concentrate on Lola on the day itself." And not overburden herself on her own birthday. Not that many of the invited guests knew that tidbit. What was fifty compared to one hundred anyway?

"I'll help you with her," Rafa volunteered. "That is, if I'm still invited. It looks like a family-only event."

"Of course, you are invited, along with four hundred people who have a close connection with Lola Naty," Vida assured him. Her grandmother had touched thousands of lives in her century of life. She and Grandda Robert had helped immigrants settle in the country legally by hiring them to work in the hotel and vineyard and sponsoring their petition for permanent residence. "You're more of a family to Lola than some of our blood relatives," she added.

"Like Tito Ollie," Carlo said. "The family playboy. He's a bit of a flake," he told the puzzled Rafa.

"Oliver is ghosting me, so I haven't included him on the guest list yet. Serves him right if he shows up next Saturday and the hotel security doesn't let him in," Vida said with relish. Without Oliver's monetary contribution, she'd been forced to dip into the contingency fund. Not cool.

"Ooh, I like it when you play contra-Vida." Carlo snickered.

"Against life?" Rafa asked, which was the literal translation of the Spanish words.

"No. In Filipino it means anti-hero," Vida said.

"A villain? You can never be that. You're the kindest, most generous person I know," Rafa said.

If the earnestness in his voice hadn't convinced Vida of the sincerity of his compliment, the admiring look on his face had. Her cheeks heated. "You're sweet for saying that, but I can be contrary at times."

"Get a room!" Carlo called out then immediately slapped a hand over his mouth when she and Rafa turned to face him. After a couple of seconds, he lowered his hand. "Sorry, I forgot you're both in a relationship. It's just that you look so good together. Like a Hollywood couple. I mean, nobody even notices the age gap. Aaand I'll shut up now." He pressed his lips together and mimed zipping it closed.

"I should get going." Rafa stood. "Thanks for dinner, Carlo. Call me if Mrs. Moore is in pain. I'll come back right away." He nodded to her. "See you later."

Vida tipped her chin at him. "See you." She kept her back turned to the front of the house, but she was conscious of his progress the entire way. There went the footsteps across hardwood, over rug, then the woosh of the pocket door in the hallway closet opening as he retrieved his jacket. The zip of boots followed by Carlo's answering wave and finally, the soft nick of the closing front door.

"See you later?" Carlo teased, wiggling his eyebrows.

Vida pointed a finger at her nephew. "You are cut off from my will. I'm giving your share to Aldwin and Badet and Ron's babies," she said, mentioning Carlo's brother and sister and the children of one of her first cousins. "That will make Eden my main heiress." Her niece, the event planner for Lola Naty's party, was the closest thing to a daughter Vida had.

"Aww, Tita! You don't mean that. I'm your favorite," he protested. "I'll keep cheering for you until the universe manifests the romance between Vida Moore Aquino and Rafael I-Don't-Know-His-Middle-Name Balmaseda," he said, throwing his arms in the air like he was releasing confetti. "Or, until I meet your mystery lovah." He brought his hands together to form a heart over his chest. "How long have you been dating him? Almost one year. Longer than any of your former boyfriends. Does Grandlola know? Is his name Mr. Snuffleupagus? Who is heeeee, Tita?" He ended the pantomime with his chin propped between his cupped hands, fluttering his ridiculously long eyelashes at her.

"I can't even with you." Shaking her head at her nephew's flamboyant antics, Vida pushed back her chair and got up. "Can you bring in Lola's barong dress for the party from the car? I left it unlocked. I'll check on her one more time, then I'm leaving for my date."

"Invite him to the party!" Carlo called out after her retreating back.

Vida smiled. *Oh, he'll be there.*

CHAPTER TWO

Rafa

Rafa draped a dark blue fleece blanket over the arm of a chaise longue, finishing his preparations for tonight's date. Winter had arrived in Napa five days ahead of its official schedule. The thermostat had read a lower-than-average thirty-five degrees outside when he came home fifteen minutes ago. It was only a few degrees warmer inside, so he had turned on the electric fireplace. It emitted a cozy warmth throughout the open living space and provided a romantic ambience as well. Its flickering red flames, combined with the blinking multicolored lights on the Noble fir tree, depicted a picture postcard scene.

He surveyed his handiwork one more time. In front of the fireplace, he'd scattered decorative pillows over the plush shag rug. A bottle of red blend from the Hacienda Luz vineyard was breathing on a side table. Beside it, he'd placed a box of chocolate nonpareils. Smooth jazz played quietly in the background. All were her favorite things.

Rafa sat down on the couch and picked up the bottle. Several of the words and phrases in the product description jumped at him. "Rich and alluring, lusciously layered, deep and complex, arouses your senses, silky mouthfeel, leaves you wanting more."

The same words could describe his girlfriend, Vida, to perfection.

Girlfriend. An awkward term, that. At almost fifty, Vida had long ago left girlhood behind. A friend, yes. A girl, no. A lover, most definitely.

Rafa returned the bottle to the table and sat back, remembering their first meeting at the beginning of the year.

He'd been driving around to familiarize himself with various routes from his house to the clinic, to the homes of the handful of patients he'd agreed to visit in his new job. A reconnaissance of sorts.

Before he'd transitioned to private practice, his final assignment for the US Air Force had been in the medical center at the base in nearby Fairfield. He'd visited Napa a number of times, but visiting and living there were two different things altogether. If he was going to be called in for emergencies, he needed to know shortcuts and alternate routes.

The name Hacienda Luz on a roadside billboard had caught his attention. Vineyard of Light, he loosely translated. The possibility of finding a community that shared his Hispanic heritage had lured him to visit the small winery.

It was raining that day, normal for the region in January. There weren't a lot of cars in the parking lot, no sight of a tour bus either. Typical of the low season. Perfect timing on his part. He'd have left right away had there been a long line.

As it was, the reception area of the visitor center was empty aside from two women. One stood in front of the white gloss counter, the other behind it, heads down, looking over a document he couldn't see from where he remained by the door. They hadn't noticed he'd come in. He'd entered just as a couple was leaving.

His eyes homed in on *her* right away. She was the older of the two, the taller, and the one who possessed an air of command he'd always gravitated towards. Her profile was to him. Black shoulder-length hair was tucked behind an ear adorned with a pearl earring. Lush lips beneath a straight nose moved as she spoke in low tones. An elegant, lean body was clothed in crisp, white, long-sleeved dress shirt and woolen gray slacks. Low-heeled black ankle boots completed the simple but sophisticated look.

She straightened, and he knew he'd been caught staring. He dragged his eyes up to meet hers. They were brown, like sleeping grapevines, and wary as befitting someone catching a stranger who'd been ogling her.

"Hello," they said at the same time.

He smiled and walked forward, holding out his hand. "I'm Rafa. I apologize for dropping in without an appointment. I was driving by, saw the billboard, and was curious about the name."

Her expression of wariness left, replaced by a warm smile that transformed her face from merely lovely to downright stunning. "Welcome to Hacienda Luz, Rafa. I'm Vida. This is Jen, our estate ambassador. We appreciate your visit on this rainy afternoon."

The hand that firmly shook his had long fingers, neatly trimmed nails with clear polish, and a soft palm. He hadn't wanted to let it go. He only did when she pulled away to point at the glass of red wine the other woman was holding out.

He'd been so engrossed with Vida he hadn't noticed the estate ambassador move to and from the bar on the far end of the room to pour him a welcome drink.

"This is our Cabernet Sauvignon from the 2013 harvest. One of our best years since my grandparents, Naty and

Robert Moore, started operations almost eighty years ago. It's a small taste of the exceptional quality of wine we produce," Vida said.

Rafa accepted the glass. "Thank you," he said to the younger woman, who smiled and returned to the bar, leaving him with Vida by the reception counter, pleasing Rafa greatly.

It pleased him even more to follow Vida to the glass-enclosed veranda with its large gas fire pit and a one-hundred-eighty-degree view of the property. Even without grapes on the vines, the colors were earthy and predominantly brown, the Hacienda Luz vineyard was a striking sight. But no matter its grandeur, it couldn't hold his attention for long. Not when all he wanted to see was Vida's beautiful face.

"Gorgeous, isn't it?" Vida asked.

There was no ring on her left finger, so he thought he'd take a shot. "Yes," he said, openly staring at her.

Her lips formed a word that Rafa couldn't hear. He could have sworn it was "smooth." He gave her a cheeky smile.

"Aren't you going to try the wine? I want to know what you think of it."

He swirled the dark red liquid and brought the glass to his nose. After an appreciative sniff, he took a sip. "Hmm. It's ripe, savory, and yet sweet. Smooth and complex. I'm enticed to find out more." He took a larger gulp, then another until he finished the glass. His eyes held her expectant gaze as he declared his final assessment. "Sexy."

Vida's cheeks turned a lovely dusky pink. Her eyes flicked to his lips. "I think so too," she said.

A deep breath and a nod of her head told him she'd had an internal debate and had decided on the next course of action. "How may I help you today, Rafa? Are you looking for anything in particular? A tour of the winery, caves, and library?" A slight pause, then her voice had gone husky. "Or a private tasting, perhaps?"

Rafa smiled at the memory of Vida's flirtatious offer. He'd chosen a private tasting. Of wine, at first. And after a couple of dates, of everything else she had offered for him to taste. She'd offered generously.

Their first meeting had been on a Friday. Since then, they'd dated every weekend, driving all over Northern California, never going farther than one hundred miles away from Napa. They'd stayed in charming bed and breakfasts until he'd bought this house at the edge of Napa Valley and American Canyon last month, on his fortieth birthday.

Vida hadn't felt comfortable staying in his one-bedroom apartment in downtown Napa. Too many people knew her there, she'd said. The risk of someone seeing them together was too great. She wanted to keep their relationship private.

It stung, sometimes, her denial of him. Like this afternoon with her nephew. She was too conscious of what people might say about their ten-year age difference and his role as her grandmother's physician. He didn't give a flying fuck. But she did, and he had to respect that. It didn't mean he would stop trying to get her to commit to him wholeheartedly.

The rumble of an engine drew Rafa's attention to the direction of the driveway. He waited for the slam of the car door and the beep of the locks engaging before he got to his feet to welcome his girlfriend of nearly one year into his home. As soon as the front door closed behind her, he was there to swing her down into a dip. Almost exactly like his timely catch to stop her from falling this afternoon.

Brown eyes the color of late autumn leaves opened wide in delight. "Rafa," she breathed.

"Hello, Vida." He drew her upright and greeted her like he would have at her house if her nephew hadn't been there.

Cupping her beautiful face between his hands, Rafa pressed his mouth to hers. Without much coaxing, she opened her lips, tangled her tongue with his. He hungered for her. It had been an entire week since their last kiss.

He could never get enough of her taste. Fruity and juicy like her family's wines. And sweet, so sweet.

She felt so right flush against him. He needed to get closer still. Skin to skin, without layers separating them. He moved his hands to her collar, intent on pushing her coat off her shoulders, but she was already shrugging it off. He loved this about them. They were so in sync. As combustible as the first time they'd made love many, many months ago. One kiss and they both caught fire.

He lowered his hands to her waist, felt for the hem of her sweater, but it wasn't there. She had changed clothes after he left her house. His hands wandered past her hips, down her thighs, and encountered satiny skin.

Rafa groaned, breaking their kiss. "You're going to kill me." He dropped to his knees and worshipped Vida with his eyes. Starting from her feet and long legs that were encased in black leather, custom-made knee-high boots. Sexy as fuck. Up the expanse of smooth skin beneath the hem of her mid-thigh, body-hugging knit dress. He skidded to a stop at the sight of two hard points pushing at the clinging material. "No bra."

"No panties, either."

Rafa's gaze flew to her face.

She was biting her lower lip, looking at the outline of his erection tenting the sweatpants he'd changed into knowing it turned her on.

He jumped to his feet and caught her hand. "Bedroom. Now."

She tugged him back. "Too far. Let's stay here. In front of the fireplace."

Rafa paused. "Are you sure? Your back. I—"

"You won't hurt me. We'll pile on the pillows. You already have them there on the floor," she said, pointing to the area rug.

He had. For relaxing. For cuddling. Nothing more strenuous than that. But she knew her own body. If she wanted to change his plans, she was welcome to it. Without further hesitation, he scooped her up.

"I can walk, you know. It's only a few steps." Her arms clinging around his neck belied her protest.

"Not fast enough." It took him four long strides before he kneeled and deposited her gently in the middle of the pearl-gray rug.

While Vida rearranged pillows under her lower back, he pulled his long-sleeved shirt over his head. He hadn't planned to start their evening this way, but he wasn't going to waste any opportunity to make love to this sensual woman who'd captivated him from the first moment they met.

"Don't take the boots off." They were a gift from him. He'd had them specially made for her.

She pulled the zipper back up and leaned back on her elbows. "No?" Her voice teased.

Rafa crawled forward, nudging her legs apart with his shoulders. "No, but you can remove your dress and let me feast on you."

"You always go for the private tasting," she said, complying with his request to undress. A quick task with the dress being her sole article of clothing.

"Only when you're the one offering." He ran his hands over the skin she bared. Touching her was an irresistible urge he never denied himself.

Vida's pulse thudded beneath the palm he laid on her left breast, arousal in every rhythmic beat. "For you alone, it's an open invitation," she said, voice husky.

His own desire ramping up, Rafa settled more comfortably between her thighs. "One I'm glad to accept." He bent his head towards her softness and, as he'd declared, feasted. Tasted and drank to his heart's content. To her satisfaction. And when she demanded for him to join her, he brought them both to completion.

* * *

Rafa traced the S curve of Vida's spine with his index finger. After eleven months of dating, he knew her body intimately. Her medical history as well.

Her scoliosis was mild—less than a ten-degree sideways curvature. She'd been managing it admirably for years with non-surgical movement therapies.

Still, his heart ached for her, for everything she'd suffered because of her condition: the separation from her parents at thirteen when they chose to leave her behind for better health care rather than take her to an uncertain situation in the Philippines; her decision to never bear a child for fear of passing it on to them—one of the myriad reasons she'd never married. The limitations to physical activities, including several sexual positions that could cause excruciating pain. The self-consciousness, at least in the beginning, about her uneven hips and shoulders.

His gift of the boots with the right foot outfitted with custom-made insoles to help reduce the length discrepancy of her legs had brought her to tears. Happy tears, she'd assured him. Grateful tears, appreciative tears. Apart from her grandparents, he was the only one who understood her, who wasn't repulsed by her physical differences.

As their relationship progressed, she'd lost many of her inhibitions. Rafa could take partial credit for that, having shown her time and again how much he desired her, all of her.

He brushed her tousled hair to one side and pressed a kiss on the curve of her neck. She responded with a slight shiver.

"Are you cold?" He pulled the throw blanket higher over her nude body.

She turned around to face him. "Not when you're here to keep me warm."

Her words filled his heart with joy. He leaned closer and caught her lips in a quick kiss. "Hold that thought," he said. He pushed to his feet and took a small gift box from the mantle over the fireplace. He'd left it there earlier, intending to give it to her at the right time. That time was now.

He returned to the rug to find her sitting up, blanket tucked under her armpits, a questioning look on her face. She stared at the flat rectangular box in his hand. The size and shape of it were deliberate choices on his part. Nobody would mistake it for a ring box. He knew Vida wasn't ready for a permanent commitment yet.

Rafa was.

Not because he was forty and tired of the dating scene. It was because of *her*. His Vida. He hoped tonight's gift would eventually nudge her into his way of thinking.

Naked, he knelt before her and laid himself bare. "I always want to keep you warm, mi Vida. Or cool if that's what you need. If you'll let me, I'll keep you warm every day and every night." He offered her the gift.

It was only a second, but he saw her hesitate before opening her palm to accept his present. A deep breath, then she lifted the lid. A soft gasp escaped her. "Oh."

Inside the box was a gold heart-topped key pendant on a thin chain. On the back of the diamond-accented stem, a series of numbers—122472—was etched. Her birthday and the code to his smart lock. Up to now, he had always come home ahead of her, had always left the door open so she could come in.

"Make my home yours, Vida. Stay with me. Not only on weekends." He rubbed his hands down his thighs, gripped with uncertainty at her lack of response.

She placed the box on the rug, picked up the necklace, and clutched it to her chest. "Oh, Rafa. It's beautiful." She raised gleaming eyes to him. In them he saw her answer.

Rafa spun away, groping for his sweatpants. He pulled them on with jerky movements. As if they were armor that could protect him from the hurt she was about to inflict on him.

He strode to the side table and poured himself a glass of wine. Downed half of it before he felt calm enough to say the words she hadn't uttered. "You're saying no."

A trail of blue fabric moved to the couch. "I want ... I can't. Lola ..."

Resentment went through him. Her grandmother. Always her grandmother.

He gulped down the rest of the wine. That was unfair. He loved the old lady too. Naty Moore had claimed him as one of her own that first day he'd visited her at her home. She'd chosen him as the replacement for her former physician who'd retired to Florida. She was one of only two patients he made house calls for.

He'd never known his grandparents from either side. They'd stayed behind in Cuba and died before his parents felt secure enough to return for a visit. Lola Naty was his grandmother now.

"This is only ten miles away. Even in the worst traffic, you can be at the hacienda in fifteen minutes if she needs you," he reasoned, facing Vida for the first time since she'd given him a non-answer.

Hand outstretched, she beckoned to him. "Rafa, please."

The hold this woman had on him couldn't be denied. He sat beside her.

"There is nothing I want more than to stay here with you. Sleep with you every night. Wake up in the morning seeing your handsome face on the pillow beside mine."

These were the words he wanted to hear. The upcoming "but," not so much.

"But the thought of leaving my grandmother alone makes me feel ashamed, makes me feel ungrateful."

She wasn't going to leave her grandmother by herself. Carlo was a registered nurse and they could always hire a caregiver when her nephew wanted some time off. They both knew that, but he couldn't say it out loud because reason had nothing to do with her reluctance to commit to him. Ultimately, she had to face her fears on her own.

He reached for her hands, the right still balled up with the key inside, and held them in his. "How long have you been taking care of her? Ten years? Twenty? I'm sure she never required it of you."

"Fifty years is not long enough. Lola Naty has been my mother since I was thirteen. Since my parents left to fight for other people instead of their only child. She's been my father too since Grandda Robert died fifteen years ago. My only parent since those who birthed me passed away. If …" Her breath hitched. "When her time comes, I want to be the last person she sees before she takes her last breath." She gulped for air, tears falling from her eyes. "If not, I will never forgive myself."

And she'd never forgive him for taking her away from her grandmother's side. He was a selfish prick.

Edging closer, Rafa shifted Vida to his lap. Stroked her hair as she wept. Comforting the families of patients after he'd given them bad news had never been his strong suit. In the military, where deaths were commonplace, keeping an emotional distance was paramount to his survival. It got even easier in private practice. More transactional, a thousand times more impersonal.

Rafa seldom offered consoling words. He never offered his shoulders to cry on. He always protected his heart.

For the woman he loved who was anguished by thoughts of a future worst-case scenario, there was no way he could be detached. The opposite in fact. He would do anything to take on her burdens, to share in her grief.

"I'm sorry, Vee," he said after she'd subsided to sniffles. "For being selfish." He raised her chin and wiped the tracks of tears from her face. "For making you cry. I hope never to do that again except for happy tears." He pressed his forehead gently to hers and looked deep into her eyes. "The offer is open anytime you want to accept it."

"I'm saying not yet." She lifted a hand to his cheek and kissed him sweetly. Pulling back, she opened her clenched fist to show him the heart key. "Put it on me?"

He did, his heart light.

Touching the pendant lying between her breasts, she asked. "Is this my birthday gift?"

He'd long ago realized that she had received combined birthday and Christmas gifts throughout her life, so he'd made it a point to give her a present every week to catch up on all the years he'd missed. Many of his gifts—custom made stuff suited to her specifications and measurements, personalized objects with her name on them, perfume, lingerie, adult toys, books, music—were here. She'd brought a lot of them over when he moved in, effectively moving in herself. It had raised his expectations.

"Yes. I'm all caught up. Happy forty-ninth, Vee."

"Thank you. I love it."

But did she love him? She never said the words, though she'd shown him in plenty of ways. Except for the one way he'd been waiting for—telling her grandmother about them. Once she'd done that, he'd have no more doubts. He'd be all in.

CHAPTER THREE

Rafa

Rafa stretched his legs under the round folding table outside the bubble tea shop, sighing in relief at finally getting off his feet. A couple of the shopping bags around him crackled as he moved. He considered himself relatively fit, but two hours of shopping at a premium outlet in the middle of the day one week before Christmas had proved him wrong. He was beat. And thirsty and hungry. Vida had told him to start without her while she went to the restroom, so he ate and drank the takoyaki and taro milk tea he'd ordered for himself.

He'd gotten used to doing all his shopping online. With only a handful of people to buy Christmas gifts for, he'd been set for a while now. But Vida had a long list, both hers and her grandmother's, what with the reunion bringing in family members they hadn't seen in a long time.

Rafa recognized a couple of the names Vida had mentioned—her cousins Sophie Palacio and Drew Hizon. "A sex podcaster and a US senator," he muttered, amused.

Vida had an interesting family. There were nurses like Carlo, chefs, a priest or two, active-duty military, politicians, and entertainers. Her own parents had been in media, deeply entrenched in the turbulent Filipino political scene during the seventies and eighties. Vida's father, Simoun, was a distant relative of the famous Aquinos that had given the Philippines two presidents. Not that she ever boasted of the illustrious connection, preferring to go by her grandparents' surname Moore.

Rafa fiddled with his wooden chopsticks as he contemplated the differences between himself and Vida. Their ages were the least important as far as he was concerned, but that was a major one for her. The family background was another, but only in terms of how extended hers was compared to his nuclear unit.

There was also the fact that she was rich, he was merely comfortable. Rafa owned his home outright, had modest savings and investments, had three sources of income—his military disability, retirement income, and his current work—and had no debts. Vida had inherited her mother's share of Hacienda Luz and stood to gain more from her grandmother.

He didn't know whether their financial gap was an issue to worry about. Not until they moved forward in their relationship. Moving in together was on hold. The next step was hers to take. He could do nothing but wait.

Rafa shook his head. Deep thoughts were giving him indigestion. He leaned to his left, searching for a sign of Vida's return. She'd warned him that there might be a line. The next restroom was all the way across the parking lot.

There! He pushed the chair across from him out from the table with his feet as he saw Vida approach. To his annoyance, a tall gray-haired man called out to her, further delaying her return. She turned and kissed the guy on the cheek in greeting.

Rafa observed the interaction, wondering at the slight resemblance between the two. An uncle or an older cousin? Lola Naty had photos of her family all over the house, but he hadn't been interested in looking at them closely unless they included his lover.

Vida wasn't smiling as they talked. Some nodding and headshaking. Another kiss on the cheek, then the old guy proceeded to his car—a flashy late model German import.

"I'm so sorry I took so long." Vida sat down and immediately reached for her Thai Green Tea Latte.

Rafa let her drink and eat some of the popcorn chicken before asking, "Who was that?"

"Oh, that's my Uncle Ion. He's my mom's youngest brother," she said, then went back to eating.

Her uncle. And she didn't think to introduce them. He was only a few feet away, but she hadn't even glanced his way when she was talking to her relative. Rafa kept his temper in check. "Uncle, not Tito?" he asked.

"That's what he prefers." Vida lifted her shoulders in a shrug. "He's the most white-presenting of all Lola Naty's children and the one closest to the Moore's Irish heritage rather than the Filipino side. He's based in Dublin, overseeing our international operations. Only here for Lola's birthday."

So, they weren't close. That mollified him somewhat.

A movement to his left caught Rafa's attention. It was Vida's uncle returning.

"Vee, I think your uncle forgot something," he said.

"Huh?" Vida turned to her right. "Oh." She glanced at Rafa, half-stood, then sat back down when her uncle reached them.

Rafa pushed to his feet.

"Vida, have you heard from Oliver?" Ion asked.

"Not since six months ago," Vida replied.

"I thought you'd know where he is." The older man ran a hand through his hair in obvious frustration.

Another of Vida's shrugs. "Sorry, Uncle."

Silence followed. Rafa cleared his throat, catching Ion's attention.

"I'm sorry for my rudeness. I'm Ion Moore."

"Uncle Ion, this is Ra … Dr. Balmaseda, Lola's doctor," Vida said, not looking at him.

"Ra as in the Egyptian sun god?" Ion held out his hand to Rafa.

He shook the proffered hand. "Ra as in Rafael. Nice to meet you, sir."

Ion glanced at his niece who had her head down, stirring the tapioca balls in her milk tea. "Good to meet you, Rafael," he said. "I'll leave you to your lunch. See you at the party, Vida."

Rafa stood there for a full minute before speaking. "Are you finished? I'd like to go home now." Without waiting for an answer, he gathered the boxes and cups.

"Yes. I'm … Yes," Vida stammered, standing up.

They threw away their trash and picked up the shopping bags in silence.

Rafa drove the twenty-four miles to his home without speaking to her. He moved her bags from his car to hers wordlessly. Without kissing her goodbye, without saying anything, he entered his house and closed the door behind him.

Listening to the growl of her car as it left, he rubbed his fist against the left side of his chest.

That had fucking hurt.

CHAPTER FOUR

Vida

Vida tucked her feet under her on the sofa and adjusted the weighted lap blanket to cover her legs. Still, goosebumps remained on her upper arms.

The whirr of wheels came furiously from the hallway. "Robert, set temperature to seventy-two degrees," Lola Naty yelled to the smart speaker. She'd named it after her husband, taking delight in ordering it about like she had her beloved when he was alive.

Immediately, the heat pump hummed and a stream of warm air emanated from the air vents in the ceiling and wall. Vida looked over her left shoulder to the thermostat. Sixty-four degrees Fahrenheit. *Ugh!* No wonder.

Vida's grandmother wheeled herself closer to the living room. "Is this how you want to preserve me, apo? By freezing me?" she asked, her voice light and teasing.

"Sorry, po, Lola. I got hot earlier and had to turn the heater off. I became engrossed in the details of Eden's plans for tomorrow and didn't realize the temperature had gone so low." Her niece had finally returned to Hacienda Luz after fourteen years and Vida couldn't have been happier. She was so proud of the woman that the once-rebellious teenager had become.

Her grandmother placed her hand behind her right ear. "Ha?"

Vida repeated her explanation, pitching her voice higher so that her *lola* could hear her better.

"Ah, menopause." Lola Naty nodded her head.

"Opo," she said in agreement, even though her gynecologist had told her she wasn't there yet. Not until a full year without menstruation. It had only been six months since her last period.

"It's so quiet here. Let's play some music," her lola said. "Robert, play 'Pasko Na, Sinta Ko' by Gary Valenciano. Loop mode on."

Vida groaned inwardly. Her grandmother's favorite was the most un-Christmassy song she'd ever heard, on par with George Michael's "Last Christmas." Lola Naty had started playing it on repeat the year Grandda had died.

The Filipino ballad, translated to "It's Christmas, My Love" in English, talked of love lost during the holiday season. The male balladeer crooned of his longing for his lover, who had left for unknown reasons. He asked why she was forsaking all the promises they'd made and forgetting all the affection and joys they'd showered on each other. He lamented his lonely Christmas without her by his side.

A lump rose in Vida's throat. Her vision blurred as she touched the heart key pendant on her throat. It was Rafa's voice singing the woeful words to her. She was the heartless woman who had abandoned him at Christmas.

Vida shook her head. Technically, she hadn't abandoned him. Yes, she'd left his house with things uncertain between them. Yes, he was angry with her. Was hurt by her. Sniffing, she brushed away the tears she couldn't hold back from falling.

They hadn't broken up yet. And they wouldn't. If she could find the words to explain, they wouldn't break up. She stared down at her empty hands. Why couldn't she explain?

"Robert, stop," her grandmother ordered from Vida's right, shutting off the music before it replayed the melancholic song. She moved from her wheelchair to the sofa.

Crying earnestly now, Vida felt herself enfolded in a warm embrace. Gentle hands brushed her hair as she sobbed.

"It's Rafael, isn't it?" Lola asked after Vida's tears had subsided.

She wiped her face with the blanket. "You know?"

"Since January. You've been talking to me about him when you thought I was already sleeping."

"Oh. Why did you never ask me about him?"

"Because I wanted you to tell me on your own. When I'm awake. Why haven't you?"

Vida felt like she was nineteen again, talking to her grandmother about the boy who'd broken her heart when he joined the Navy.

"At first, it was because I wasn't sure how long we would be together. None of my previous relationships lasted longer than half a year. You like him as your doctor. He's really good to you. If we break up, I didn't want you to fire him."

"And then?"

"Well, you know … The age difference. He's ten years younger than me."

"So what?"

"I don't want to be called a cougar or Mrs. Robinson." A ridiculous excuse.

Lola made a sound of disgust. "Why do you care what other people think? Does Rafael care?"

"No." He truly didn't.

Her grandmother *tsk*ed. "It's your parents, isn't it? They abandoned you and you haven't been able to trust anyone not to leave you."

Bingo. "I've gotten so used to keeping men at a distance and protecting my heart that I don't know how to stop." Nobody had ever persisted in getting closer. Nobody had worked harder to make her fall for them. Except for Rafa.

"I know Rafael loves you. Even my fading eyesight can see how tenderly he looks at you. Do you love him?"

Vida didn't hesitate. "I do."

"So, tell him. That's all you need to do. You might not believe this, seeing as I'm turning one hundred tomorrow, but life is short, my child. I'm only lucky. You might not be. Live and love today. Tomorrow may not come."

That almost brought the tears back. "Please don't say that. Tomorrow has to come so you can have your noche buena party."

"I will cancel the party if you don't go right now and reconcile with Rafael. He's the best doctor I've ever had. He's going to help me live twenty-five more years. I have to beat Iska."

Vida laughed and hugged her grandmother. "I love you, Lola." Could it be that easy? Just say "I love you" and everything would be all right?

"I love you too, apo. Now go! I'll call Carlo so we can practice our dance one more time."

Vida went.

* * *

Peering at the house from the driveway, Vida looked for lights, for movement, for anything that would indicate that Rafa was home. Her car clock had said she'd arrived at five thirteen, around the time they usually met for their weekend date. He always showed up before her. Maybe he was already inside. The garage door was closed, which didn't tell her anything.

"There's only one way to find out, Vida," she admonished herself. "Go." She squared her shoulders and walked up to the front door. Touching her heart key pendant like a talisman, she punched in the six-digit code that was the date of her birth. She released the breath she'd held at the sound of metal retracting. Grasping the doorknob, she twisted and pulled. The heavy door opened with a slight creak. Two seconds later, she was in.

The living room was dark. The tree lights were off, the fireplace unlit. Vida shivered, despite her woolen coat. There was no warmth, no welcome here like the previous week. Her shoulders fell.

She turned to go just as the front door flew open.

"Vida? What are you—"

Rushing to him, she threw her arms around his neck and kissed him. Her heart leapt with joy when he responded, kissing her back like he'd missed her as much as she'd missed him.

She drew back, breathing heavily. "I love you, Rafa," she said. "I love you. I told Lola Naty about us. Carlo knows too, and soon the entire Moore family will know. I love you, and I'm sorry I took so long to say it. Took so long to tell my family about us." Her heart thumped hard against her chest. "I love you." Once she'd said the words, she couldn't stop.

Rafa pressed his forehead to hers. "I love you too, mi Vida. That's all I wanted to hear."

She didn't deserve this man's generosity. "I was scared. I've been waiting for so long for someone to fall in love with. I spent most of my life wondering where he is, who he is." She held his gorgeous face between her hands. "I know now. You're here. It's you."

"It's you as well for me." He lifted her in his arms. "Hush now. I want to make love with you. You can tell me more later."

She did. Much later.

~*~*~*~

CHAPTER FIVE

Vida

"Shameless. Flaunting her affair with a younger man in public. And during mass, too," a nasal voice brayed from the front of one of the arched pillars on the side of the vineyard's Spanish-styled non-denominational chapel. Vida had stationed herself and her grandmother inside the covered patio to protect them from the cold while they waited for Rafa to bring back the special golf cart for wheeled passengers. He'd had to drive one of Lola's contemporaries to the hotel to rest before the party. The poor lolo was over a decade younger than her grandmother, but much frailer.

"Hush, Mitch. You're being a bitch. Oooh, that rhymes," another voice, a more pleasant one, said delightedly. "Why do you care? They're both single."

"The cougar is what? Forty-seven, forty-eight? And he's in his mid-thirties," Mitch continued.

"Really? They look the same age to me. Early forties. Doc has gray on his temples. A silver fox. Ms. Vida is not too bad. She's slim and her skin looks smooth, and not in the injected kind of way."

Vida stiffened at the mention of her name. She gave her grandmother's wheelchair a little push, wanting to get away from the gossiping women, but her lola stayed her hand.

"He's a ten. Why is he dating a four like her? She's plain, flat-chested, and she lists to one side." Mitch the

Bitch made an *ee* sound as if she was leaning sideways to demonstrate Vida's uneven posture.

Vida looked down at her white pumps. She had been running late and had forgotten to transfer her insoles from her boots. So yes, she listed to the right.

"You're just green with envy, Ms. Grinch. What happened? Did you throw yourself at the handsome doctor and he shot you down?"

"He looked right through me. As if I wasn't even there!"

"Hahaha! Serves you right. You're just bitter. You should go to confession. Maybe the priest can pray over you and perform an exorcism."

"Oh, my! Father Nick. *Rawr.*"

Their voices faded, heels clicking on the cement as they walked away.

"Apo, go look," Lola ordered, her voice pitched high. "See if you recognize those women. Find out who their parents are. I will scold them later. They are not raising their daughters right."

Vida sighed inwardly but complied. She saw a blonde and a redhead getting into a golf cart. Both wore red coats. Their accents were common US English, so they could be from anywhere. She was sure they were neither family nor hacienda employees.

"I don't know them, Lola."

"What? Why are they here if they're not invited to my party?"

"Probably a member of someone's entourage. We have politicians and celebrities on the guest list. You saw Drew earlier," she said, mentioning her cousin Drew Hizon, one of the US senators from California. They'd been catching up with him and his fiancée, Gel. "Also, if they're related to us, they know to call me ate or tita." As the oldest granddaughter, most of the younger generation addressed her with an honorific.

"*Hmph*. That Mitch is maldita. She's a mean girl. If I were her boss, I'd fire her."

Vida would too. How dare she call her a four!

"I like the other woman. I'll find out who she is, where she works, and recommend her for a promotion or something."

Lola nodded in agreement.

"Oh, here's your novio now."

Rafa braked in front of them and lowered the ramp from the center of the four-seater cart. "Your chariot awaits, milady," he said, assisting her grandmother into the vehicle and locking her chair in place. Vida sat beside Rafa in the front.

She warmed at her grandmother's use of the Spanish word to refer to Rafa in relation to her. Mi novio. My groom.

Not that they were going to get married anytime soon. This afternoon was the first time they had presented themselves to Lola as a couple. At four, one hour before the anticipated "midnight" mass, Rafa had shown up wearing her gift: a blue barong Tagalog—an embroidered long-sleeved formal shirt that matched her terno dress.

Lola Naty was effusive in her approval and claimed credit for bringing them together, although of course she wasn't. They'd met before they both knew her grandmother was Rafa's patient.

To say that Vida had glowed during the entire mass was no exaggeration. They'd held hands throughout the service and hugged during the peace greeting portion. The heart key necklace he'd given her was prominently displayed by the sweetheart neckline of her Filipiniana dress. Her earrings and bracelet, his fiftieth birthday gifts to her, completed the set.

Yes, she'd flaunted her younger lover in public. It was Christmas Eve today. Her birthday. A milestone event. She had the right to celebrate it the way she wanted. She'd wanted to show Rafa off, so she had.

Watching him as he eased the vehicle to a stop in front of Lola's house, assisted her grandmother in alighting, and transferred her to Carlo's care, Vida counted her blessings. Lola Naty had made it to her one hundredth birthday. She'd made it to her fiftieth. Both made her happy. Being out in the open about her relationship with Rafa and feeling secure about his love for her made her ecstatic.

Tonight, only her family would know that Vida, too, was celebrating. She'd made it clear to Eden and Norah that she wanted no part of the spotlight. It didn't matter to her. She'd already received all the greetings and the gifts she needed. She was content.

"Vida." Lola addressed her once they arrived in her room. "I'll send Carlo to fetch you when the beautician and hairdresser are done with me. It shouldn't take long. I only want baby powder on my face and for them to put on my tiara."

"Opo, Lola," Vida agreed absently. Hers would be fast too. All she needed was a light hairspray and a long-lasting lipstick and she was fine.

After a quick chat with her aunt Nancy, who was there to retrieve a pair of earrings from Lola's collection, Vida stepped out of her grandmother's bedroom and pushed the door of her own room across the hall open. As they pre-arranged earlier, Rafa was already there. It was the only place in the entire vineyard they could have privacy. Both Hacienda Luz and Bahay ni Lola were packed with relatives and guests.

"You okay?" Rafa asked.

"I'm good. Why do you ask?"

He sat beside her on the edge of the clothes-strewn bed. "You were quiet during the ride back here. I thought you might be angry about the woman who flirted with me at the chapel. I can assure you that I—"

"Ignored her. I know." She laced their hands together and gazed up at his worried face. "Rafa, there will always be a Mitch out there. Someone who wants you for themselves, who thinks you're the prize you obviously are and that they deserve you more than I do." She brought their joined hands to her lips and pressed a kiss where their knuckles entwined. "They will catch me at a bad time. When my back hurts or when I'm hit by a hot flash. I can't promise never to feel insecure. I'm only human. But I can promise—no, I *do* promise—to trust you. To trust us."

He pressed his forehead to hers. She loved it when he did that.

"Do you know how beautiful you look right now? How sexy you are to me always? I'm tempted to keep that door locked and undress you and spend all night looking at you wearing only my heart keys." His voice had turned gravelly. "God, Vida. I want you so much." He captured her mouth in a searing kiss that she returned with equal fervor, matching him stroke for stroke. If this were their usual Saturday, they'd be kissing for hours. Tonight, this would be their only chance for intimacy until the end of the party.

Mouths fused, they tumbled down onto the bed. One second, they were kissing, the next Rafa was springing off her with a muttered curse. The stiff pleated material of her butterfly sleeve had dug into his cheek.

Loud raps on the door had Vida sitting upright so fast, she felt a twinge in her hips.

"Tita Vida, Grandlola wants to know if you're coming," Carlo yelled from outside.

Rafa snickered. An answering laughter bubbled up inside her. She choked out, "In a bit," before she dissolved into belly laughs.

"Why are you laughing?" Carlo's aggrieved voice receded as he moved away from Vida's door. His next words were shouted from across the hall, obviously meant to be heard. "Grandlola, why is Tita Vida laughing?"

Rafa stood up and helped her to her feet. "Will you be coming later?"

She laughed. "You'd better make sure I do. It's still my birthday." His chuckles followed her out the door. In Lola's room, she met her grandmother's twinkling eyes with a wide smile of her own.

* * *

Rafa

Rafa crouched down in front of Naty Moore, fingers on her wrist. Her pulse was steady, but it was obvious from her pale face and the slump of her shoulders that her energy was flagging.

She and Vida had been greeting well-wishers, accepting gifts like the tortoise from Sophie and her boyfriend Travis, listening to speeches, and watching slideshows, karaoke, and dance performances for over two hours now. They'd reconciled with the prodigal Ollie. Eaten the sumptuous feast Ruby had prepared. Posed for thousands of pictures. And she'd led that boogie like a dancing queen half her age. But she *was* one hundred years old. It was past nine. Time to wind this party down for the guest of honor.

"How are you feeling?" he asked his patient.

"Like I'm still ninety-nine years old," she said with a sass he'd come to expect from her.

A soft hand settled on his shoulder. Vida had returned from giving instructions to the event planner. She bent down to fix her grandmother's rhinestone tiara in the shape of the number 100 and smiled fondly at her. "Are you ready for your big moment?"

"Ready. Vida, roll me to the stage."

He pushed to his feet and got out of the way. The ladies entered the center of the stage to thunderous applause, prolonged by the arrival of a cake and champagne from the other side, wheeled in by Ruby and another chef. Rafa sang along to "Happy Birthday" and clapped when the centenarian blew out her single candle, also in the shape of her age.

Accepting the microphone from her granddaughter, Naty Moore launched into her speech.

"My heart is full of love and gratitude. Thank you all for coming to my birthday party, and thank you to everyone who helped me reach this special milestone that very few achieve. To my family—my children, grandchildren, and great-grandchildren—thank you for arranging this party and for your love and support. To my doctor, Rafael Balmaseda, thank you for keeping me alive. To Carlo, apo, thank you for taking care of me in my home. To all the staff of Hacienda Luz, thank you for many years of service to me and my family. We appreciate you all."

Applause greeted every name Lola Naty uttered, with calls of "We love you!" from those who were mentioned. She continued after a lengthy pause to wait for the crowd to quiet down.

"Today is a special day. In the Philippines, where I was born, it's already the day we commemorate the messiah's birthday. Happy birthday, Jesus."

Greetings of Merry Christmas in several languages rang out. "Maligayang Pasko! ¡Feliz Navidad! Nollaig Shona dhuit!"

Lola held up a hand to call for silence. "But the most important reason why December twenty-four is the best day is because I share this birthday with my namesake, my granddaughter Vida Luz."

Vida leaned down to kiss her grandmother's cheek while the gathering sang a fresh round of "Happy Birthday to You." When she straightened, Rafa saw tears in her eyes. She hadn't been expecting to be included in the spotlight.

"Today, I'm one hundred. Vida is fifty. I wish for her to have the love and friendship I had with my Robert for the next fifty years." Lola Naty covered her microphone with her hand and looked up at Vida, who nodded in answer to a question he couldn't hear from where he stood.

Rafa's pulse raced when she walked towards him with love in her eyes, holding out her hand. He laced their fingers together just as Lola Naty spoke again. "Rafael, I trust you to make my birthday wish come true."

"I'll do my best," he vowed, his eyes on Vida. She mouthed "I love you." He tugged her close to his side and whispered, "I love you, mi Vida."

There was applause while Lola Naty finished her speech, but he barely heard it. He wanted to whisk Vida away from here. He wanted to tell her the depth of his love beyond the words he already said, his happiness at her public acknowledgment of their relationship. But he couldn't. He had to wait until Lola Naty left.

That wouldn't be for a long while yet because there were more pictures to be taken in all possible combinations. He and Vida with her grandmother. Naty Moore with all her living children, with each of their families, with her grandchildren, great grandchildren, the entire clan, Hacienda Luz staff, and on and on.

After the photos, she spent another half an hour saying goodbye to departing guests beside the big Noble fir tree in the lobby. Those who were staying at the hotel returned to their tables. Carlo accompanied Lola Naty back to her house, finally leaving Vida alone with Rafa.

They moved to the back patio of the hotel, which was blessedly empty of people. A space heater blew out warm air, which kept Rafa in his thin barong and Vida in her short-sleeved terno from suffering the winter's cold. Music drifted out from the ballroom through well-placed speakers. A ballad was playing. He now recognized the song as "Pasko Na, Sinta Ko" after hearing it sung numerous times throughout the night.

Rafa held out his hands to Vida. "May I have this dance?"

She flowed smoothly into his arms. They swayed together for a few beats before she spoke. "I have something to tell you."

Rafa felt a flutter in his stomach. He braced himself for whatever was coming. "Yeah?"

"I'm moving in with you." Vida's face lit up with a huge smile.

Elation filled him. "You are? When?"

"Tonight. I want to wake up on Christmas morning with you."

He kissed her. He couldn't help himself. "Merry Christmas to me."

"Merry Christmas to me, too. You're the best combined birthday and Christmas gift ever!"

THE END

ABOUT MAIDA MALBY

Filipino American author Maida Malby crafts foodie, multicultural, and contemporary destination romance stories filled with heat, sizzle, spice, and a whole lot of love. She is a founding member of the Kwentitas, as well as an admin and member of select writing groups and romance book clubs. Her To-Be-Read Mountain and book reviews are featured on her website maidamalby.com. Subscribe to her newsletter (maidamalby.com/newsletter) to receive updates on upcoming releases, book promotions, signing events, and advance review copy opportunities.

Booklist:

Boracay Vows - books2read.com/Boracay-Vows

New York Engagement - books2read.com/NewYorkEngagement

Global City Tryst – books2read.com/GlobalCityTryst

Singapore Fling – books2read.com/SingaporeFling

19th Hole Fiesta – books2read.com/19thHoleFiesta

Forevermore – books2read.com/Forevermore

Island Kisses – bookfunnel.com/s61awj72kz

Lovelock Freeway – books2read.com/LovelockFreeway

Love at the Fiesta – books2read.com/LoveattheFiesta

Social Media:

Facebook - @MaidaMalbyAuthor

Instagram - @maidamalbyauthor

Threads - @maidamalbyauthor

LinkedIn - MaidaMalby

Twitter/X - @MaidaMalby

TikTok - @MaidaMalby

Pinterest - MaidaMalby

My Only Love

MAAN GABRIEL

My Only Love

MAAN GABRIEL

Blurb:

He's on his way to the White House. She's fighting for women's rights on the streets of DC.

Ten years ago, Drew and Angelica broke off their engagement while in law school. They both attribute their failed relationship to young love and ambition. But when Drew begs Angelica to attend his grandmother's 100th birthday and pretend for one week that they are back together, sparks fly between them. Is it pretend when the feelings from the past never truly went away?

The thing is, Angelica doesn't want to be Senator Hizon's number one. Selfish as it may seem, she wants to be his only one – his only love.

Content Notes:

Mention of death of a parent

Profanity

CHAPTER ONE

Washington, D.C.

More than ten years ago

"Our love is stronger than your fear," Drew declared with conviction.

His eyes said it all, but his shaking hands proved he was as frightened as I was.

"I love you," he whispered, his arms around my naked body. It was hard to speak my heart because I had so much at stake: my heart, my self, my dreams. "This is real life now," he added, "I can't wait to spend the rest of my life with you. Just you."

"You're just saying this now," was my response. This, after I'd said yes to his proposal a week ago.

"It will never change. My love is bigger than who I am. It defines me as a man, as a human being. My heart belongs to you, Gel. You'll always be my number one."

Number one. For some reason, his words didn't sit well with me. Did this mean I would always need to fight for first place? What if number two did things better? Would I lose my spot?

I could feel tears forming in my eyes, a choke in my throat, because though I love this man with all my soul, it will take more than his heart to reassure me.

* * *

Present Day

"Love … is a sham. Love is a sham," I say under my breath like a chant. I remind myself of this every single day.

When you fall in love early in life, chances are it will not make it past your prime. Life will consume you, ambitions will redirect you, and love—yeah, it takes a back seat.

That is the story of my life with Drew—Andrew Emmanuel Moore Hizon, the illustrious thirty-six-year-old senator from California. So, when I received a call from him last night, ten years after our painful breakup, all the suppressed feelings didn't just come tumbling in. They frightened me, again. Why does he need to talk to me after all these years, anyway?

Sitting by myself at a Georgetown bar, far from the Capitol and from prying eyes, my palms sweaty amid the cold winter weather and my insides a mess, I wait uneasily. My cheeks are still cold from my walk from work, hoping the chill in the air would relax my nerves some. It didn't.

Instead, my hands tremble incessantly. I've not seen this man in a decade except for accidental flickers on television, which I almost always turn off immediately.

As if perfectly timed, I turn my head toward the door, and in he walks. The world stops as I process this, seeing him again—looking perfect in his dark blue suit, royal blue tie, and that flawless body still the same from when he once was mine.

Mine?! I roll my eyes at this thought. He looks exactly as I remember—chiseled jawline, perfect cheekbones, and amazingly bronze skin thanks to his Filipino roots. He bites his lower lip upon meeting my eyes.

I sigh. The sight of him still takes my breath away. Like I'm back to that unsuspecting law student that I was, idealistic to a fault, thinking that love could withstand the undetermined current of living. I smile and give him a small hand wave. Now, I'm self-conscious. I check my newish dark suit that I paired with red pumps. It's not bad, but it's not strikingly attractive either. Oh, well. I roll my eyes again. "Here we go," I huff under my breath, the chant still lingering in my head: "Love is a sham ... a sham ..."

"Hey," he says softly, stopping next to me, uncertain. We try to kiss each other's cheeks, stumbling like idiots. We both laugh at this. Nervously, of course.

I can see it in his eyes. His molten amber-brown eyes were—are—my kryptonite. They made—make—me react with an uncontrollable desire to have more of him. I shake my head to reset my thoughts.

"Hi," I respond. He pushes a stool next to mine, sits down, and loosens his tie. His movements seem casual, but I detect trembling in his fingers. Or am I just imagining things?

"You must have been really surprised to hear from me last night," he begins.

"Yeah. So, what's up? What can a famous senator from California need from a lowly nonprofit lawyer like me?" I try to tease, though I'm shaking inside.

"Well ..." He gives me a sideward glance before turning his gaze on the prematurely holiday-decorated liquor cabinet in front of us. The Christmas spirit is already making its way into town, and holiday songs are playing on the radio, which I'm not particularly enthused about. "How about we get something to drink first?"

"Sure," I say, but the truth is, I really just want to know what he wants, be done with it, and not see him again for all eternity.

Drew, his air of authority obvious, waves at the bartender, who immediately stops what he's doing upon recognizing the man next to me.

"What are we having tonight, Senator?"

"I'll have Jack and Coke. Gel?" he asks, turning to me. He still calls me that. Gel, short for Angelica. He once said my name was too long to enunciate, especially when we were in bed together doing pleasurable things. My heart does a quick tumble against my will. *Be still, you jackass.*

"Malbec."

"Wine?" the senator asks, surprised. I raise both my eyebrows to confirm. I'm sure he was expecting me to ask for beer. I was, after all, the beer queen in law school, chugging pint after pint without a care in the world.

I don't know that person anymore. Ten years is a long time for someone to stay the same. I've changed, and so has he. Up close, I can see the fine lines at the corners of his eyes and a few white hairs on his temples. It adds to the senator brand, actually. He looks better with them. On him, they are not flaws but marks of experience. When men age, they are considered distinguished veterans, but with women—we're just plain aging. I huff.

"On it," the bartender says as he leaves us be.

"So, Lola Naty is celebrating her hundredth birthday on Christmas Eve," he says, veering toward me, speaking of his maternal grandmother.

"Wow!" I've always wondered how she's been all these years. That woman was impressive. A force. The first time I met her, there was this certain air of munificence about her. She has seen many things—both good and bad—and experienced many lives. "How's she doing?" I ask.

"She's actually great. Strong. And still very sharp." He smiles at this, his adulation for the old woman obvious.

"I'm glad. She's always been so nice to me, treated me like one of her own. She'll always be special to me. You should give me her address, and I'll send her a little something on the big day," I say with a sincere smile.

"Well, that's why I called. She ..." Drew looks unsure, and this man became a senator because he was—is—always sure about what he wants. "She would like you to attend her party in California next month."

With a frown, I jolt backward in surprise. I've not seen her or any of Drew's family for over ten years.

"Well, I kind of ... I don't know how to say this ... insinuated that we got back together," he says and looks away immediately.

"Andrew!" I snap. And he folds and shrinks like a young boy, head bends down and hands firmly on his lap. "And your parents?"

"They were so happy when I told them," he whispers.

"Why would you do that after all that we've been through?" I jump off the stool and am ready to go when Drew takes my arm gently.

"I'm so sorry." He gets up, his six feet three inches towering over my five-two frame.

I'm fuming. This is unhinged and unacceptable.

"I really am. It was the only thing I could say to make Lola happy. If you could only have seen her face when I told her, them. My mom. God!" He turns around, raking his fingers through his hair in frustration. "My mom cried. She was so happy, she cried. I can't get out of this lie without hurting anybody."

"You're a true politician, Drew. You sold this idea to your family, pulling me into your mess. Unbelievable! What do you expect me to do?"

"Show up, pretend with me for a couple of days. Just pretend you still love me."

My heart skips a beat when I hear this. "I'm not going to demand further explanation about why you disappeared from my life, but I'm begging you to at least do this for me," he adds in a whisper.

'Love is a sham. A sham.' I chant again in my head.

I said this ten years ago. I say it again. And yet, why the hell is my heart doing backflips right this minute?

CHAPTER TWO

"The nerve of that man!"

Bless my roommate and best friend, Arlene, because she will say whatever I want to hear. I called her earlier tonight as soon as I walked out of that dark basement bar and told her everything—with a lot of cursing. Now, we're both slumped on the floor in our tiny apartment by the Wharf on the southwest waterfront in Washington, DC, and I'm emotionally spent.

"The nerve," I whisper, finally calmed down.

The thing is, Andrew Hizon's family are the kindest, most considerate, and generous people. When my dad got into an accident while Drew and I were still together, and we didn't have enough money to pay the medical bills, his mom showed up at the hospital and took care of everything. It wasn't just the money she provided; she gave me everything I needed to carry on. She embraced me like her own, she loved me. And I loved her. I loved them all.

And now that I'm all alone since Dad succumbed to cancer three years ago, I don't know if I have the capacity to open my heart again. I can't get hurt again. It's the reason I've been very careful this past decade, because no one will be there to catch me when I fall.

But, having been raised in a Filipino household, I know the importance of *utang na loob,* indebtedness. Its value is not lost to me. They carried me when I was lost and alone, and I am in debt from my soul. With them, I saw the beauty of family—what a true, big, rowdy, fun, food-loving, generous Filipino family is all about. And family to the Moore-Hizon clan isn't just blood; it's heart.

"What are you thinking?" Arlene asks, waving her hand in front of my face, pulling me back to the present.

"One week. I think I can do this for one week," I tell her—and myself—with a frown.

"So, you're thinking about it?" Arlene sighs and leans back against the coffee table, crossing her arms in front of her.

"They were nothing but kind to me. I owe them this, at least. I'm not going to do it for Drew, but I'll do it for his family. The first time I met Lola Naty, she hugged me so tight I cried. I've never been held with so much love, like I was her own grandchild, like I was her *only* grandchild. It stayed with me." I hug myself, remembering the warmth of her embrace.

I lift my eyes to meet my best friend's, and I see worry. I worry too.

"Drew is not just some man, Ange. You guys were engaged before the tragic end."

The tragic end—of almost losing myself, of losing him to someone else, of running away broken—nearly killed me, yes, but it also opened a path for me to work at our London office.

That night is still vivid in my head. That exact moment when I realized I needed to run or lose it all. I'd just had a big fight with Dad about a job I wanted, my dream job, and so I ran to Drew to seek refuge. Instead, I saw him carving his own future, his own ambition with someone else.

By the door of the rowhouse he shared with his friends, Drew stood in the dark with the woman I despised the most: Kate Maxwell. She was as driven as Drew, well-connected, and from a powerful political family in California. She had seen an ally in him. You could smell both their ambitions a mile away.

How can there be three people in a relationship? They were perfect for each other. That was when I realized I needed to find my purpose and myself, to understand where Drew fit into my plans and not the other way around. I didn't want to be Drew's number one, I wanted to be his only one. The next day, I accepted a job offer and flew to London without looking back.

Kate Maxwell is now Senator Hizon's communications director, running his office, running his life. I've heard she's more powerful than his chief of staff.

A deafening boom of thunder rattles the night, and a flash of lightning surprises us both in our twelfth-floor space.

"The sky is frightened, Ange."

"And in mourning too, I guess." I let my lips curve upward, managing a weak smile before bending my head to my knees.

The intercom buzzes. Arlene sighs, gets up, and answers the call.

"Who is it?"

"Drew. It's Drew." The voice from the small white box crackles. I pull my head back in attention.

"What the fu—What do you want me to do?" Wide eyed, Arlene silently mock-screams in panic after releasing the TALK button.

"Gel, I know you can hear me. I'm not asking for myself. It's for Mom and Lola. Yeah, and my sisters too.

They miss you. A lot. I know lying to them is on me, but can you at least reconsider? Please?"

I let the silence after his plea simmer.

"Buzz him in," I finally tell Arlene. Her eyes widen some more, giving me an anxious, questioning look. I nod at her to confirm my decision.

I get up from the floor, still wearing my pajamas, and wait for him by the door. Arlene runs to her bedroom, wincing as if in agony.

Finally, there is a knock. Arlene, running from her room with a jacket on, opens the door. She looks at me in panic, turns to look at Drew and then back at me.

"I'll leave you guys to it. I'm walking the dog," Arlene blurts.

"You guys have a dog?" Drew asks in surprise, forehead creased with worry. "You're allergic to dander."

"It's the neighbor's." Arlene hurriedly walks out and slams the door shut behind her.

Drew is soaked and dripping wet in our tiny wood foyer. He pulls his jacket off and loosens his tie before removing his shoes. I run to the linen closet to get him a clean towel. When I hand it to him, our hands touch briefly, and we both feel the static shock that sends us jolting backward.

With no bra under my flimsy white pajama top, I can feel my nipples coming to life. Drew notices too and takes a good look before lifting his eyes to meet mine. I know that face so well. It's the face he makes when desire starts to consume him—the face that once excited me, sending heat to my center. I shake off the feeling.

Instead of breaking away, Drew takes a step forward toward me. I don't move. We are inches apart, and his scent—of clean ocean and mint, unchanged since the last time—sends me down a dangerous rabbit hole. I sigh, catching my breath.

"You made a mistake walking away from this ten years ago," he whispers close to my ear. The hairs at the back of my neck rise.

This closeness is so intoxicating that I close my eyes to steady myself. Instinctively, I put my hand on his arm and he grasps it. I slowly open my eyes, and he is as drunk as I am with desire. Mine, pent up for ten long years.

To feel his hands again on my body, his fingers inside me, his lips on my breasts, his body beneath mine in ecstasy. The thought makes me shiver. I can still remember his face when he was on the verge of losing it, of my giving him pleasure, the power I had over his desires. It was mind-blowing. We were so good in bed together, so good that there was not a single day in the three years we were together that we didn't have sex.

Some days, we were so drunk with desire we couldn't get enough of each other and would end up doing it more than twice in one round. It was like food I consumed and water I needed to survive. And I could have it anytime, anywhere I pleased. In the bushes at midnight, the stairwell midday when classes were in session, the metro bus on its last run. I was a different woman. I had needs, and I conquered them. And I did it all with this man, standing so close to me.

I could have it again. Right here. Right now.

Then there is a snap, and I'm back in my senses. I jump away from him instantly.

"Give me details. What? Where? Who do you want me to be?" I can still feel my knees shaking. I steady myself by walking toward the kitchen counter and leaning my hip against it. Thankfully, Drew maintains the distance and stands where I left him.

"Everyone wants you to be you." His eyes bore into mine as if seeing into my very soul.

"Why am I being pulled into this lie, Drew? Justify this to me. Make me understand."

"Besides the fact that my grandmother probably has only a few years to live?"

"Exactly. Why lie?"

"Because for the past ten years, I've tried so hard to make her proud of me, but all she talks about is my failure to keep you." There is a pained expression on his face, and his eyes droop in shame and regret. We are both silent for a long hard minute after this honest declaration. "I just want to make her happy," he adds in a whisper.

"You're a member of the United States Senate, Drew. That's something to be truly proud of."

"Don't get me wrong. She is proud. It's all she talks about in front of family and friends. But in private, all she talks about is you."

"Why?"

"Because, apparently, it was the only time she saw me … free."

~*~*~*~

CHAPTER THREE

Drew and I are in the business class section of the redeye flight to San Francisco. He pointed out when he emailed my flight details that not a single cent spent on the plane tickets came from the United States government or the taxpayers of California. He knows how meticulous I am about these things.

Also, I despise lying. Agreeing to this means I'm breaking all my rules and almost everything I believe in. *For what again*? I've been asking myself this from the moment I agreed to this ridiculous idea.

"We have to have rules, Andrew." I whisper as soon as the light goes out in our cabin after dinner.

"Andrew, really?"

"Whatever. But we need ground rules," I insist.

"Okay. Whatever they are, I'm game." He smirks at this.

"Drew, please take this seriously."

"There is nothing about you that I don't take seriously, Gel," he says with sincerity, and there goes my silly bitch heart again doing backflips.

"I don't know about that, but let's start with this. The only lie we will tell on this trip is that we're back together and nothing else. We won't concoct any stories about our reconciliation. Agreed?" I ask pointedly.

"Sure. But what are we going to say?"

"That we met at the bar in Georgetown like we did, and that was that."

"People will want to know more."

"And you're not going to give them anything. Understood?" I lean down to get a notebook and pen from my purse on the floor.

Rules: No More Lying, I write on a clean new page.

"Fine," Drew concedes.

"We're not going to sleep in the same bed."

"We're going to sleep in my old room at my parents'."

"You sleep on the floor."

"Fine."

Never Sleeping in One Bed. Ever, I add to my list.

"No over-the-top public displays of affection."

"That will expose our charade. We used to be all over each other. We have to act like we used to. We can't bend on that," Drew argues, leaning over to look at my list.

"Fine." I see the justification in this, quite honestly. My cheeks heat up at the thought of our hands on each other around his family. I'm already traveling across the country, so I might as well go all in, rather than fail in front of his mother and grandmother.

"Next?"

"No sex, no matter what." I say quietly for fear that our neighbors on the next rows will hear us and our ludicrous scam.

"Whatever."

No Sex, I add to the list.

"Next, let's not hurt each other." I say this as slowly and as quietly as I can.

We both agree to this.

"Don't ever fall in love again." I can feel my hand tremble on my lap. Again?

"That doesn't … really …"

"Apply?" I am curious.

"… go away."

* * *

The cabin is dark and quiet, and everyone is fast asleep except for a few who are working on their laptops, Drew included. My chair is fully reclined, and as I lie on my side with a blanket to my chin, I watch him.

Did he just admit a few minutes ago that he still loves me? I sigh as I remember his face, his head angled sideways in an out-of-character coyness, his lips red and kissable. *Kissable, really?* I want to smack myself on the head.

He slowly turns around to face me, his face illuminated by the tiny pen light on the side of the chair.

"You're still awake?"

"Yeah."

He reclines his chair to match mine, turns off his light, lies on his side to face me, and pulls the blanket over his body. Our faces only a few inches apart, I can see his clearly, with the light from the next row bouncing off his amber eyes.

"Thank you for doing this," he says, looking straight into my eyes as if searching for a chance to see my heart again.

"I'm doing it for your lola and your mom. They were kind to me."

"They loved—love—you."

"I knew that." I say this with sincerity because I felt it. It was the kind of love I never got from a mother I never met, a family I never knew, and a father who was distant and always out working to put food on our table. The pain is still as raw as when I was young, and the memory of the Hizons' love is still as fresh as the moment they took me into their arms.

"Gel, I know this is the last thing you want to hear right now. But I … I never, not once, have ever taken you for granted. I know that seems hard to believe because of what you thought you saw." His voice is so soft that I wouldn't have heard it if I'd been an inch farther away. "I was never given a chance to explain. And I was angry."

"That's in the past. We've both moved on." It's the least I can say. I am not ready to argue right now. I just want to enjoy the peace and quiet of this ride and, for a few hours, live in a dream bubble where Drew and I are okay. "We've made something of ourselves. And that's what's important, right?" I smile.

"Are you happy?" he asks a few minutes later.

It's a loaded question.

"I'm all right. Life is peaceful. Calm. No drama, no roller coaster of emotions, no hot and cold. You?" I pull the blanket up to cover my mouth, hoping to hide the quiver of my lips.

"I don't think I have time to be happy. I've been working too hard. Mom asked me to take this week with the family as a break to reflect. I don't even know what that means."

"I know. And I think that's okay."

"Is it, though?"

I really don't know. After moving back to D.C. to take care of Dad, following four years in London, I didn't really have a moment to think about myself or my happiness or ask the universe why my heart had stopped beating. I existed.

"I have very high expectations of happiness," I say. "I try to be more strategic about the things I do in my life. I don't need the mundane or the temporary or instant gratification. I don't like taking any more chances or risks. So, maybe happiness is not at the center of my world, but I'm at peace with everything else. And I think that's important."

"I like that." His eyes are glued to mine. And I can't get lost in them anymore because I might want that happiness I can't maintain. I close my eyes to avoid his gaze, and I know he's still staring at me. I can feel it. I can feel him. My heart beats, knowing he's close by. And I don't remember my heart beating like this in the past decade.

I stay still for a long time, hoping he will turn and let me be. I pretend to sleep. I can't talk anymore. I might say something I'll regret later. He doesn't move. For more than half an hour, we stay like this.

"I hope it goes away, baby. I hope I can let go," he whispers and brushes a stray hair off my face. I don't open my eyes because what he said is the same hope I've had for as long as I can remember.

CHAPTER FOUR

When Drew and I emerge from the arrival gate, I see them all—his mom, his dad, and the girls—holding a big banner that says, Welcome Back, Angelica! I hold it in, willing myself not to cry.

"Ange! Oh dear, sweetheart!" Drew's mom, Nancy—the only mother I've ever known—rushes to me for a tight embrace. His dad, Bert, welcomes me with open arms. And the girls—Cindy and Laceley—drop the big banner and jump right in to welcome me back. This is the only family I've ever had.

"What am I, chopped liver?" Drew complains, following it with a thunderous laugh. Nancy hugs her son. I see in my periphery that she has given him a small pat on his head as if to say, "Well done." Though he smiles to acknowledge it, there is sadness in his eyes. I understand this because slowly I'm feeling that same sense of gloom. The lie.

When Cindy and Laceley pull away from me, they start jumping up and down. Both in their early twenties, they did not try to hide their excitement and relief. I know how Drew loves his little sisters, and how they both adore him.

"We're going shopping later today, and we're going to choose the most beautiful dress for you. You'll look like Cinderella at the ball," Laceley declares. And in a lot of ways, she's not wrong. I will be that girl who, at the stroke of reality, will go back to a life that does not include Drew or any of them.

"Let's go get some breakfast at Bruno's." Bert gathers the crowd to the exit, pulling my rolling luggage behind him. "We've missed you around here, Angel. Welcome back home."

When my dad passed away three years ago, Nancy and Bert sent me a check for a substantial amount. It's still in my closet somewhere, uncashed. How can they welcome me with open arms when I rejected them for years? Unguarded, I feel Drew's hand on mine. He probably noticed that I am shaking.

"You okay?" he asks when we're finally alone behind the excited group. I nod.

I can't speak right now because if I do, I'll bawl. We may be pretending to be what we are not, but my love for these people is real. And despite all the years that I tried to forget them, I know my love is still here.

* * *

Nancy insists on paying for a blush-colored gown with subtle silver sequins and beads sprinkled all over the fabric in flower silhouettes. It's the most beautiful dress I've ever seen. We even find the perfect silver strappy sandals to go with it.

"Tita Nancy, please let me pay," I say in front of the cashier.

"I've missed you. Now that my eldest daughter has returned home, I'll lavish you with everything I missed doing the past decade. You wait and see what I'll do to my grandchildren. I'll spoil your kids rotten," she says. I almost choke up, but cover it with a light laugh.

Nancy hooks her arm through mine as we walk away from the store.

"So, tell me. How did it happen this time? I'm excited to know. Drew has been moping around for a decade now, and when he called me last month to tell me that you're back in his life, he was so happy." Nancy says.

"We bumped into each other at a Georgetown bar." I offer, smiling widely. This is the story, as promised. We don't need to lie.

"I bet he gave you a long spiel. Oh, I remember him and the girls practicing those lines for years. I'm sure it melted your heart instantly." She puts her arm around my shoulders and pulls me to her for a half embrace. "I'm just so glad you're back in his life. It was hard, the first few years after you left for London. By that time, he was done with law school and had started clerking for Senator Foster. He said that job was perfect because it kept him busy, and the pain was easier to handle. He was like a zombie, and we were all worried about him."

"It hasn't been easy for me either." I give her a subtle, sideward glance. This is not a lie.

"I know. I heard. There was a point when Dad and I wanted to intervene. Fly to London and beg you to take him back. He was such a mess, it terrified us. But I also know Drew. I knew that he would find his way back to his dreams and ambitions. And to you."

His ambition was the reason things went south for us. Seeing him with Kate that night was the final nail in the coffin. I don't think Drew understood that I was not willing to take a back seat, that I would not give everything up when he decided to go into politics. When I told him about the offer in London, he cringed.

He likes to be loud and proud, and I like to play behind the scenes. I couldn't just be standing next to him in a powder-blue dress, smiling at his constituents while inwardly cursing every minute of it.

"The people of his district love him. He's doing a great job," I say, beaming for Nancy.

"There were conversations about the White House someday, Ange. But this is a decision you will make as a couple."

The White House? I want to tell her that after Christmas Day, I will never be part of his or their lives. I'll make sure I hide in the shadows again. I'll make sure we never ever cross paths. I feel a sharp jab in my heart at this thought, and, instinctively, I put my hand over my chest. I've protected this part of my life so well. I can't let them all in again.

"I'm sure in time we will have to talk about this. But for now, we just want to be surrounded by love and family." I immediately wonder if this is considered a lie. Guilt jumps straight to my gut.

"You're right. It's the reason you're perfect for Drew. You know how to put structure into things—whether it's work, life, or love. He needs you in his life."

"I don't think he's that helpless." I laugh. "He became a senator without me." He became a senator because Kate was standing next to him, I add in my head.

"How many times did he call me to ask if he should reach out to you for advice, for guidance? He's been very lost,"

I look away as she says this. But how about me? Who gets to understand me? I don't have a mother who has my best interests at heart. No father to stand up for me and support my dreams. No big family to hold my hand. I crawled to survive the last ten years.

"And I know it's not been easy for you either. We're here for you, Ange. Please know we will forever be here for you."

"I'm sorry for not saying goodbye."

"Many times, I just wanted to call you and tell you that you're my daughter too—regardless of your relationship with Drew. I wanted us to have a relationship. I missed how you used to call me just for simple things like what color dress to wear or lipstick to buy. Little things that mother and daughter share." I see tears forming in her eyes. "But you're here now. Back in my life, and I plan to spoil you rotten."

We turn the corner to meet Cindy and Laceley at a dessert shop where they had sent a text earlier to say they were stopping for ice cream.

When we walk through the door, I see another person sitting next to them. The lighting is softer inside, and I wait for my eyes to adjust. When the third person turns around, I drop my haul on the floor in utter surprise. It's the same woman I saw Drew with on his porch the last time I saw him.

Kate Maxwell.

~*~*~*~

CHAPTER FIVE

By the time dinner is over, I have a raging headache. Although Kate the bombshell declined the invitation to join us, that didn't help with my anxiety. Seeing her today, fitting into this lovely family that once was mine, makes my blood boil and my head explode.

Are they carrying on an affair behind his family's back? What am I, a decoy? Was this the plan all along?

"Are you okay? You look a little pale," Drew whispers to me, trying to go unnoticed by his loud, boisterous, but utterly beautiful crew. Seeing Nancy cleaning up while Bert playfully pokes her waist and the girls running around showing off their shopping haul, smiling and laughing, is the only consolation I have for seeing that woman again.

"I'm fine. Jetlag, maybe," I say. It's almost midnight on the East Coast. He puts his arm around my shoulder and pulls me closer to him.

I stiffen. And I can tell that he feels it. He immediately drops his arm and looks at me apologetically. I shake my head to tell him it's okay. His touching me is okay—as long as it's in front of his family. It's in the rules.

"You kids look tired. Head on up to bed, and we'll clean up here," Nancy says, looking at Drew and me lovingly with a hopeful glint in her eyes.

I get up, gather some dirty dishes, and walk toward the kitchen. When I reach the door, Bert grabs the load from my hands with a wink. "Let me get these, and you get your sleepy head up to bed," he jokingly orders.

"Your bedroom is clean, sheets are new, and the remnants of your high school life are gone for good." Nancy laughs as she says this. "But, it's quite tight in there now because we can't move the treadmill or the Peloton. Too heavy for Dad's back, and mine too. And the girls ... don't even get me started on that."

"We got here just a few days ago. We're tired from school," Laceley complains.

"We tried to push it as far into the corner as we could, but there's really not much floor space. Sorry, lovebirds," Bert says apologetically. And that is going to be problematic, seeing how our deal was that Drew would sleep on the floor.

I sigh again, tired, restless, anxious.

"We'll manage." Drew responds with a forced smile, and I can tell that he's thinking of the exact same thing: Where is he going to sleep tonight?

Standing on either side of the queen-sized bed, Drew and I look at the tiny space. Sure, if we were romantically together, this would be perfect—but we're not. And we made a deal. I lift my head up in frustration, but at the same time, I feel my nerves doing some sort of party within me.

This is not something to be freaking excited about, I tell myself and whack my forehead with my palm.

"That bad, huh?" Drew asks, eyeing me closely.

"Huh?" I ask, pretending not to understand the question. He doesn't realize that I am trying with all of my might not to jump him. The X-rated things that are parading through my head right now are just downright embarrassing.

"To be this close to me again."

"It's not that."

"Then what? It's only for a few nights. On the night of the party, I'm sure we'll get one of the honeymoon suites at the hacienda." He says this with irritation, which I sense he is trying to tamp down.

"The deal." It is the only thing I can come up with. Otherwise, I will have to either be painfully honest or lie— neither of which I plan on doing.

"I'll take a shower, and we'll sort this out when I get back. I'll use the bathroom down the hallway, and you can take the one right here." His voice is now devoid of irritation and sounds sad.

Or perhaps, this is all in my head. I turn around, stamping my feet, and march away.

Think of Kate. Kate, Kate, Kate, I tell my freaking heart. For all I know, I'm here because they didn't want to tell his parents about her yet.

When I come out of the bathroom, Drew hasn't returned from his shower. I look around, remembering the many times I've been here, making love with Drew at every angle, even on top of the window rail where the rest of the neighbors could have seen us were it not two in the morning. It had been one of our bests. I almost broke the window, pushing myself backward in pure, unadulterated ecstasy.

Drew could take me there anytime, any day, wherever. I can feel an unwelcome stirring between my legs, and I shake it off. This is not a great time to be remembering sex with Drew—not with us sharing a bed in a few minutes.

And then he walks in, naked to the waist, hair dripping wet, looking oh   so delicious. I could just lose myself, pull him into bed, and ravage him. But where would that take me tomorrow when we wake up?

I turn away from him instead, but I can feel the heat rising inside me, stirring further, my need potent. I might have to take another shower. I roll my eyes at this.

"You can sleep on the bed with me," I offer before I can stop myself.

"Thank you. Otherwise, I'll have to sleep on the couch in the family room."

"You don't need to do that. It's fine. Like you said, it's only for a few days." As I say this, I know those will be very a trying few days for me, sleeping next to the man who can turn me on quicker than anything in this world. Drew is a stallion in bed.

Geez, where did that thought come from? I whack my fist against my forehead again, harder this time.

"Are you sure?" he asks gently, like walking around eggshells.

"Yes." My voice is firm. "Turn off the lights when you're ready for bed," I say.

I hear a snicker, but I don't turn around to look. My willpower is being stretched thin.

"Just like old times, I see."

"What do you mean?" I say nervously under the covers.

"You always ask me to turn off the lights before jumping into bed with you. It means …" He stops mid-sentence. It means we are going to have a quiet dark night of unfiltered lovemaking. "Do you ask them to do the same?"

"Them?"

"Your lovers after me?"

I don't answer this. There were a few, of course. I tried to lose myself in the arms of whoever could help me forget about this man next to me.

But my heart had frozen. Only just a few weeks ago had I started to feel it beating again.

"Oh, yeah. Sure," I respond, hoping it ends the conversation.

"How many?"

"What?"

"Lovers."

"A few."

"Are you trying to hurt me even more?"

"I'm trying to do nothing. You asked a question, and I answered." Then, I turn around to sit up and face him. "How about you? How many lovers have you had after me? Is there one you're keeping from your family right now, Senator Hizon?" A vision of Kate walking in on us right this minute appears in my head. I close my eyes and shake it off.

"I'm not seeing anyone right now, if that's what you're implying," he sternly responds to my pointed question.

"Are you sure? I have a feeling you're not telling me everything." I can hear my voice rising. I stop myself before his family hears us.

I'm not doing this for Drew, I tell myself again. I'm doing this for Lola Naty. And yet, why is the thought of Kate and Drew together still making me burn in anger?

Slowly, Drew joins me in bed. I turn away to face the window. Drew and I were an explosion of atoms, pure chemical, live-wired attraction. I can feel his heat, his naked body next to mine, though we are still a few inches apart.

This is going to be a long night.

* * *

It's still dark outside when I open my eyes.

Drew is looking straight at me. There is softness in his eyes, and a slight curve to his mouth, last night's argument forgotten.

I rub my eyes with the back of my hand to help me wake up, a little embarrassed to be so close to this man again. There is no denying that he still holds my heart, no matter the years and distance apart.

"We've already broken one of our rules," he whispers. "Shouldn't we break more?" His voice is soft and intoxicating.

My heart, overpowering my will, slowly commands me to touch his bare shoulders with my fingers. I do it lightly at first, uncertain, my movement awkward.

Gently, he covers my hand with his and pulls it to his lips. I close my eyes as I feel his breath on my fingertips. I can almost taste it, taste him, the pure pleasure of it all.

"Can I come closer?" he asks and I nod, passion bubbling within me. I move my leg on top of his, and I feel a tiny shiver from him.

I swallow hard, not knowing what to do next, and when he bends down his head and lowers his lips to mine, I am gone. We meld gently and slowly, trying to remember our movements, trying to relearn what we've lost.

But as my heart beats next to his, I know that no distance or years can make us forget. I still remember his lips savoring mine, slowly, gently, and as he bites my lower lip with his teeth, I am beyond redemption.

"Gel," he says under his breath. I hear the power it has on him, my name. And for one quick minute, I let him overpower me too.

His hand moves down my shoulder to my waist, lingering there before his fingertips make their way into my pajama top to my breast. "Gel," he says again. I tug him closer to me, and then I let my hunger be known, playing with his lips with my tongue. I see him open his eyes in surprise before offering me a mischievous grin. His eyes gleam with freedom and excitement, and I move my lips to his nose and then his eyes and then his temples. He pulls me in closer, his erection touching my thighs. I feel myself soaring with need, a place I want to reach, a point to ecstasy I haven't experienced in ten long, painful years.

I reach for my panties and push them down, ready to take a chance, when his phone rings on the bedside table.

"Let it," he says, moving his mouth toward my neck and down my shoulder. The ringing stops before it starts again a few minutes later.

"Answer it. It might be an emergency." I lightly push him away, getting us both back to reality. When he reaches for his phone, it's Kate's face on the screen. What can that woman need at five in the morning? Immediately, I get up and head to the bathroom.

* * *

It's been a few days since the night that almost got us.

Drew made an inane excuse, telling his parents that the bed hurt his back, and he's since been sleeping on the family room couch. No one is suspicious, especially since Drew's hands are always all over me when we're with the family.

It's freezing this time of year in DC, but the weather here is perfect. I get dressed and plan to go for a walk around the neighborhood. Drew walks in after helping his dad build the new shed in the backyard while I'm putting my shoes on.

"You going with the girls somewhere?" he asks with a creased forehead.

"Nah. They already left for the bakery. I'm just going for a walk."

"Can I join you?" We've not been alone since our close call, and this makes me feel a little awkward.

"Sure. I guess."

The sun is bright, and the heat penetrates my skin like fire. In a few minutes, we need to pack up to head to the hacienda for the party tomorrow night. I have yet to see his family, and if I'm being honest with myself, I'm truly glad to have this chance again.

To see Ate Vida, his eldest cousin, the one other person who has known my pain from the moment my heart broke. Vida was the voice of reason, but my pain, and ultimately my fear, ate me up inside.

Fear. If only I could let go of it, if only I could forget the searing agony at the very core of my soul. If only I were brave enough to take a chance on love. But alas, even I know I'm not capable of that much strength.

"Thank you for doing this," he says after we're out of earshot of his father, who waved us off.

"You're welcome,"

"I think it's time we talked about the past."

"I don't see any reason for that now."

"You didn't give me a chance then. You disappeared."

"You could have come after me. You didn't. And that's okay."

"Whatever you saw, it wasn't what you thought."

"I don't want to go there again. It's one episode of my life I'm trying to forget."

"You'd rather forget what you think you saw than know the truth?" His voice is solemn as he says this.

"The truth? It depends on whose."

"Shouldn't I be given a chance to speak my truth?" he asks.

We walk side by side in silence. And in his senator role, Drew speaks to people we walk past or waves to those who eagerly acknowledge him with a smile. He is their senator, after all.

"Can I ask you a question, Drew?" I say a few minutes into the walk. I'm trying to shield myself from finding an excuse to believe him.

"Sure."

"Does Kate know about our deal?"

"Yes," he finally responds.

"Why does she have to know?"

"Because she'll protect me if something goes wrong."

"What will go wrong?"

"She'll be able to work on what I can say and show publicly. For instance, this walk, I should have checked in with her first," he admits, and this breaks me inside.

"She will always be part of your life."

"She stood by and believed in me when no one did."

I nod. Kate deserves Drew's loyalty for all the years she stood by him.

"Then why am I the one walking with you here, and not her?"

"It's complicated, Gel."

I got my answer. Even then, though I may have been his number one, I would never ever be his only one.

CHAPTER SIX

Drew and I end up being assigned one of the suites at the hacienda's hotel, just like the other guests who live out of state or out of the country. It's also where the hairstylists and makeup artists who are getting us all dolled up for tonight are staying.

As the stylist is putting the finishing touches on my hair, Laceley walks into our suite with Kate.

Three more days. As he promised, I will fly out on the twenty-seventh, and he will stay until after the new year. Three more days of lies.

I remain seated in front of the floor-to-ceiling mirror while the hairdresser adds more pins to the back of my hair, styled simply in a low, tight bun. I steal a look at Kate.

She wears a long lime-green gown with a low-cut neckline that accentuates her perky bosom. Her golden hair falls to one side, while the other is clipped perfectly with a pearl hair pin. Her makeup is dazzling in hues of green and pink, unlike mine, which I purposely want to be light and subdued. I can't compare my tiny little button to her straight nose, my big brown eyes to her blue ones, or my boring black hair to her beautiful blond tresses.

"Is Drew here?" she asks no one in particular, sashaying her luxurious beauty across the room.

"I'm here." Drew emerges from the bedroom, in the middle of putting on his cufflinks. I quietly blow a breath at the sight of him. He looks good. Perfect. Perfect for television. *For the White House.* He not only has the looks for it, but he also has the heart. Kate will be perfect by his side every step of the way.

"Hey, Drew. With the guest list, it's likely there will be photographers in the lobby leading to the ballroom. I just want to make sure you and Angelica are aware. You'll probably get a few snaps, and a reporter might have some questions about who she is."

"Tonight is about Lola. I'm not in Hollywood, Kate."

"Well, you in politics is the closest D.C. will get to Hollywood. It's like you're melding them together."

"And I don't like that," he responds. Kate immediately walks toward him and starts helping with his cufflinks. She gets him, understands his ambition like I never will. I can see a comfortable dynamic between them, and I don't know if I'm the only one who does.

I turn to Laceley, who starts looking through the makeup on the table next to me, oblivious to her brother and Ms. Maxwell. Drew doesn't even notice me.

To my surprise, Kate walks toward me with a smile.

"What earrings are you wearing?" she asks. And as if timed perfectly, Nancy walks in with a small pouch and hands it to Kate.

"Here. These are Mama's. She would be happy to see them on Angelica tonight." Nancy says. "They were her mother's," she adds, helping Kate with Lola Naty's earrings.

They are by no means fine jewelry or precious stones, but they're gold, vintage—over a hundred years old—and delicate. And I fear that if I wear them tonight, on this very special occasion, I'll be committing the biggest betrayal of all. I look at Drew, who gives me a weak smile, understanding what's going through my head.

"Are you sure? I think you should wear them instead, Tita Nancy," I say.

"No. These are yours to wear for tonight. Mama once said, love for blood is a given, but love for those we chose to be in our lives, we have to give our all." She offers me a reassuring smile full of motherly affection. My heart skips a beat.

After Kate fastens the second earring, she steps away so I can see my reflection in the mirror. The earrings, though small, add sparkle to my image.

Nancy stands right behind me, her hand on my shoulder, with Drew on the other side. And I feel I am one of them again. Like I belong. I smile at Nancy and then at Drew—and with all my effort, I keep my tears from falling.

* * *

Tonight is a spectacle.

Everyone is in their best Filipiniana couture. Laughter is abundant and food aplenty. A fine selection of the all-time Filipino favorites like lumpia, pancit, chicken wings marinated in adobo sauce, and the highlight of the menu, positioned around the main hall, are lechon, roasted pig carving stations. The dessert buffet is a feast for the eyes as well as the palate, the lavish purple ube cake its major attraction. All prepared by Drew's talented cousin Chef Ruby Moore.

The music is a beautiful fusion of the past and the present, a Grammy-winning band delivering the performance of their lives. This is not just a party. Tonight is a celebration of a life well-lived by a Filipina woman who created a close-knit community and has touched so many lives. Mine included.

I sit alone at our table, soaking it all in, enjoying the moment. Sophie, Drew's famous podcaster cousin, is gracefully floating across the room. She looks at me and beams in recognition. She was so young when Drew and were together. I smile right back with warmth in my heart. And there is Eden standing by the door, trying to look invisible and yet watches the goings on with trained eyes, running the party like a master. I miss these girls. I miss them all so very much. Then my attention veers toward Drew, dancing playfully with his sisters—not the handsome senator, but the grandson, the older cousin, the son, the brother. My supposed lover. I smile at this, letting myself pretend for a second that this is my reality—that I am happy.

I let my imagination take me.

By this time, I'm married to Drew. Perhaps we have a young daughter, playing and dancing with her cousins on the dance floor. I may well be pregnant again. And I am happy with my career. Drew and I are more in love, and each day is a gift—at night we make love to exhaustion, and in the morning, we are a senator, a lawyer, and loving parents.

If only there was a straight line from points A to B—a line that did not include doubts, insecurities, and fear— perhaps that would be the life I'm living today. But dreams and reality don't usually match. It's the reason I limit my expectations—or avoid them altogether.

"Penny for your thoughts." Bert, in his dashing barong Tagalog, pulls up a chair and sits next to me with a bottle of beer in hand.

"Hey. Are you having a good time?" I ask, jumping out of my reverie.

"A great time. And you?"

"The best," I gleefully reply, widening my smile.

He snickers in response. And in some ways, I feel he is reading me—reading this, Drew and me together right here. I've seen his stolen glances the past few days—and in them were questions.

"This is a lie, isn't it?" he finally asks, angling his head in sympathy, changing the mood.

"What do you mean?" I try to conceal the truth.

"Drew asked you to lie for him after months of his grandmother and mother giving him a hard time about settling down." He offers the truth that I can't reveal, and I don't know how to answer this. I promised not to create more lies. I give him a weak smile to confirm his suspicions.

"I'm sorry." I concede.

"I'm not mad. I knew from the moment I saw you at the airport. I can tell that you've been holding it all in. Look, I promised Drew that I would never get into his affairs unless he asked. But for what   it's worth, I want you to know that Drew worships you."

I take a sip of my wine and play with the glass on the table, rolling the bottom mindlessly, trying to find the right words in response to this declaration. Bert and I have always been honest with each other. To him, I was his eldest daughter, someone he could have honest conversations with when the girls were barely teenagers.

"I didn't think love was enough back then. We were young. Barely out of law school. That life was tough. We were like zombies just trying to make it out alive. Drew and I, we were each other's reprieve. But …"

"But when it came time to face the real world because you both were getting out of school, you got scared." It isn't a question. Bert is blunt like that.

"I was terrified."

"I figured."

"But so was Drew. During the months leading up to my leaving, he was not himself. I felt he'd made a mistake proposing to me."

"That, I can promise you, is not true. To this day, no other woman can measure up to who you were, who you are in his life."

Then who is Kate Maxwell? I want to ask, but I don't.

The woman runs everything for him. From where I'm sitting, I can see that Drew can't survive without her.

"There's been no one else since you, and this worries his mother and grandmother. He couldn't pick himself back up for more than a year after you left. To them, he's not some hotshot senator. He's just a son and a grandchild," Bert adds.

"I'm sorry."

"You didn't do anything wrong. This is life, right? It's just funny that we're sitting next to each other after all these years. There must be something to that."

"Maybe." Or maybe not.

We both find comfort in quiet, so we let the silence linger between us. In fact, we were once each other's introvert buddies at big family gatherings like this.

Finally, the dance music stops. Drew turns around to look for me, and when he finds my eyes, he smiles and saunters rhythmically toward me. His smile widens when he sees his dad.

"Just like old times, I see," he jokes, giving his dad a small pat on the back.

"Yeah, I guess. Now that you're here to keep Angelica company, I better find your mom for my obligatory dance." Bert stretches his legs before standing, taking a quick swig of his beer. "You two should dance. It will make Mama happy." He then walks away with a wink.

As if on cue, Adele's song "Someone Like You" starts to play.

It is the most heart-wrenching song. When I moved to London, it played over and over on radios, in bars, in stores—just about everywhere. It made my sadness all the more unbearable and my tears a nonstop current. Just like Adele, I wondered if I would ever find the same kind of love again. But years have passed, and though the ache lingers, the pain isn't as raw. We've moved on and made something of ourselves. That is something to celebrate tonight.

"Lola would like to see us." Drew stands and offer his hand.

I take his hand, and we walk pass the dance floor. I see Bert staring at us with a knowing expression.

"He knows. Your dad knows," I finally say when I put my hand on his arm. To my surprise, his nearness almost takes the breath out of me, jolting me backward.

"Are you okay?" Drew immediately steadies me by gently taking my arm. "What did he say?"

"That he knows we're a lie."

"We may be a lie, but this, right here, is not an act. There will always be love between us, Gel. I'll always have that for you. I hope you know that," he whispers, pulling away sideways to look straight into my doubtful eyes. "I know you know. We're connected like that."

And I do know. It is perhaps the reason why we can't be friends, why we can't be in each other's lives, because it's either all or nothing. It's the kind of passion we had when we were young. It's the kind that's been bubbling between us the past few days.

We stop a few feet away where Lola was watching us. I nod in acknowledgment and she smiles warmly, happiness obvious upon seeing Drew and me hand in hand. I let Drew's hand go, and I walk toward the woman we are celebrating tonight. I bend on my knees in front of her, and immediately, she presses her hand on my cheek. I can feel tears forming in my eyes as in my heart. This love, I feel it. I feel them all. No longer an outsider in my own life. I am part of this. At least for tonight.

Lola gently pulls my chin toward her, and gently whispers, "You made me so happy tonight, iha. Thank you." My tears, which were threatening to spill seconds earlier, is now running rivers down my cheeks. "You go kids dance the night away and do so for yourself, not for me." She then gently kisses me on my forehead. And bending down, Drew kisses Lola on hers.

When I get up, Drew takes my hand again and leads me to the dance floor, our eyes on each other. There are so many questions I am not ready to answer tonight. And just like Lola instructs, I will dance the night away for me, for us.

"Drew," I say as we make it to the dancefloor.

"I miss how you say my name like that." He twirls us slowly to a dark corner of the dance floor. "Like you'll be saying my name like this through the night." He chuckles nervously, trying to make light of the situation.

The few glasses of wine I had tonight are making their way to my brain—in a good way. Not drunk, but light and free and strong and determined. Like I can take on the world. I laugh along with him, bending my head backward, exposing my neck close to his lips.

When I flip back, there is no humor in his eyes. I know what that means. The same feeling I have right now. I let my lips land near his chin—close enough but not touching it. He sucks in his breath and pulls me closer. His body still feels rock-hard, and I can only imagine what pleasure it could give me if I let it. The memory of a few nights before enters my mind.

The music stops, but we stay that way. Holding each other. Holding on. Tight.

"Pasko na, sinta ko ..." It's Christmas, my love, the next song begins. Drew and I both understand Tagalog, and this Filipino Christmas song is hitting us straight in the heart. It tells of someone searching for his love who left him behind, of broken promises and regrets.

'Am I ready to say goodbye again after this?' I ask myself, pulling back, staring straight into Drew's solemn eyes.

I can sense it. The buildup. The need. There is anticipation now. Something that has suddenly pushed a button. We gaze into each other's eyes as we walk slowly back to our seats.

When Drew lightly brushes his finger on my arm, I almost jump back, recognizing the desire in my core.

Before we even reach our table, I grab his hand and pull him out of the ballroom. The festive atmosphere, with hundreds of guests celebrating, makes it easy for us to slip away unnoticed.

I feel bold all of a sudden. I blame the wine.

I want this, right now. Tonight is my only chance. Screw the rules.

When we turn a corner, I see a quiet spot away from the crowd. I lean against the wall, making sure a thick pillar is concealing us, and then I pull him close to me, his body pressing against mine.

"Gel—"

"Kiss me," I whisper, my fingers brushing the side of his neck, about to pull him to me. Tonight, I am stomping on my fear. Ready to be brave.

And his mouth finds mine. Fire.

When I open my lips, his tongue enters immediately. No permission necessary. Tonight, he's got me. No interruptions will dissuade me.

Playfully, I join him moving in and out, like a dance. Or a war, a battle over our desires. I feel his hand holds tightly on mine and the other firm on the arch of my back, pressing me even closer to him. I come up for breath. In his eyes, I see not just desire but something else. Something I want to say is forever.

"What are you doing to me?"

"Tempting you to take me to bed."

"The rules?"

"Tonight, fuck the rules."

* * *

As Drew takes me there, tears roll out of my eyes. The pleasure of our coupling is more than physical. I take him in, swaying with the rhythm of his need and mine, and then I explode in a million pieces.

"Drew!" I scream, and he pulls up to see my face. He kisses me all over, holding on to me as I shake underneath him. I grab his shoulders, and he holds the rhythm.

I move more aggressively this time for him. And when he makes it there, arching backward, I stare at his face, taking it all in, letting myself believe that even for a millisecond, that for one night, he is mine again.

"No regrets," I say under my breath. "No regrets."

CHAPTER SEVEN

I never said I was brave. If I were, I would have walked through the storm with Drew. I would have fought heroically. But alas, I admit, I'm a coward.

He looks peaceful in the golden sunlight of breaking dawn peering through the window, his arm around my waist. I've been watching him sleep for the past half hour, his hair beautifully disheveled and his face devoid of emotion, debating whether to stay and fight for him or run away again.

Love is a sham. You may feel it, but it doesn't necessarily translate to reality. Drew said from the get-go that this was pretend. If love was   important, then he would have fought for it a long time ago.

I never doubted his love—but it was an inconvenience for us both. Love made me weak, and I couldn't afford that. And love, should we so choose, would only hinder Drew from making bold, ambitious decisions on his own. I don't want that. He needs to share his brilliance with the people of California, and later, with the rest of America.

There it is again. The overwhelming feeling of defeat on my chest, a welling up of both fear and pain—the high of our lovemaking gone. My tears are threatening to spill because it hurts to love.

It hurts to love Drew. I've felt it before, and I feel it now. I first have to conquer my personal demons before I can allow myself to love completely.

I control a sob and slowly move his arm away from me. I pack as quickly and as quietly as I can, and then, as if history were repeating itself, I walk away, this time leaving not just a piece of my heart, but all of it.

* * *

"… three, two, one. Happy New Year," I whisper into the cold, quiet apartment, a glass of red wine in hand, watching the ball drop on Times Square on TV, alone. Arlene is at a party somewhere in Dupont Circle, but I decided to stay home. I am not in a particularly partying mood.

My phone buzzes on the table, and I almost leap in anticipation.

"Happy New Year!" It's a text from Arlene with a photo of her and her hot new boyfriend, Carlos. "Nothing?" is the next message. I know what she means. Asking if Drew or anyone from his family has reached out.

"No. I don't expect them to. And Happy New Year to you and Carlos."

Exactly ten years ago, my world was shattered.

Drew and I had our biggest fight. A few months before then, I'd had a job offer from Women Fund International, a nonprofit with headquarters in London. I received the call months before I was set to finish law school. It was a dream come true for a poor girl with nothing and no one rooting for her.

"I don't want you to be alone in this world, Angie," my dad said when I told him about the job and the choice I needed to make. "I want you to be with Drew. It's hard not to have someone." I could tell that he was speaking from experience.

"Dad, this is a job offer of a lifetime."

"Drew can take care of you, anak." He sighed, eyes sunken, looking tired after having just finished a long shift two hours after the country rang in the new year.

"All my life, I've done nothing but compromise," I said.

"Why is this any different?"

"Because I want this, this job, Dad, for me."

"You can find another job. Don't rock the boat, Angie." I could sense his frustration. "You've been lucky to be given opportunities like this. To be able to go to law school for free and work toward something."

"Then why are you asking me to give it up?"

"All I'm saying is not to give up on Drew. I don't want to leave you alone in this world without family."

I had run home to talk to my father that night because I was afraid of making a mistake. And instead of backing me up, telling me my dreams were important, he wanted me to cower and choose Drew.

To choose to be a wife and not a lawyer, a job I'd dreamed of since I was a young girl with no prospects. It broke my heart. It broke me. No one took my dreams seriously. I knew I couldn't be with Drew because I would only despise him day after day as his wife.

But I cowered. I ran to him that night to make peace, to declare my undying love, to make passionate love with him so we could live happily ever after. But fate intervened. In fact, truth be told, I should have thanked Kate Maxwell for making the decision easier for me. Finding her on my fiancé's darkened doorstep was enough motivation for me to leave on the next plane to London.

The look on Drew's face when I screamed told he didn't know me enough.

"This isn't you, Gel. Don't make a scene," he said, walking toward me with Kate not far behind.

"Actually, Drew, this is the real me. Surprise! I'm insecure, selfish, and lost. The more I love you, the more I lose myself," I blurted out truthfully.

"Gel, you know you'll always be my number one."

"Stop saying that, Drew. Just stop. Right this minute, I need to be your *only* one."

"Gel, Kate and I are—"

"Yeah, I know. Planning to save the world." We were all quiet for a long second before I finally made my decision. "You have to let me go," I said with a quiver in my voice, and then I ran away, braving the storm.

And he did let me go.

And he never came after me.

* * *

"What are you talking about? Of course that bill needs to pass. We're talking about women's health. We're talking about women's right to health care!"

I slam the phone hard on the cradle, fuming. It's been a busy couple of weeks, and I've been working ridiculous hours since the holiday break, which I'm grateful for. I lower my head to my desk and cradle it in my arms in frustration. I need to be in a meeting at the Rayburn Building in a couple of hours, my hair is a mess, my suit is all wrinkled, and my eyes look like I haven't seen sleep in days.

"Are you okay?"

I jerk my head up and see someone familiar, yet someone I can't seem to place, looking gorgeous in my office doorway. She seems misplaced in this musty room full of old folders and bundles of papers.

"I was going to ask you for coffee, but it looks like you need something stronger," She says with a smile, her red lips curving upward with finesse.

Kate Maxwell is in my office. Kate Maxwell with her long legs in a red suit and black stilettos. Kate Maxwell with her gorgeous hair and big blue eyes. Kate Maxwell who looks like a goddess next to a pauper like me.

"Hi?" I don't know what else to say without sounding rude. She laughs.

"I'm sure you're surprised to see me here. I don't blame you."

"What can I do for you?"

"I've seen you around the Hill, you know. And I tried each time to make sure Drew doesn't bump into you." My heart skips a beat.

"I don't know what you need. But I don't really want to be part of your play," I snap.

"Well, you kinda got yourself into this because you agreed to Drew's play. Now I have to pick up the pieces."

"Today is not a good day for any more battles. Can you come back another time?" I stand up.

"Oh, goodness, I'm not here for a fight, Angelica. I'm here to try to be your friend. I'm sorry if I come off too strong. I need it for my job. I guess it doesn't always translate well into my personal life."

"Not to be rude or anything, but I don't think I have time for this today."

"Are you still in love with Drew, Angelica?"

There is a long, deafening silence while I simmer over this question.

"I don't know this man. It's been a long time."

"And yet I saw the sparkle in your eyes when you two were together. Was that a lie?" She steps into my office and closes the door behind her. "That man is going to be a candidate for the highest office in this country someday, Angelica, and it's my job to make sure he's happy."

"At whose expense?" I ask with sheer force.

"No one's. I was hoping for a happy ever after. A true love story," she says.

"And so why are you here?"

"Because, well … you are Drew's world. Without you, he falters. It's the reason why I try to keep him away from you."

"I don't know what you came here to achieve, but I'm not going to fall for this."

Kate drops her purse on the floor and takes the sole chair across from my desk, crossing one leg over the other as she looks around, taking it all in. I've seen a lot of these political operatives, and I can tell she's already coming up with a strategy on how to position me next to her boss. And then her demeanor changes—power tripping gone, just one woman in front of another.

"I was in love with Drew for a long time. But more than my love for him, I believed in him as a public servant. He has the heart to serve the people of California. I admired that, and I still do. To be honest, I think I mistook it for love. Most importantly, his heart will never be anyone else's except yours. You. We were never in a relationship, but yes, I will admit, I tried to kiss him that night, which he stopped before anything further happened."

I take my seat slowly, looking into this woman's eyes, and, surprisingly, I see sincerity. But again, she is a political operative, so what do I know?

"And then, I wondered, did you run away because of me, or because of what you saw? It wasn't just a misunderstanding, was it? And you can lie to yourself all you want, but we both know—woman to woman—that you were frightened of losing yourself because of Drew's ambition. You weren't willing to give yourself up. And that was when I realized how much I liked you. You walked away from the love of your life because being you was more important than being Drew's wife. I respect that. I would have done the exact same thing. But you've already made something of yourself. You've helped a lot of women fight, not just for their rights, but for themselves. Yes, I've followed your career. And so maybe, just maybe, it's time to give your heart a break from hurting and just love. And be free."

She knew. She knows.

"Loving doesn't make you weak. If done wisely, love can make you strong … stronger."

"How can you speak of love like this when you, yourself, are single and serving the senator from California with all of your time?"

"I just got engaged to my girlfriend of three years, Angelica. Drew doesn't know it yet. You see, through the years, I learned to set my heart wild and free while doing the thing I love. Life isn't flat and one-dimensional. Life should be filled with corners and angles and layers. They make life more meaningful." She stands up, ready to leave, but turns back to face me. "One other thing. If you become first lady, you can change the lives of not just a small fraction of women but of every woman in the world. You can shape that narrative and actually be the vessel of change you want to see in this world. Think about that."

"Why are you doing this?" I ask.

"Aside from making my job easier? Well, Drew is different when you're around. He's light. He's happy. He deserves that too. Drew deserves to be happy. So do you."

~*~*~*~

CHAPTER EIGHT

By the time I step out of the office, the sky has fallen. The winter storm has shuttered the entire District, and the snow is almost five inches high. It's exactly the same gloom I feel after Kate's visit. And absentmindedly, without checking the weather this morning, I left the house with only black tights and ballerina flats, so walking home is not an option.

I pull out my phone to call an Uber. Just as I expected, the rate has tripled because of the weather, and no one is taking my request. The street is empty in front of my office building. It's almost ten p.m.

I spin in place, deciding which way to go, debating whether to brave this storm or cower in the office where it's safe and comfortable. I almost laugh at this. Even the weather is playing with me. I zip my red coat all the way to my chin and pull the heavy faux-fur hoodie up to protect my head.

"Decide, Angelica, decide!" I fume under my breath.

My phone suddenly buzzes in my hand. Drew's face flashes on my screen. With trembling hands, I almost drop the phone in the thick snow accumulating in front of me. I don't answer, shoving my phone back in my purse. I start walking toward my apartment, anxiety taking its toll.

"What do you think you're doing?" a voice shouts from behind me.

I freeze. It's the voice that's been inside my head for the past decade and all the more vividly in the past few weeks.

I continue walking forward, ignoring him. "Gel, it's freezing, and you're not even wearing proper shoes."

I stop.

Slowly, I turn around to face him. My heart warms at the sight of him. He looks fragile tonight. Vulnerable.

We are still a few feet apart, and yet I feel his heart on mine, putting weight on me, pinning me down. Suddenly, I can't breathe. I put my hand over my chest and start rubbing it. I watch Drew follow my hand with his eyes.

"I still make you feel trapped?" he asks uncomfortably, his eyes glued to my hand attempting to appease my frantic heart, stepping forward and immediately retreating again. "I thought ten years was enough. But I see it wasn't time you needed. It was to get away from me." His voice breaks. He bends his head, shoulders sagging, before raising it again to hold my gaze.

The crack in his voice betrays his pain. I instinctively want to run to him, to comfort him. Instead, I stand frozen in place.

We stare at each other for what feels like forever. My tears gather in the corners of my eyes.

"I see that now," he finally concedes before turning to walk away.

I suddenly feel cold inside, as if I am being torn to shreds. My heart has decided to double the tumble. With every step Drew takes, widening the distance between us, it hurts with a feeling so potent I can feel my heart breaking bit by bit.

Then I panic. For whatever it's worth, we have to clear it all tonight and maybe, just maybe, we can both finally move on. And be truly free.

Free. If I hold onto this love and never fully live it, will I ever be free?

I take a step toward him, about ready to run.

"Drew!" He continues walking. "Drew, you scare me." My hands ball into fists. "Loving you frightens me. I can't be with anyone who has so much power over my heart. I can't love anyone more than I love myself. I don't want to be like Dad."

He stops mid-step but doesn't turn around. Suddenly, the snow starts to fall more heavily, blanketing the tops of our heads.

"I had to learn to stop compromising, because it's all I ever did." I let the tears fall down my cheeks this time, showing my true self, standing naked, baring my soul. "I promised the universe so many things that eventually hurt me because I wanted someone so badly—for Mom to stay, for Dad to work less, for you to stand next to me forever, for your family to accept me as their own. I kept telling myself that I was willing to give up something, anything, so I could have everything else. But, is that how I should live? Why do I need to compromise on things I deserve?"

"You don't need to. Not with me. Never with me."

"Kate—"

"We both know what you saw was nothing but a trick of the eye that you exploited to justify leaving, leaving me, breaking us. What compromise did you have to make for that?"

"I compromised myself—and I was done compromising."

We let the snow fall, silence slicing between us. We hold each other's gazes, the need to be accepted, heard, and understood palpable.

Finally, he closes the distance and moves swiftly toward me. I clasp my hands to stop the tremors.

"You will always have me," he whispers. "You don't need to lose anything, especially yourself, for my love. Gel, you've had my heart from the time we first met to this very moment. And I am willing to compromise, to give it all up just so I can love you again. For you to let me love you again. And if you don't love me enough, I have all of mine for both of us."

"Why?" I have to ask. I don't understand why he loves me so. My mother clearly didn't, and my father barely spoke to me. So why does he love me like this?

"You have to know who you are, Gel."

"I don't think I'm enough—for you, your family, your dreams ..."

"Angelica, you are plenty enough. The past ten years have been a blur. I was just existing, and for the first time, at Christmas, you made me feel alive again."

"Drew—"

"I love you more than my ambition. I love you more than my dreams. I love you more than anything in this world before, or now, and for years to come. You have to know that. I can't go back to living without you. I love you. I love you so much it hurts not to see you smile or hold your hand or simply breathe the same air you're breathing."

"Drew."

"I will do anything to make you want to be with me again, and I will wait until you're ready to love me. It will be my life's work to wait for you to love me again."

Does a love like this truly exist?

"You've always had my heart. It's in your hands right now. It's the reason I tried to run away ..." I stammer as I speak.

"Will you give me a chance again?" The pleading in his eyes pulls me in. I need to be brave this time around. I need to understand that loving Drew doesn't mean loving myself less. In fact, letting myself love him again means I am finally winning.

Is it time to stand up to my demons and finally conquer my fears? Is it time to give my heart a reprieve, to let it run wild and free, to beat with joy—and though uncertainty is a given in this world, should I just embrace it and be happy? Truly happy. No questions. No buts. Just be.

"Yes." I whisper into the wind. I see Drew's surprised, happy face take this in.

"And spend the rest of our lives together, for real this time?"

"Yes," I say.

Suddenly, the doors of a car parked a few feet from us fly open. I turn to see Nancy and Laceley and Cindy, and then there's Bert, who is looking at me guiltily, excitedly getting out of the car.

"Give her Lola's ring now, Drew!" Cindy screams, jumping up and down.

"Now!" Laceley echoes.

I look at Nancy's expectant face close to tears, her hands over her mouth in nervous anticipation. I turn back to look at Drew, now on his knee deep in the snow, a small box in his hand.

"Angelica Patricia Mendoza, you are the reason I am on this earth. I believe that, and I'm not kidding. I can't imagine my life without you in it again. With all my heart and my soul and all of me, which you own, I ask if you'd be willing to stand next to me, not just as my wife, but as my partner and my equal. Will you marry me tomorrow at noon?" And then he opens the box to show me Lola's ring. But I snap it shut immediately. And everyone gasps. I pull him up to face me. Everything around us goes quiet, and everyone seems to be holding their breath.

"Drew. I don't need to see the ring to decide. This is not a compromise to get the better diamond. I will marry you, with or without it." A click in my heart, a clarity in my head, and just like that, I feel free. This time around, I feel confident in my response.

"Cindy, Kate said to take a photo as soon as she says yes," Laceley cajoles her sister.

"But she hasn't said yes yet," Cindy protests, holding her iPhone steadily toward me and Drew.

"Angelica, sweetheart?" Nancy says, and I turn to her. Tears are streaming down her cheeks. "Will you take us all as your family? Because we truly, truly, want you in ours, anak." A mother I yearned for and thought I never deserved. A father who speaks to me. And sisters who will forever be mine. And then, there's Drew, who—and though for years I refused to admit this—is a big piece of my joy.

"Yes!" I burst into tears, and Drew reaches out to me and takes me in his arms, holding me so tightly, so strongly, I don't think I'll ever want to let go. "Yes. Yes, to you all."

"No compromising," Drew whispers in my ear. "We shouldn't compromise for love. You'll always have me, Gel, and as you can see, my entire family wants you in their lives just as much as I do. You are not just my number one. You're my only one. My only love."

"I deserve you," I whisper close to his ear.

"You do. And more, my love. And more."

THE END

ABOUT MAAN GABRIEL

Maan Gabriel is a mom, wife, dreamer, writer, and advocate for women's stories in literature. She earned her BA in communications from St. Scholastica's College in Manila and MPS in public relations and corporate communications from Georgetown University. She has lived in Manila, Brussels, Dakar, and Mexico City. During the day, she works in strategic communications. Gabriel, along with her husband and son, currently calls suburban Washington, D.C. home.

Booklist:

After Perfect

Twelve Hours in Manhattan

Pasko Na, My Love

Forevermore

Love at the Fiesta

Social Media:

Facebook - @MaanGabrielAuthor

Instagram - @maan_gabriel

Twitter - @MaanGabriel

ALSO BY THE KWENTITAS

Forevermore

You are cordially invited.

The Moore family requests the pleasure of your company on a starry harvest night, rich with tales of passion, magic, and love.

Our beloved Filipino American family hosts a gathering at Hacienda Luz this autumn for another grand celebration – Vida and Rafa's long-anticipated wedding. As promises of fidelity and infinity fill the air, ten couples live and relive intimate stories that attest to the true meaning of happily ever after.

Love at the Fiesta

Return to Hacienda Luz—the world of *Pasko Na, My Love* and *Forevermore*—as the beloved Moore family opens the gates once more for a dazzling Santacruzan Fiesta in the heart of Napa Valley.

For two vibrant days, the vineyard comes alive with music, food, pageantry, cultural traditions, and unforgettable moments beneath the spring sky. But amid the beauty and celebration, hearts are on the line.

Some will fall in love.

Some will fall back in love.

And some will risk it all for the love they've been waiting for.